UNCHARTED PASSAGE

By the Author

Come and Get Me

Heart 2 Heart

Heartland

Uncharted Passage

UNCHARTED PASSAGE

by

Julie Cannon

2008

UNCHARTED PASSAGE

ISBN 10: 1-60282-032-5
ISBN 13: 978-1-60282-032-6

This Trade Paperback Original Is Published By
Bold Strokes Books, Inc.
New York, USA

First Edition: October 2008

Credits
Editors: Jennifer Knight and Stacia Seaman
Production Design: Stacia Seaman
Cover Design By Sheri (graphicartist2020@hotmail.com)

Acknowledgments

My thanks to everyone behind the scenes at Bold Strokes Books, especially Jennifer and Stacia, who have once again made this a work I am proud to put my name on. Sheri has once again weaved her magic making this cover extra special for me.

Thanks to L, A & E for letting me wade through millions of gallons of water last summer on our vacation in one of the most beautiful places on Earth.

On December 9, 2004, an earthquake measuring 9.0 on the Richter scale triggered perhaps the most destructive tsunami in history as it rolled across the Indian Ocean, devastating coastal communities in a dozen countries and leaving millions homeless. Waves as high as 50 feet (15 meters) in some places traveled as far as 3,000 miles (nearly 5,000 kilometers). A variety of reputable sources have reported the death toll as anywhere from 175,000–275,000 people. According to an HBO documentary, 176,300 bodies were recovered. Two years later 50,773 were still reported missing. One third of the victims were children.

Dedication

For Laura—I'd do it all over again.

Chapter One

Khao Lak Beach, Thailand
26 December, 2004

Salt water burned her skin raw and churned around her feet as she clung precariously to the branch. The noise was deafening. She rested her cheek against the rough bark and closed her eyes, too exhausted to move any higher, at least for the moment.

She tried to gather her senses. The last sane thing she remembered was lying on fine white sand with a cold drink in one hand and a hot woman in the other. It was her third day on Khao Lak Beach, a pristine paradise on the southwestern coast of Thailand, and she was looking forward to another afternoon of casual flirting leading to a warm, tropical night tangled in the sheets, definitely not alone.

Finding herself clinging to a tree was not what she'd had in mind.

There had been no warning. First came the rumble, a crescendo of sound growing louder and louder until the softly cresting waves along the shore receded and an ear-splitting roar announced a thirty-foot wall of water bearing down on her. Before she could move, she was swept off her feet and carried inland along with everything that stood in the water's path. Beach chairs, umbrellas, uprooted trees, and entire buildings rushed past like twigs bobbing in runoff from a hard rain in a street gutter.

But this vast tide of destruction engulfed more than sticks and leaves and the occasional unlucky bug. Dogs and cats panicked in the brown murky water. Farm animals landed on the roofs of buildings. However, it was the people Hayden would never forget. The bodies of the already dead as they floated by, and the desperation on the faces of those fighting for their lives. And the children. They had absolutely no hope against the surge of millions of gallons of water thrust upon the beach by the tsunami that rolled across the Indian Ocean. Those bodies, those faces, would forever haunt her dreams.

Nothing had prepared Hayden Caldwell for this. A graduate of West Point and several Army survival training schools, she was seldom overwhelmed, but she'd never had to fight the unstoppable power of nature. Liquid dripped into her left eye and Hayden was surprised when she touched the area and found her fingers covered in bright red blood. It was only then that she noticed the throbbing above her left eye. Gingerly, she explored a gash that was about an inch long and ran through her eyebrow. Before she had a chance to dwell on her injury, a movement caught her attention. The water was carrying someone directly toward her.

Hayden judged the distance and knew that if she could reach out and grab an arm, the flailing swimmer might have a chance. Or Hayden could be pulled from her precarious perch and they both could die. She had a split second to make her decision. Instinct won out, and she grabbed the victim's arm. A sharp pain pierced her shoulder at the sudden jolt of weight. She was strong from her habitual trips to the gym, but for a moment she almost let go. Dark, frightened eyes locked on hers and Hayden tightened her grip on both the victim and the tree branch. Both arms felt as though they were being ripped from her shoulders. Every breath burned her chest. With the strength she had left, she lifted. The drag was intense, but the raging water finally released its prey. The victim, a woman, dangled barely conscious above certain death. Hayden didn't know if she had the strength to lift her onto the branch.

"Wake up," she bellowed over the roar. "You've got to help me." She was rewarded when the dark eyes opened once more. "That's right, stay with me. Can you move? Can you grab a hold of this branch?"

The woman was naked, her clothes torn from her body by the force of the water. She blinked a few times and spotted the branch. Hayden shouted encouragement as she reached up. The muscles in her arm screamed for relief. When she thought she couldn't stand the pain any longer, the woman got both legs around the branch and pulled herself up. She did not let go of Hayden's arm, but the insistent pressure was gone.

Emily Bradshaw hugged the branch, breathing heavily. She was aware of a hard texture pressed to her cheek, but her mind was still bobbing in the water. The feeling reminded her of drinking too much and falling into bed, swearing the bed was moving. She was afraid to open her eyes in case she was hallucinating and the woman she had clung to was a mirage and she was still being thrashed about in the raging water.

"Mary Mother of God."

A cry drew her fully present and she opened her eyes. Two children no more than three or four years old were headed right toward them, perched on what looked like the remnants of a door. Her rescuer prayed again and scurried farther out on the branch. Emily watched in disbelief as she hooked her legs around the branch and hung upside down over the raging water. Before Emily had a chance to move, the woman scooped up both children in her arms as their makeshift raft slammed into the tree, shattering into pieces.

"Help me." Hayden didn't know if the woman she'd rescued was conscious. In her current position, she wouldn't be able to lift both children onto the branch, but she could not fathom letting one of them go. They were amazingly calm as they clung to her arm like stripes on a candy cane.

Hayden's thigh muscles had begun to cramp when she heard a thin voice insist, "Give him to me."

Emily summoned her remaining strength and reached down to grip the child closest to her. Dragging him up and gripping him firmly, she shimmied back to the hollow where the branch intersected with the tree trunk.

"You're okay, buddy. Stay right here and hang on to the tree. I'll be right back." With one last look at his pale, frozen face, Emily retraced her path.

She almost lost her balance as she reached down for the girl, swinging precariously over the raging water below. Saying a silent prayer, she gripped a small arm and yelled, "Got her."

Hayden breathed a sigh of relief. Her muscles threatened to give out when she tried to lift herself upright, but then her hand was grasped, giving her the leverage she needed.

When her rescuer was safe on their perch once more, Emily shifted the little girl from her arms and placed her behind the boy. She scooted behind both children, forming a cocoon around them as they leaned into the tree. A pair of strong arms slid past her to wrap all of them.

From behind her a voice rasped, "Thanks." Warm breath blew in Emily's ear. "I didn't think I could hold on."

"But you did. You were very brave." A question about their mysterious rescuer passed quickly through Emily's mind. Who would risk their life for a complete stranger? And then do it again for two more? Who was this hero?

The body pressed against her back was warm and solid, and Emily felt safe for the first time since she was swept out of her chair on the beach. With a long sigh, she let her head relax sideways on the sturdy bicep near her cheek.

"We're going to be all right," Hayden said as the woman in front of her shivered.

She sounded far more confident than she felt. Everywhere she looked was water, demolishing all in its path without regard to size, shape, or inhabitants. With the exception of the one they were perched in, almost every tree was ripped out of the ground. Moving closer, she enclosed the woman and two children in her arms. The girl was crying quietly. The sight tugged at Hayden's heart.

"It's okay, sweetie. You're safe now. Nothing's going to hurt you. We're going to take care of you." She continued saying soothing words, and almost immediately, both children fell into exhausted sleep.

"What are we going to do?" The woman in front of her spoke quietly.

Hayden didn't answer. What was she supposed to say? Given the circumstances, it seemed ridiculous to say they were going to be fine. It wasn't going to be that simple. Far from it.

The water marked a steady upward progress on the trunk of the tree as if claiming its stake. Hayden watched doggedly, unable to measure time except in the passage of debris and bodies, until the water slowly inched down and began to recede.

Chapter Two

Teetering on the precipice between wakefulness and slumber, cocooned from the world, Emily was slow to surface. A vague memory of a woman with desperate green eyes floated in and out of her mind. Emily tried to bring the image into sharp focus before it faded away, but in doing so she became more conscious and grimaced as she tried to move. Every bone in her body ached. Something hard pressed against her back and her ass hurt. When she finally forced her eyes open, she was disoriented.

The pale walls of her hotel room were gone, supplanted by the naked glare of daylight. Emily blinked in case she was still caught up in the remnants of a bad dream. She noticed the eerie quiet. There were no sounds of birds squawking or dogs barking, or the constant hum of people carrying on their everyday lives. As if on cue, her memory unlocked, and every sight and sound came flooding back. With it came an intense awareness that she was alive. Naked, in a tree. With strangers.

Destruction spread as far as she could see. Trees ripped from the ground lay strewn across the landscape like matchsticks. Building materials littered the area like confetti, a door here, a window over there. A sheet of plywood with stenciled letters lay propped against a car that was embedded in mud, the only thing visible its hood and headlights reflecting the midday sun. A piece of mangled corrugated steel waved in the soft breeze like a flag erected after a long, bloody battle. Emily squinted recognizing one of the chairs that had been lined up like perfect solders around the hotel pool earlier that morning.

Her stomach churned, and she whispered, "Oh, my God," when she realized that the shapes she thought were more debris were actual bodies. For some inane reason she started counting and vomited when she got to twenty-three.

"It's okay."

Startled by the voice behind her, Emily wiped her mouth with the back of her hand.

"I feel like throwing up, too. It's pretty awful."

"What happened?" Emily knew the answer but couldn't stop herself from asking.

"It must have been a tsunami." Hayden had read about the massive waves but, like most people, had never come close to experiencing one. That had changed hours ago, at least she thought hours had passed. It could have been minutes. She'd lost track of time, guarding the three people she'd saved and waiting for the water to recede.

"A tsunami? That's incredible."

Hayden suppressed another bout of nausea. While her neighbors on the tree limb slept fitfully, her analytical mind had worked overtime to piece together the chain of events. "There must have been an underwater earthquake somewhere that triggered it. A fairly large one, to cause the wave that could do this kind of damage."

"I went down to the beach after breakfast," Emily said. "I'd just gotten there and I was trying to decide whether to get in the water first to stay cool, or wait till I got hot and then jump in. I remember seeing the water recede and I thought it was kind of strange that the tide would go out that far, almost to the reef. Hundreds of yards. All the seashells were exposed, and it was quiet, kind of like it is now. The next thing I knew I was in the water." She shivered as she realized just how narrow her escape from death really was.

Immediately a pair of tanned arms wrapped around her and a soft voice tickled her ear. "Are you cold?"

"No, just a flashback." The hands moved slowly up and down her arms in a gesture of comfort that felt like a caress. The air was still. The only sound was the soft, rhythmic breathing of the children in front of them. Emily shuddered again and leaned into her rescuer's comforting embrace.

"It's okay." The voice behind her was low and reassuring. "You're in shock. We all are."

Emily nodded, knowing if she tried to speak she would sob. She let herself relax, and for few minutes she didn't move. Slowly she became aware of the source of the two hard buds pressed against her back and realized she wasn't the only naked inhabitant of the branch. She started laughing.

"If you can find some humor in this situation, please share it with me." Hayden held her breath, hoping it was humor and not hysteria that was causing her limb partner to laugh.

"Well, usually when I'm stark naked in a woman's arms, we've at least exchanged names."

Hayden wasn't certain she'd heard correctly. "Excuse me?"

"I said I usually know the name of any woman I get naked with." Emily was amazed that her sense of humor could survive in such a bleak situation. She bit her lip when she realized what she'd just said. If this woman was straight, she might just toss her off the branch. Somehow Emily doubted it.

Her neighbor chuckled. "Usually?"

"Well..." Emily didn't get a chance to qualify her statement.

"I'm Hayden," her rescuer said. "I'd offer to shake your hand, but the angle's awkward and we'd probably fall out of the tree."

"I'm Emily."

"It's a pleasure to meet you, Emily. Do you come here often?"

Emily laughed. "I hope that's not the line you use to get a woman naked." She felt the nipples against her back tighten even more.

"No, I'm usually much more suave, but considering the rather compromising position we're in, I thought I'd just jump to the chase."

From her position behind Emily, Hayden had an unobstructed view of a pair of perfectly shaped breasts. Her hands tingled when she imagined how they would feel, and her lips ached to cover a tattoo of red lips on Emily's left shoulder. Chastising herself for having such thoughts in an extremely serious situation, she moved back a little and immediately missed the warmth of Emily's skin.

Obviously misunderstanding her withdrawal, Emily extended the space between them. "I'm sorry if I offended you. My mouth gets me in trouble all the time. I didn't mean anything by that. I'm just...uh...look, forget I said anything."

"I'm not offended. On the contrary, I was hoping I'd have a beautiful woman in my arms this afternoon. This wasn't exactly what I had in mind, but it's certainly going to make a great story at parties."

Emily expelled a breath she didn't know she was holding. She turned around as much as she could, wanting to see the woman who'd saved her life. Clear green eyes looked back at her. Their faces were close enough that Emily could see the dark flecks that surrounded Hayden's pupils. Short blond hair framed a face with just enough laugh lines to signify experience but not enough to give away her age. Strong cheekbones gave her face character, and at this moment she was smiling.

"You're hurt." Emily touched some dried blood over her eye. Fire burned from her fingertips and cascaded through her body. Mistaking the heat for fever, she settled her palm on Hayden's furrowed forehead. The skin felt cool but heat coursed through Emily again. Her eyes locked with those of her rescuer. The fever was inside her.

"I'm okay, just a scratch."

Before she could stop herself Emily dropped her gaze to the chest that had provided such comfort and safety. A bikini tan line accentuated the pale mounds of two perfectly formed breasts. Pink nipples came to immediate attention and Emily's mouth dropped open. She was no stranger to bare breasts, but the ones in front of her were the most beautiful she'd ever seen. She had to clench her fists to restrain herself from caressing them.

Time stood still. Hayden couldn't look away. Emily's fingers felt feather light and soothing. Desire flared to life and Hayden saw it mirrored in Emily's eyes. She was unprepared for the strength of her own reaction. She'd had been instantly attracted to many women, but this was something different. It went deeper than the pulsing between her legs. It gripped her stomach like a hard fist. But this was not the time or the place to explore the feeling further.

Several moments passed before Hayden finally spoke. "Everything else all right?" She wanted to take Emily and make love to her under the afternoon sun for hours.

A flush of embarrassment ran up Emily's neck. Mortified at what she'd just done, she didn't know what to say, so she said nothing.

Hayden's eyes burned with what Emily could only describe as desire. Finally, she bridged the awkward silence. "We'd better get out of this tree and take these kids somewhere safe."

The children must have heard her reference because they started to stir. Emily dragged her gaze away from Hayden's and caught their attention. "Hey, guys, time to wake up." She spoke quietly so as not to frighten them and gently touched their shoulders. "My name is Emily. Can you tell me your name?"

"Victoria." The voice was soft and weak.

"Victoria, that's a mighty big name for such a little girl."

"My name is Jake Nathaniel Hight and I'm five years old. My sister is only three. She's the baby of the family."

Emily smiled at the grown-up way the boy talked.

"I am not a baby, I'm a big girl." She pronounced girl as if it were "gurl."

Emily breathed a sigh of relief that the two children appeared to be unharmed by their ordeal. "Well, you two are really brave."

"I'm brave just like my dad. He's a policeman."

Watching the exchange, Hayden quickly took inventory of their situation. With the exception of losing their clothing, they were all very lucky to have escaped serious injury. Hayden panned the horizon, not recognizing any landmarks. None were left standing. Buildings had been obliterated; their foundations remained as if ready to be used again. The lush green vegetation of Khao Lak that had not been uprooted and carried away lay limp, bent over from the force of the raging water.

Glancing up to the sky, Hayden judged the time of day to be early afternoon. Out of habit she looked at her left wrist and cursed herself for leaving her TAG Heuer watch in the safe in her hotel room. The large timepiece looked out of place with her bikini, and there was no reason to wear it while on the beach. It was not as if she had appointments to keep.

The sun was beating down and it wouldn't be long before they were scorched. They all needed fresh water, and clothes to protect their skin from sunburn. It didn't take more than a fleeting look to know that finding what they needed to survive was going to be a challenge.

Hayden forced a casual confidence that revealed no sign of her darker thoughts. "Hey, guys, my name is Hayden, have either of you climbed a tree before?"

❖

Hayden was thin, but not what Emily would classify as skinny. "Strong and lean" was the phrase that jumped to mind. She moved with the ease of someone very confident in her athletic ability. She climbed effortlessly down from the tree, then helped the children onto the ground and looked up expectantly at Emily.

Feeling self-conscious because of her lack of athletic ability as well as her nakedness, Emily steeled her nerves and grabbed the rough trunk. Hayden was directly below her and would see everything she had to offer as she shimmied her way down. Afraid to make eye contact, she inched her way to the ground in a state of disbelief. How in the hell did she end up in this surreal moment? All she wanted was a week of uninterrupted one-on-one time with her girlfriend, holding hands on the beach, rekindling their dying romance. Instead, what she got was an ugly fight with Michelle, an empty seat next to her on the plane, and seven days alone on the beach.

She certainly wasn't prepared for this. Nobody could be prepared for this. It wasn't as if she should have packed for a tsunami. Julia said all she needed was a bikini and sunscreen. Oh my God, Julia. She would be frantic when she heard the news. Her good friend had been here before and knew how secluded Khao Lak was from Phuket. The remoteness was what drew Emily here in the first place, and now she wondered how long it would take for them to be rescued.

Sensing Emily's discomfort, Hayden gave her a chance to collect herself once she'd reached firm ground. If she were honest, *she* was the one who needed time to collect herself. Her heart beat wildly in her chest and her hands were shaking. Emily scaling the tree was the most erotic thing she'd ever seen. Her body was perfect. Hayden had envisioned the long legs and arms wrapped around her instead of the tree trunk. As Emily's backside inched closer, her fingers had tingled with the desire to touch the exposed flesh. By the time she hit the ground, Hayden's knees were weak with desire.

Embarrassed by her lascivious thoughts, Hayden forced her attention to the daunting task in front of them. "Help will probably come to the beaches first. The sun will set over there," she pointed across the devastated landscape, "so that's the direction we should go."

"Do you know where we are?" Emily felt more composed than she'd been a few moments ago. She rubbed her arms where the bark had scratched her, and her actions drew Hayden's attention. Her breath caught at the look of unbridled desire on Hayden's face. Their nakedness was unsettling, and a long since forgotten throb of desire settled between her legs.

"No, and there are no familiar landmarks to go by. Absolutely nothing looks like it did this morning, but I know the beach is that way."

A pair of small hands grabbed her leg tightly. "I don't want to go to the beach." Jake's voice shook.

Hayden knelt down so that she was eye level with the boy. "I know, I don't want to go back to the beach either." She caught a surprised expression on Emily's face and wondered what it was about. Did Emily think that just because she was butch, she wouldn't know how to comfort a scared child? She remembered as a child when she was frightened all it took was a few kind, straightforward words from her mother and she felt better. "But that's where the people are that are going to help us."

His chin started to quiver. "Is that where my mommy is?"

Hayden scooped him into her arms. "I don't know, but I bet she's looking for you and your sister. What do you say we go and find her, okay?" Hayden had minimal experience with children and even less with ones the ages of these two. She didn't know what to do with them, but she did know they would have to go slow and rest often.

Jake's bottom lip trembled and a tear slipped down his cheek. "Okay. Is my daddy there too?"

Hayden couldn't answer his question but instead pulled

him closer, and he laid his head on her shoulder. "Hey, big guy, everything's going to be all right. But I'm gonna need your help. Do you think you can help me?"

The youngster's eyes lit up. "My dad always lets me help him when he's doing something really important."

"Well, then I know you can help. Let me tell you what I need you to do." Signaling Emily and Victoria to follow, Hayden started walking in the direction of the beach.

Emily was surprised how easily she let Hayden assume the lead in their journey. In her everyday life as a teacher, she was the planner, the one in charge—she had to be with a room full of first graders. She hadn't started out wanting to be a teacher. She was going to be a world-renowned scientist like her parents. Her life had been mapped out for her from the very beginning and she blindly went along, ever the dutiful daughter. It wasn't until Julia dragged her along to a school for the homeless that her company was sponsoring that she found her true calling and her backbone. It had been a downhill slide with her parents ever since. The latest argument was over this trip. They were furious with her when she had told them of her plans to go to Thailand over Christmas, insisting that family should be together during the holidays. Their emotional blackmail used to be effective, but in the past year Emily had drastically changed. She was restless, tired of settling, of going along to avoid an argument.

She was definitely not a follower, and certainly not one that would willingly be led across this disaster to God knew where with a stranger in charge of her destiny. Oddly enough, she was comfortable in this role with Hayden and knew instinctively that they would be safe as long as they were together.

"Here, try these." Hayden handed her a bundle of clothes. "Sorry, it's the best I could do."

While the three were resting Hayden had gone scouting ahead and had stripped three of the dead. Besides the fact that it wasn't easy to concentrate with Emily's naked body constantly within arm's reach, they were all at risk of extreme sunburn if they didn't get some clothes on. Her feet were sore from walking in the mud and debris, and she was thankful she hadn't stepped on anything more dangerous than a piece of cement. She'd found a loose-fitting pair of shorts for herself, and a man's shirt that was missing the top three buttons.

Emily appreciated the tantalizing view of her breasts the damaged garment provided. Hayden looked sexier in the shirt than when she had nothing on. As she sorted the clothes for herself and the children, Emily shuddered and tried not to think of where the garments came from. Emily stepped into the shorts, thankful they had a drawstring she could cinch tight enough to keep them from sliding down her thin hips.

The clothes and flip-flops for the children were way too big. Hayden tore the bottom off her shirt and made makeshift belts to keep the garments from dragging on the ground.

Looking down at her T-shirt, Emily started laughing. It was emblazed with a surfer riding a giant wave. "Pretty appropriate, don't you think?"

Heat exploded in her veins when Hayden's eyes landed on her chest. She felt her nipples harden, and Hayden's eyes darted back and forth between the two protruding buds.

"Uh…" Hayden's mouth was so dry she couldn't have said anything even if she could think of something. She was leaning over as she helped Victoria dress, her face in direct line with Emily's breasts. If she leaned forward just a little she could…

"Owie!" Victoria shrieked.

Instead of reaching out and touching Emily's breasts, Hayden was squeezing the child too hard. "Sorry, sweetie." She gently rubbed the little arms. "Okay, everybody ready?"

Hayden took the lead, Victoria grabbing her hand and holding it with strength Hayden never would have imagined the little girl had. They trekked on in the direction of the beach. Rescuers would follow the path of the water searching for survivors along the way, and sooner or later they would meet up with them. Hopefully sooner, Hayden thought. They were hot, tired, and thirsty.

Chapter Three

"Are those people dead?"

Hayden faltered at the young boy's innocent question. They had been walking for an hour, and during that time she had lost count of the number of bodies they passed. She didn't know why she was counting. Maybe it was the training that had been drilled into her to keep track of details. Maybe it was because she was trying to wrap her mind around the magnitude of the carnage. The most disturbing were those buried in the mud with only an arm or leg protruding as if reaching for heaven. It was late afternoon, and the heat of the midday sun had started to take its toll on the dead, spreading stench and the threat of disease.

Hayden glanced at Emily. "Do you want to take that one?" They'd fallen into a natural rhythm of taking turns answering the boy's questions.

"Not on your life." Not that she wouldn't have, but the sound of Hayden's voice as she answered Jake's questions gave her a sense of calm. Hayden was a tall, strong woman with a hard edge, yet when she spoke to the children, her voice was soft and calm and always at a level they could understand.

"Thanks, you're gonna owe me big time for this one." The relaxed banter between the two of them was surprising. Here they were in an obvious life-or-death situation, and they were chatting like old friends. They hadn't shared any personal information, but it was as if they had known each other for years.

Emily teasingly bumped Hayden with her shoulder as they sidestepped a car mangled by the water's force. "I already owe you my life, I can't get any deeper in debt than that."

Since she had defied her parents, quit her job, and was now doing what *she* wanted to do, Emily hated being in debt to anyone for anything. Surprisingly, she was okay with this form of debt. If not for the woman walking beside her, in all likelihood she would be one of the bodies they passed. Emily still couldn't believe it. She wondered if her parents were worried about her. They were news junkies with CNN blasting through the house every waking moment. Surely they'd heard about the disaster.

"You don't owe me. It's what anyone would have done." Hayden recalled having this conversation shortly after she plucked Emily from the water. "I will collect on Jake's question, though. Don't think you're getting out of that one."

Emily grinned, lightening the mood. "If I'd known you were that easy, I would have had you rescue me years ago. It would have saved me a lot of grief and heartache."

Hayden's stomach tightened at the thought of Emily experiencing any kind of pain. There was something about her that made Hayden want to protect her. She knew it was silly; Emily was a grown woman, perfectly capable of taking care of herself. Hayden wondered what kind of pain she was referring to. Did she have a difficult childhood or unceremoniously get her heart broken? She stopped as an overwhelming desire to keep her safe washed over her. The silence was deafening, and a shroud of death and destruction hung over them like a cloak.

Emily continued on a few steps before realizing Hayden had stopped. "What is it? Do you hear something?"

"No, it's nothing." Years of experience had taught Hayden it was usually not in her best interest to openly talk about her feelings. She had been in the Army for twenty-three years, way before "don't ask, don't tell" was the military's position.

At the look on Hayden's face, Emily lightly touched her arm. "Hayden, what is it?" Her voice was soft and caring, her eyes encouraging conversation.

"If I would have known you needed rescuing, I would have been there." Hayden had no trouble speaking the truth but tried to keep it light.

"That would have caused quite a scene. If you rode up on your white horse and carried me away, my parents would have shit." Emily grimaced at exposing the little girl in her arms to her language.

"You didn't get along with your parents?" Hayden picked up Jake and started walking again.

"I did until I grew some balls and started to live my own life." Emily suppressed a shiver, remembering the ugly confrontation she had with her parents when she told them of the change she was going to make in her life. Raised voices, angry words filled their house for the better part of an afternoon. But she held firm and was proud of herself for remaining so. "I was the prodigal child of two geneticists. My mother won the Nobel Prize when I was eight. I knew in no uncertain terms that I was expected to exceed the accomplishments of my parents."

"And did you?" Hayden sidestepped a pile of lumber beaten into matchsticks by the water.

"Oh yeah, did I ever. Ever heard of the Ashley Institute?" Emily continued when Hayden shook her head. "Not many people have. It's a world-renowned think tank. They offered me a research position after I got my Ph.D."

"And you didn't take it?" Hayden prompted. She could tell that Emily was intelligent, but never would have expected a Ph.D.

Emily tasted the bile in her throat. "No, I took it, all right. I worked for six years with the greatest minds in the world."

"So what happened?" Hayden shifted Jake to her other arm.

"I decided I wanted to teach homeless kids." Emily recalled the day she'd accompanied her friend Julia to a homeless shelter.

There she found children of all ages thirsty for knowledge, eager to learn everything about the world around them but unable due to their social conditions. Emily was soon spending all of her free time with the children, teaching them everything from their colors to Christopher Columbus and quickly discovering a love for teaching children.

"And that's bad because…?"

"Because I quit the Institute. My parents have never forgiven me. I'm a professional embarrassment to them." Even now, two years later, Emily still felt the sting of her mother's comments. One time when she was meeting her mother for lunch, as she approached the table, she overheard her mother on her cell phone telling someone that her daughter *teaches the snotty-nosed kids of worthless parents*. The comment had been a blow that Emily never told her mother she had overheard, but it had definitely cemented their wounded relationship.

Anger welled up inside Hayden and she would have strangled Emily's parents if they were in front of her right now. "You could never be an embarrassment."

"Tell that to my parents. They certainly think otherwise." Emily didn't even try to keep the bitterness out of her voice.

"I'm sorry." Her response sounded hollow.

Emily stopped, tears choking her. The gentleness in Hayden's voice was something she had not heard from her own parents since she quit the Institute, and hot tears burned her cheeks.

"Hey, I'm sorry. I didn't mean to make you cry."

Emily immediately buried her face in Hayden's neck and sobbed. Her head fit perfectly under Hayden's chin and a sense of déjà vu floated over her, as if Emily had been there forever. It felt right. She felt powerful and would do everything in her power to keep Emily safe. She held her close, and a little hand with chipped pink nail polish reached out and patted Emily on her back.

"It's okay, don't cry." Victoria offered her own form of comfort.

Hayden's arms were safe and Emily expelled the long-held pain over her parents' betrayal in sobs that racked her body. Several minutes later she dried her tears. "I'm sorry. I don't know why that happened. I'm not usually like this, I don't know what came over me." Embarrassed, she turned away.

"Hey." Hayden didn't let her escape. "It's okay. We're in a stressful situation here and our emotions are a little raw."

"I've never told anyone about what happened. Not even Julia, a friend of mine who took me to the shelter in the first place." Emily wiped her face with her free hand.

Hayden's heart ached at the pain that was reflected in the brown eyes pooling with tears. "I'm honored you shared it with me."

Tears barely held in check threatened to spill over from Hayden's gentle tone and soft eyes. One lone tear had a mind of its own and slowly trickled down her cheek.

Hayden's hand shook when her thumb wiped the tear from Emily's face. The skin was so incredibly soft that Hayden was overwhelmed with the need to touch it again. This time the backs of her fingers gently caressed the check now free of any evidence of tears. Red lips beckoned to be kissed and Hayden slipped her hand to the back of Emily's neck, her eyes never leaving the moist lips.

Unconsciously, Emily licked her lips and desire flared in Hayden's eyes. Emily was simultaneously frightened and thrilled at the intensity she felt in Hayden's arms. She wanted to be kissed, no, she *needed* to be kissed by this strong stranger, the sensation so powerful it frightened her. She leaned forward to meet Hayden's lips halfway when a sound penetrated her foggy head. She jerked her head back.

"Did you hear that?" Emily scanned the horrific scene in front of her, swearing the sound she heard came from somewhere to her right.

Caught up in the desire to kiss Emily, Hayden took several seconds longer to gather her wits. "What?"

"I heard something, I know I did. It sounded like someone moaning, and it was coming from over there." Emily started in that direction but Hayden caught her arm to stop her.

"Wait. You stay with the kids, I'll check it out." She'd heard the sound and knew whoever it was must be severely injured. She wanted to spare Emily additional horror, and the children certainly didn't need to see it either.

The tone of Hayden's voice left no doubt as to her seriousness, and Emily was too tired to argue. She set Victoria on the ground and took hold of Jake's hand to keep him next to her.

Hayden gingerly stepped over debris as the moaning grew louder with each tentative step. Her stomach clenched as she passed a wheelchair stuck in the mud a few feet from an elderly man showing no signs of life. The sound returned, this time near her feet. Hayden moved a large piece of corrugated metal, hot to the touch from the metal baking in the sun. What she saw no one should ever have to see.

The child was not more than a year old and still securely strapped in her stroller. Her yellow sundress was soiled with dirt, and the matching yellow bow in her hair stood out like a beacon of daylight. She looked like she was simply sleeping, like she had probably done many times before, but Hayden knew otherwise. A leaf was covering one eye, and Hayden's hands shook as she removed it, quietly saying a prayer.

The child's mother moved, startling Hayden, and she jumped. "Jesus." Hayden reacted and knelt beside the woman, who moaned again. "It's okay, I'm here." Hayden's EMT training kicked in and she noted that the woman's breathing was shallow and quick. Her head lay in a pool of blood and Hayden suspected she had a severe injury to the back of her head. Her pupils were dilated, her skin clammy. A cement block too large for Hayden to move covered the woman from her breasts to mid thigh. There was nothing Hayden could do for her, and it was only a matter of time before she succumbed to her injuries.

"My baby?" the woman asked, spitting blood as she coughed. "Is my baby all right?"

It was then that Hayden noticed the woman's hands were wrapped tightly around the handle of the stroller like an umbilical cord to her child. Hayden fought down the nausea that was threatening to overtake her. Large, hopeful eyes looked up at her, piercing her soul.

"Is my baby okay?" she rasped in desperation.

The woman grasped Hayden's hand with more force than she thought was possible. It tore at her heart that the woman was more concerned with her child than her own injuries. The love of a mother for her child was never ending. She swallowed hard and lied.

"She's fine." Peace replaced panic in the woman's pleading eyes. They closed and the woman took one last ragged breath. She died holding Hayden's hand.

Hayden stumbled back to Emily and the children, the image of the woman and child burned in her brain forever. She was numb and didn't feel the piece of exposed metal scratch her leg as she passed. Her mind was focused on getting back to the soft, peaceful eyes beckoning to her fifteen yards away. Those eyes were drawing her into warmth and understanding. Step after step took her closer to home.

As Hayden gingerly threaded her way across the dangerous terrain, Emily silently thanked her for insisting she stay with the children. She didn't know how much more death she could take. She had no way of knowing what Hayden had found under the debris, but by the dazed look on her face it had been disturbing. The pain drew Emily the last few steps and she gathered Hayden into her arms.

With one hand on Hayden's back and the other tangled

in her hair, she murmured soothing words to the woman who had been so strong for them. Her heart ached and she wanted to protect Hayden from the world's ugliness and felt helpless that she couldn't, that they were walking through it.

Hayden struggled with her emotions, fighting the urge to stay cocooned in Emily's arms. An unfamiliar sense of peace settled over her and if she were to die at this moment, she would die happy. She'd come to Thailand seeking escape from her life for a few days. She wanted nothing more challenging than deciding which swimsuit to wear that day.

Hayden was career Army, from the tips of her highly polished shoes to the sparkling insignia on her collar. A graduate of West Point like five generations before her, she knew when she was eleven years old that her father would make her the general he never was.

She knew she was different from the other little girls in the neighborhood. When most of her friends were talking about boys and getting married, Hayden was dreaming of commanding troops into battle and riding in a tank. When other teenage girls were earning extra money babysitting neighbors' children, she was practicing parade march and reading books on military strategy. She never wondered which parental gene she had inherited. She was her father's daughter.

It was several years into her first assignment and out from under his constant scrutiny when she realized that she definitely was just like her father. She found that she liked women and embarked on her first affair with a nurse at the ripe old age of twenty-six. She'd never looked back, preferring her women with no regrets and few entanglements.

Lately, however, Hayden had been plagued with a vague sense of anxiousness. The normal routines and structure that she usually thrived on were now more choking than comforting. The clear purpose of her life had turned foggy. The responsibilities that filled her days and were once challenging now were simply an annoying nuisance. The prying eyes of her "Big Brother," the

U.S. Army, had burned a hole in her back that no salve could soothe. The weight of masking who she was beneath bureaucracy, regulations, and conduct becoming an officer was crushing the life out of her, and she didn't know what to do about it.

Warm breath tickled her ear, bringing Hayden back to the present. As much as she didn't want to, she straightened and stepped out of Emily's arms but could not look at her. She squared her shoulders, her military training too much a part of her DNA to lie dormant for long. "Let's go."

They picked their way through the debris, carrying the children for the remainder of the afternoon. The change in Hayden's demeanor after her discovery troubled Emily. The casual chatting and near banter they shared earlier in the day had vanished and Emily missed it. Hayden had moved Jake to her shoulders, her gait more determined than before. She kept her head down, glancing up only occasionally to check their route.

"Hayden, your leg is bleeding." Emily hadn't noticed the injury before, but the dried blood on the outside of her leg could not be missed.

Finally Hayden stopped. She glanced at her leg. The cut was about two inches long but not deep. Blood welled in a slow trickle. "It's just a scratch." Her voice was flat. "We'll stay here for the night."

Hayden plucked Jake from her shoulders and set him gently on the concrete slab that would be their bed for the night. Hayden recognized the structure as one of the few houses made of block on the beach, and had a fleeting thought of the children's fairy tale *The Three Little Pigs*. This house still had its roof, which would keep them dry from the nightly rain, and the three sides that remained would ward off any chill. She had been looking for a place to spend the night, but every structure they passed didn't look safe. The tsunami had knocked down walls and roofs, often leaving only the foundation as evidence that a building was even there in the first place.

Most troubling was the need for fresh water. Large bodies of water were everywhere, some spanning several hundred yards, but they sampled the first one they came upon and almost gagged from the salt water of the Indian Ocean. Remnants of the tsunami filled buckets and tires and anything that could hold water, but whatever fresh water there might have been in the area was now contaminated. Several times the children had asked for something to drink, and Hayden was concerned that they were all becoming dehydrated in the warm, humid conditions.

"Don't go too far," Emily cautioned the children needlessly. They had not drifted from their side since Hayden plucked them from the water. Emily reflected on the resilience of children. She had seen children in the most challenging situations, and despite their socioeconomic conditions they were always ready with a smile and for an adventure.

"I'm gonna look around a little bit. If this was a house, maybe there's some food the water didn't wash away. We need water and something to eat if we're going to make it back to the beach." Hayden frowned, realizing this was the first time she questioned if they in fact would make it. She brushed the thought from her mind.

"Okay, I'll see what I can find too. There's got to be something around here. A can of soda or, God help us, a bottle of water." Emily's mouth was parched from hours in the sun and the children had been dangerously quiet.

"Be careful, there's glass and nails everywhere," Hayden said, dodging a broken window as she spoke.

Still distracted, Emily wasn't paying attention to where she was going and ran directly into a jagged piece of rebar sticking out at an odd angle from a block of concrete. "Shit!" she exclaimed, grabbing her thigh, the blood seeping from between her fingers and dripping down her calf. It started to burn and she battled a wave of nausea.

"God damn it, Emily. I said be careful," Hayden barked. Her heart raced at the sight of Emily's blood, and she ran to her side and knelt in front of the wound. "Jesus." The gash was just above her left knee and was about three inches long and deep. Hayden's hands shook as she fought her natural instinct to touch the gash, not wanting to add to the germs that were already teeming inside the wound.

"Christ, Hayden, it's not like I did this on purpose," Emily snapped. Hayden's anger confused her and she momentarily forgot the pain in her leg.

"Do you have any idea how dangerous a cut can be in these conditions?" The wound bled profusely and Hayden looked around, searching for something to clean it. Finding nothing even remotely dirt free, Hayden gave up and concentrated on the amount of blood flowing from Emily's leg.

"Of course I do, and I could say the same thing about you." Emily pointed at the cut on Hayden's leg. "Do you think I want to get some kind of infection? Jesus, it could kill me!" She hated it when people thought she was stupid.

Hayden's blood ran cold at the thought of the possible consequences if the wound could not be kept clean. She'd barked at Emily out of fear that she was seriously injured. As it was, the cut was deep but the bleeding was flushing out some of the germs. Hayden just hoped it was enough.

Another sensation gripped Hayden, this one frightening her almost as much as imagining Emily falling ill. Hayden's chest heaved from her shallow breathing. She forgot all about the wound, her concentration directed to the feel of the soft flesh under her hand. It was begging to be touched like fine silk cloth or the soft petal of a rose, and Hayden was powerless to fight the desire.

Hayden couldn't think, couldn't breathe, and couldn't react to anything but the sensation of Emily's skin under her fingers. She was consumed by the hard muscle covered by tanned flesh. Emily's legs were like Emily herself, strong and powerful. Hayden's face was eye level with Emily's crotch and she swore she could smell her arousal. Her own arousal skyrocketed. She had touched more women than she could remember, but none with the reaction she was having with Emily. It shook her to the core.

Warm cascades of liquid flowed through Emily's body, each wave mirroring the soft caresses up and down her calf. Stroke by stroke, the passion in Hayden's eyes burned brighter, and Emily had never felt so desired. Hayden's hands caressed her body while her eyes embraced her soul. The unspoken connection with Hayden was powerful. She'd experienced the hands of many women, but none had touched her like this.

"Hayden." Her voice shook. She didn't know if uttering Hayden's name was a question or a plea. Her body was screaming, her senses on fire. She wanted Hayden to touch every inch of her body. She wanted to feel Hayden's strong body on top of her. She needed to feel Hayden quivering under her touch. Emily wanted to be consumed by her.

Unsettled by her attraction to Emily, Hayden dragged her attention back to the wound in front of her. It was bleeding steadily, and Hayden tore the bottom off her shirt and wrapped it around Emily's leg.

"You're bleeding pretty good, but for now that's good. It'll help cleanse the wound of germs. It looks like a clean cut and can probably be stitched up pretty good when we get back. You'll probably have a scar, but it'll be another good party story." Hayden tried to inject humor to deflect the tension that surrounded them. She stood.

The abrupt change startled Emily and she staggered back. Hayden caught her arm before she tumbled over any more debris. "Are you okay?"

"It hurts, but it'll be all right." Actually, it hurt like hell, but she wasn't going to complain. "Thanks. You've come to my rescue again. You'd better be careful, a girl could get used to this." *And I am definitely that kind of girl.*

"Yeah, I know what you mean," Hayden mumbled more to herself than in response.

Luck was on their side and Hayden found two bottles of Coke

that had somehow not broken half buried in the mud. She thanked God they had screw tops and not the pop tops that required a can opener. She handed one to Emily and the other to Jake.

"Just a little bit now. Don't drink too much, your sister needs some too." The little girl was grabbing at the bottle before her brother had taken it from his mouth. She took a few quick swallows before Hayden took it from her and replaced the cap.

Hayden's change of subject didn't skip by Emily. She also didn't miss her unselfishness with the kids. She'd carried the children most of the day, sometimes one on her shoulders and one in her arms, and had always made sure they had what they needed. Her dedication and sacrifice for their survival intrigued Emily. Her friends were more concerned with the strength of their morning latte than with anything else. Suddenly it all seemed so immaterial. Her stomach growled.

"While, you're at it, I'll take a grilled chicken sandwich with Swiss and just a touch of spicy mayo."

She was rewarded with a twinkle in Hayden's eyes. "White or wheat?"

For some reason Emily suddenly felt giddy. "Wheat. And no tomatoes, I love tomatoes, just not on my sandwich."

The smile that followed made her legs weak. Hayden was not just the strong, competent hero she owed her life to. She was also funny, charming, and breathtakingly attractive. Emily scolded herself for her lascivious thoughts. They were in the middle of God knew where, having survived a horrific natural disaster, and here she was thinking about sex. How twisted was that? The object of those thoughts held out a large can of beans and a can of chicken soup, both of which miraculously had pop tops. Emily recognized the familiar label and her stomach growled again.

"I never thought a can of beans could look so good."

"My thoughts exactly." Hayden lifted the can of soup. "I can't remember the last time I had chicken noodle soup. Even cold, it's got to be good."

Hayden sat on a block with the children on either side of

her. Emily sat across from her and opened the beans. "Sorry, I couldn't find any silverware."

Emily chuckled. "I think we'll manage, won't we, kids?"

They shared the food, eating the beans with their fingers. Emily noticed that, as with the soda, Hayden gave more to the kids than she took herself. Her generosity stirred something deep inside. She had to be as hungry as Emily, and she was using all her strength, but she still put herself last. Emily wondered where that self-sacrifice came from. Was it instinctive or acquired? Whatever the explanation, her actions spoke louder than words. Hayden was a person of character.

"You need to eat something," Emily prompted her softly.

"I'm eating." Hayden tried to sound casual but didn't think she was successful.

"Yeah, four bites for them, one for you. That's eight bites to your one. I don't call that eating."

"You say tomato, I say tom-ah-to." Hayden mimicked the British accent with added emphasis. She was hungry, but it was more important to her that the children and Emily got enough to eat.

"I say bullshit," Emily countered.

"Emily, please. I'm fine. I'm really not that hungry." Her stomach decided at that moment to refute her last comment.

"Uh-huh. Here." Emily held out a serving of beans on two fingers. Hayden hesitated. "Eat it."

Hayden knew when she was beat and leaned forward. She took Emily's fingers into her mouth and their eyes locked.

Emily's mouth dropped open at the sensation of her fingers in Hayden's mouth. She repeated the offering, her hand shaking as she waited for Hayden's tongue to curl gently over her fingers as she accepted the food. Hayden's eyes darkened and Emily found it difficult to withdraw. Her fingers were still being sucked long after the food was gone.

Desire shot through her. How could something as innocuous as eating pork and beans be so erotic, especially under the circumstances? Where had her mind gone? The same place as her common sense and reasoning—somewhere behind her, both literally and figuratively. Her body was hot with arousal and she craved the feel of Hayden's strong arms around her. She wanted to know what it was like to make love with her. Somehow she was certain it would be intense, powerful, and like nothing she had ever experienced. She shuddered, wondering if they would survive this nightmare, and when Hayden finally pulled away, Emily was afraid that she might never get the chance to know.

CHAPTER FOUR

The sun set quickly, and without the competing glow of streetlights, the stars seemed ultra-bright against the dark sky. Victoria lay in blissful sleep with her head in Hayden's lap. Hayden leaned against a wall stripped of any ornaments, her legs stretched out in front of her. She was exhausted but knew there was no way she'd get much sleep tonight with Emily sitting next to her.

She couldn't resist asking, "Who's waiting for you back home?"

Emily's voice was soft and was a caress in the darkness. "The usual. Mom, Dad, some friends."

"Anybody else?"

"No, not really. How about you?"

"The same." Hayden was typically evasive when anyone fished for personal information.

"Were you on vacation here?" Emily heard a movement, but it was so dark she couldn't see if Hayden nodded or shook her head. "Sorry, I didn't hear you."

"Yes. You?"

"Yeah. I needed to get away," Emily replied vaguely.

She certainly hadn't planned on coming alone. The trip was supposed to be an opportunity to rekindle the passion that had been dormant for several years with her partner Michelle. At the last minute, Michelle had canceled, making some excuse about her job and an unexpected deadline. Emily was angry, hurt, and suspicious, but she refused to play into yet another of Michelle's ploys for attention. She came to Khao Lak for their second honeymoon alone.

"That's why everyone comes to paradise," Hayden said. "It's the perfect escape."

She never tired of the Southeast Asian land famous for its warmth, hospitality, cuisine, and Buddhist culture. The beach villages of Thailand openly welcomed gay and lesbian couples. This was one of the few places she could simply be herself. On each trip she visited a different beach community. This was her first time to Khao Lak.

"What are you running from?" Emily asked bluntly.

Hayden hesitated. Emily was closer to the mark than she was comfortable with. "Who says I'm running from anything? Maybe I'm just on vacation."

"Something tells me a woman like you doesn't *simply* go on vacation." Emily wondered where that observation came from. She didn't know Hayden enough to know one way or another what she did.

"A woman like me?"

Emily cringed, caught on her own words. The night was eerily still. Thankful for the darkness that hid her embarrassed flush, she said, "Well, you don't seem to be the type that does anything simple. What I mean is that you seem very intense, so I thought you probably do everything with equal intensity."

Her thoughts instantly careened into fantasy. Intense sex with Hayden. She could almost feel their bodies moving together. The image made her break out in a sweat.

Hayden chuckled. "Actually, you're right. I'm not real good at sitting around and watching the air move."

"Then why the beach? There's not much more going on here." Emily paused. "Other than the possibility of getting killed in a natural disaster."

Hayden didn't try to keep the smile off her face. "Pretty girls."

"Excuse me?"

"Pretty girls. Lots of them. I come here to fuck myself silly for a week. Then I go home."

Hayden gasped at the candor of her comment. She knew what her intentions were coming to the beach, but normally she would never share the truth with anyone else. Maybe it was the anonymity of the darkness, or maybe the sense of freedom that made everything else superfluous and immaterial. They were two people thrown together for survival, and the usual social conventions felt completely irrelevant.

"And were you successful?" Emily had no idea why she asked; she didn't want to know the answer. A surge of jealousy flashed through her at the thought of Hayden with other women. It was her body she wanted Hayden to touch, caress, and, yes, fuck.

"I'm not sure I want to answer that question."

Hayden was not ashamed of her life or her sexual experiences, but for some reason she didn't want them out for display in front of Emily. She had opened the subject and now she wasn't sure how to step back from her disclosures. Regret washed over her. Why hadn't they met at the beginning of her stay and not now, toward the end and in the middle of a catastrophe? Emily was witty, intelligent, and beautiful. She would have been the ideal companion for a week of mutual pleasure. Assuming she had holiday flings, and Hayden couldn't imagine why a woman would travel alone to a Thai beach for any other reason.

Emily confirmed her assumptions by noting, "With that body and your charming smile, I think I can figure out the answer on my own."

Hayden acknowledged the dry compliment with a lingering stare, enjoying the smooth contours she could make out in the darkness. "So what are you running from?" she asked, turning the question back to Emily.

"Nothing. Absolutely nothing at all."

Emily reflected on her relationship with Michelle. She didn't know when everything had started going south. She suspected the demise of their connection was just a case of two people growing in different directions. She had once loved Michelle deeply, but the past few days on the beach confirmed what she'd known all along but hadn't admitted to herself. She doubted Michelle had realized it either. Somewhere between boarding the plane and her third application of sunscreen, she had finally accepted that their relationship was over, and had been for a very long time.

"You'd better get some sleep," Hayden said, concerned with the resignation she heard in Emily's voice. "Tomorrow's going to be another long day and you need your rest."

"What about you?"

"I'm exhausted. I'll have no trouble falling asleep."

Emily shifted to get comfortable and the movement sent a searing pain into her thigh. "Ouch, shit that hurt." Hayden's hand landed on her arm, sending a jolt of awareness of how much she wanted Hayden's touch and just how alone they were under the stars.

"What is it?"

Her concern warmed Emily, but at the same time she felt guilty. The bleeding had stopped over an hour ago and Hayden had checked the injury. It looked red and angry, but that was to be expected. Hayden was the one shouldering all the responsibility of getting the four of them to safety, and she was complaining about a little cut on her leg. She made a mental note not to call attention to it again.

"It's nothing," she said. "Just bumped my leg, that's all."

"It's going to be stiff and sore in the morning. You'll have to take it easy."

"I'll be all right."

Emily slid down, curling on her side on the hard floor, using her arm as a pillow. She heard Hayden settle behind her but before she had a chance to dwell on how it would feel if Hayden were curled up against her, she fell asleep.

Listening to the soft sound of Emily's breathing, Hayden wondered if she'd done the right thing stressing that the wound was minor. In this heat with the filthy conditions, infection was almost inevitable, and without antibiotics an infection could grow rapidly worse. Within another day, Emily might not be able to put any weight on her leg. Hayden would carry her the entire way if she had to, but she suspected she would meet with resistance. Emily was strong and would never allow it.

Hayden wondered what to do. She would have to treat the gash somehow, without drugs or equipment. It needed antiseptic, probably stitches, and Emily should have a tetanus shot. Surely the outside world knew about the disaster and aid teams were already arriving. She needed to reach help as soon as possible or the consequences could be dire. Ulceration, gangrene… amputation. Even worse, blood poisoning. Left untreated, a wound like Emily's could be fatal.

She forced herself to stay calm. It was one thing to consider a worst-case scenario, another to make herself crazy with worry. Emily and the children were counting on her, and that meant keeping her fears to herself and making them feel confident. She could have a breakdown another day.

Hayden took several slow, deep breaths and moved in closer to Emily. Carefully, she slid an arm over her waist. She half expected to be pushed away, but Emily didn't stir. Feeling strangely content, Hayden settled against her. For them to meet like this and for her to have the feelings she already had toward this woman was unsettling. But she couldn't afford to overanalyze. She had more important things to do. Like save their lives.

❖

Hayden was jolted awake by a flailing arm. Emily was obviously having a nightmare. She sat up and leaned over her to try to wake her when Emily's elbow connected just above her left eye. It was the same place she was cut during the tsunami and the cut reopened, blood pouring down her face.

"Shit." She cupped her hand to the painful area. Sticky liquid warmed her fingers and she wiped it out of her eye to no avail. More blood simply took its place and she finally closed her eye to the assault.

Emily writhed beside her, moaning and saying things that told Hayden she was dreaming of being in the water again. "No!" she shouted. "Somebody please help me."

Her hands were reaching out like they were when Hayden first saw her. Hayden ached to comfort her, but she had to stanch the flood of blood into her eye. She tore the remaining piece off the bottom of her shirt and pressed it to the cut. Pain shot through her head and a wave of nausea rolled over her. Feeling better after taking several deep breaths, she wrapped the cloth around her head, tying it a tight knot. Her head pounded, but at least the blood had stopped running down her face. She leaned over Emily again, this time keeping an eye out for flying elbows.

Hayden sat up and pulled the sleeping woman into her arms. "Emily, hush, it's just a dream. You're okay. I'm right here." She repeated the soothing words several times before Emily fell back into a deep sleep. Emily cuddled into her like she had been doing it for years, her hand cupping Hayden's breast, her injured leg slightly bent at the knee. They sat that way a long time, Hayden's back against the wall, Emily in her arms, before Hayden finally fell asleep once more.

When she woke a few hours later her eye throbbed and her butt hurt from sitting on the hard floor. During the night Victoria had crawled next to her, placing her head in Hayden's lap. Gently

Hayden smoothed the dark hair away from the little face, and she felt Emily stir. She couldn't see Emily's face but her heart rate increased nonetheless.

Suddenly feeling awkward, she cleared the frog from her throat. "Good morning."

The first evidence of sunrise peeked over the horizon the same instant Hayden spoke, and Emily wasn't sure which was brighter. She wasn't aware when during the night she had moved into Hayden's arms but it felt good. She fit perfectly in her arms and felt cocooned from the world. She was warm, and if not for the ache in her leg and the hard ground, she could stay in Hayden's arms all day.

"Good morning." she replied shyly. She had been watching Hayden stroking Victoria's hair and cheek for several minutes, intrigued by her tenderness toward the children.

Hayden was physically strong, but it was her emotional strength that drew Emily. In the past eighteen hours she had witnessed indescribable destruction, countless bodies and limbs protruding from mud and debris. It was more than Emily could handle, and she'd fought tears and breaking down several times throughout the day. Just when she thought she could not take another step or pass by another body, Hayden would suddenly appear beside her, taking her hand as they continued on. Emily had also taken her turn to carry Victoria most of the day. She was too small to traverse the difficult terrain. Jake was able to maneuver a little better but there were several times when Emily was exhausted from carrying one child or the other that Hayden carried them both. She never once hesitated to offer a hand for support, utter a soothing word, or say something to make the children laugh.

Her mind flashed back to the several times yesterday she had caught herself watching Hayden move effortlessly through the carnage. Her body had unmistakably responded to the sweat gleaming on hard muscles clearly defined by Hayden's sparse clothing. The visceral reaction to Hayden shocked her.

"Sleep good?" Hayden asked.

"You're joking, right?" Emily had discovered early on that Hayden had a wonderful sense of humor. As her laughter filled the quiet morning, Emily was shocked to realize she wanted to wake up to it every morning.

"I think the kids are the only ones who got any kind of decent sleep." Hayden ran a hand over Jake's tangled hair. The boy had crawled up next to his sister and was snoring quietly.

"There's something to be said about the innocence of youth." Emily's relationship with her parents, her breakup with Michelle, and the tsunami were a far cry from the happy ignorance of her younger years. Being a grown-up brought adult problems, challenges, and pleasures. One of those pleasures was how she felt right now in Hayden's arms.

"The innocence of youth," Hayden mused. "I remember one summer I had a lemonade stand. It was really hot and my mother let me use the card table and I practically dragged it the entire way to the sidewalk. I made a little sign, had a full pitcher, a few cups, and I was ready to go. I honestly thought I was going to get rich. I mean, I had the inventory and the advertising, what more did I need? I had what people wanted, it only made sense that they would flock to my stand. I'd have cars lined up and down the street." She chuckled as if the scene were yesterday.

Emily felt Hayden's laugh deep in her chest. "And were they?"

"No, we lived on a dead-end street. Silly me, I think I sold three glasses. One to my mother, one to the next-door neighbor, and one to the mailman. That was my first and only foray into self-employment."

Emily pictured a much younger Hayden sitting in a chair behind her lemonade stand waiting patiently for customers that never came. She felt a pang of sympathy and snuggled closer. "How old were you?"

"Eight."

Her father had been midway through a two-year deployment

to Korea. She and her mother could not accompany him and had remained behind in San Antonio. Their house was on a quiet street in a middle-class neighborhood, but unfortunately there were few children her age on the block. That was okay with Hayden. Her father's career kept them on the move and she had suffered far too many tearful partings from friends she became close to. As a result she kept herself detached enough that she wouldn't get hurt when it was time to pack up and move to another base.

She became a voracious reader of military strategy dating as far back as Napoleon. This made her feel closer to her father when he was away, and their letters were often filled with discussions of battle tactics. Her father had developed her ability to analyze a situation from every angle and think through a course of action. She was grateful for that now.

Hayden tightened her arm around Emily and brushed aside strands of soft brown hair tickling her nose. It felt natural to hold her. They stayed that way for several minutes, neither of them speaking. The sun had risen over the horizon and Hayden watched the rays crawl across the floor. There was no way she could ever have imagined herself with a beautiful woman in her arms, two children practically in her lap, sleeping on a cement floor in the middle of a natural disaster.

The children roused before Hayden could reflect on her feelings any more. A sense of emptiness washed over her when Emily slowly disengaged herself and sat up. Their eyes met and Emily's smile was gentle and warm, if a bit shy. She looked sleepy but sparkling, and she was absolutely beautiful. Hayden wanted to wake up to those vibrant brown eyes every morning. Her thoughts must have been mirrored in her face, because Emily's expression changed. Her pupils darkened and desire flared in her eyes.

The sun chose that moment to break above the horizon and cast its first ray on Emily's face. Hayden stopped breathing. A master photographer could not have staged this image as perfectly as Mother Nature. Emily was the most magnificent woman she had ever seen. The sun spread a radiance on her face that warmed Hayden to her core. She memorized every feature, from the small scar almost completely hidden in her right eyebrow to her softly parted lips, burning the image into her subconscious.

Hayden knew she would remember this moment for the rest of her life.

CHAPTER FIVE

Lunch passed with nothing filling their bellies other than a few sips of the soda they'd found the day before. The children were listless and stumbled so often they could only maintain an erratic pace. After a few frustrating hours, they lay down in the shade created by the only wall left standing of a building destroyed by the water. The youngsters immediately fell asleep and Emily felt her eyes grow heavy. She wasn't sure how long she had slept when she jolted awake by the sound of unfamiliar laughter.

Two men stood over her, one quite a bit heavier than the other. They both wore dirty, tattered T-shirts and no shoes, but it was what she saw in their pants that made Emily's blood run cold. Both men had erections. Their intent was clearly visible in their eyes. Frantically, she looked around for Hayden. She had grown accustomed to her always being nearby and felt vulnerable without her. The children were still sleeping a short distance from her. *My God, the children. Please don't let them see this. Don't let them be hurt.*

Emily struggled to her feet and limped to move protectively in front of them. Her leg ached, the inflammation around the wound making the skin tug painfully. The taller man stepped forward and grabbed her shirt, tearing it as she fought him off. He wrapped a hand around her neck, choking off her scream, and pushed her back against the wall. Emily tried desperately to jerk away, her fingernails scraping skin while the vise on her neck tightened. The man assaulting her screamed something in Thai. His spittle covered her face. Lights flashed behind her eyes and she knew she was on the verge of blacking out when she heard a scream of rage and her attacker's grip relaxed.

He turned just in time to ward off the first blow. Emily was engulfed with relief and fear. Once again, Hayden was rescuing her. She caught a flash of movement as Hayden pivoted and swept the man's feet out from under him. He fell heavily, the breath knocked out of him. The second man charged at Hayden with both fists swinging. Hayden stepped between him and Emily and smoothly blocked the blows, countering with two swift punches of her own. Both connected with the soft cartilage of the man's nose. He screamed, reeling backward, blood pouring down over his lips and chin.

Emily's attacker staggered to his feet with a loud grunt. Before he could refill his lungs, Hayden struck again with a roundhouse kick to the side of his head. He dropped like a rock, unconscious. The second man quickly lost interest in defending his buddy and fled.

Sagging back against the wall, Emily croaked, "Hayden," and reached for her.

But Hayden stood frozen over the unconscious man, her body emanating menace. She was going to kill him. Right here, in front of the children.

"No." Emily stumbled forward. "Hayden, don't."

Hayden jumped when Emily touched her arm. She was ready to strike but immediately dropped her fists when her eyes lifted to Emily's face. She seemed to relax in increments, her muscles releasing the tension that had bulked up her physique during their defense.

"Hayden, it's over. He can't hurt us now." Emily spoke softly, fascinated by Hayden's transformation from warrior to guardian. With each breath that lifted her chest, the rage in her eyes cleared and the softness returned to her naturally rugged face. Her hands opened and closed into tight fists until Emily took hold of them.

Hayden stared down at the strong fingers tightly gripping hers. She felt like a woman at sea thrown a lifeline and being drawn back to safety. The irony of that feeling struck her forcibly. Emily was the one in danger. That indelible image flashed again, of Emily pressed against the wall with that filthy hand around her throat. Thank God she'd heard her cry out.

Hayden forced herself to calm down. She couldn't think about what might have been. Emily needed comfort, and the children awoke looking confused and upset, obviously sensing something was wrong.

She squeezed Emily's hands. "Are you all right?"

"I'm fine. A little shook up, but I'm not hurt. Really, he didn't hurt me."

Hayden searched her eyes, looking for any sign that she was not telling the truth. What she saw tore at her insides. Pain and fear were struggling to surface, but Emily was forcing them to remain at bay. At that moment Hayden realized just how strong Emily was. During the course of her military career, she'd seen men and women trained to withstand the horrors of battle and captivity collapse under less stress than Emily had experienced in the last two days. But Emily was not going to become a victim. She was smart and strong, taking responsibility for herself and those around her. When she was faced with adversity she simply refused to fall apart. Instead she grew stronger.

Hayden knew very little about her, only fragments of her background. She wanted to know more. She wanted to know everything. The thought shocked her. Like everything else that had happened since the wave swept her away, this urge was a first.

❖

"You're very quiet this evening," Emily said.

"Just a little tired, I guess." Hayden finished settling the children on a bed of muddy palm leaves and joined Emily several feet away.

They had stopped for the night next to a partial wall, all that remained of a red brick building Hayden thought she recognized as a small souvenir stand she'd passed a few days ago. If she was right, they were only about a mile from the beach where help surely had arrived by now. They were tired and dehydrated, and if they didn't get Emily's leg looked at, and drinks for the children… Hayden shuddered at the thought, then looked up as she recognized a sound she hadn't heard in days. The birds had returned, and their chirping and squawking were the only other sounds in a world that had fallen eerily silent.

"I keep thinking about what would have happened if I hadn't come back in time." Hayden could not keep her voice completely even.

She was still cursing herself for leaving Emily and the children alone. During their long, slow trek for the rest of the day, she could think of nothing except "what if?" Anguish swept over her every time she let her mind play out the possibilities. She realized she'd been brooding and uncommunicative for hours, unable to give voice to the fears that plagued her.

Holding everything in, being strong, keeping up a confident front—that was how she handled a crisis. Cool and calm was what she was trained for. In her world, people expected self-control, and no one would read anything into long silences and lack of chitchat. But Emily was a civilian. From her uneasy glances, Hayden could tell she wasn't sure how to respond.

She rubbed the tight muscles in the back of her neck and tried to come up with a casual remark that would restore normality. "Damn, I think I've pulled a muscle carrying the kids."

Emily moved behind her immediately. "Here, let me."

The response was not exactly the routine sympathy Hayden had expected, and the first touch of Emily's hands sent a shock through her. "You don't need to," she began, but Emily was determined.

"Relax. Let me take care of you for a change." Her strong fingers gently kneaded the tight muscles in the back of Hayden's neck, working magic on each knotted cord.

Hayden made herself relax, dropping her chin to her chest, suddenly realizing just how keyed up she was. She closed her eyes, melting into the sensation.

Emily's voice was soothing but insistent. "Stop thinking about it. You did what had to be done."

"I shouldn't have left you. Not even to go scout. I should have waited till everyone woke up." Hayden leaned into each stroke. "I keep thinking about what would have happened if I hadn't come back in time."

"But you did, that's all that matters."

"Those men, there was no doubt what—" She stopped, choking at the thought. They were still out there, and part of her wanted to hunt them down and break their necks.

Emily frowned, feeling Hayden stiffen again. They both knew what would have happened to her this afternoon if Hayden hadn't returned when she did. Emily suppressed a shiver. She would have been raped. For some reason, Hayden was more disturbed by the possibility than she was.

"Nothing happened," she said firmly, wanting to put the whole episode out of her mind. "You can't feel guilty over this. It is what it is, and most importantly, what it wasn't." She continued pressing her thumbs into the muscles on the side of Hayden's neck while her hands slipped further down the front of her throat and across her collarbones. Back and forth she went, each trip slightly lower than the last. Hayden's breath caught and Emily leaned over and whispered in her ear, "Relax."

Hayden's skin was hot under her fingertips, and she felt the shallow rise and fall of her chest. Her breathing had changed. Emily watched her fists slowly close and knew the effect she was having. Sometime in the last few minutes the massage had switched from soothing to sensuous, and Hayden's reactions set off explosions in Emily's body. She hadn't intended to seduce Hayden, but she certainly wanted her now.

She wanted her here and now in these primitive conditions under the stars. Hayden excited her, challenged her, and brought out in her feelings she didn't know she had. Hayden was her savior, her protector, and her hero. She fleetingly thought of Michelle and just as fast the thought left, no longer an important factor in her life.

Emily's hands began to shake and she couldn't take her eyes off the vein throbbing on the side of Hayden's neck. She wanted to taste Hayden's skin and feel the life pulsing under her tongue. Finally she couldn't wait any longer and lowered her head.

Hayden moaned when Emily's lips touched her skin. They were as soft and warm as she imagined they would be. She'd known immediately when the massage turned from therapeutic to something much more, and had done nothing to resist. Emily's fingers were soft and her skin was on fire. Stroke after stroke Emily fanned the flames, caressing her neck, whispering in her ear, dropping light, moist kisses. A shiver ran down the length of Hayden's body and curled her toes from the skill of Emily's tongue. She turned her head and was rewarded with Emily's lips seeking hers.

Passion and pent-up desire exploded at the contact and she pulled Emily into her lap. Their kisses were hot and fevered, Hayden wanting more than their lips would allow. She couldn't get enough of the feel of Emily's body, and she broke their kiss long enough to drag Emily's shirt over her head and toss it aside. She cupped Emily's breasts and deepened their kiss, tweaking an erect nipple. Emily moaned into her mouth, letting their breath mix into one.

Hayden was out of control with desire for her. Fighting back the familiar tingling of impending orgasm, she lay her down and covered her body with her own. Emily lifted a leg and wrapped it around Hayden's, effectively trapping her where she was.

Hayden groaned and pressed her hips into Emily, seeking release. A scuffling noise made her hesitate. She looked over her shoulder at the sleeping children. She didn't want them to wake up and see what they were doing but she didn't want to move any farther away from them either.

"The kids."

Emily's heart exploded. Hayden's concern for Jake and Victoria touched her deeply, and she cupped her face in her hands. "They're out for the count. I don't think anything will wake them."

She needed to feel naked skin against her own and grabbed the back of Hayden's shirt, tugging it over her head. Hayden's kisses were hot; her hands were everywhere. She slid her hand down the front of Emily's shorts and Emily arched in anticipation of her touch and was not disappointed. Hayden grasped her firmly and Emily bit her tongue. Hayden ground her hips again and Emily smiled at the reaction she caused. She expected Hayden to kiss her again, but she froze at the sound of a murmur from several feet away.

Emily glanced at the children again. "Trust me, Hayden, they won't wake up."

Hayden looked deeply into Emily's eyes. It was dark, very dark. The only light coming from the full moon cast an iridescent glow on Emily's face. She was beautiful, and Hayden did trust her, with everything she had. She kissed her again, and the way Emily responded to her touch was the most exhilarating experience she'd ever had. She often had women in this same position, but this time it was different. She wanted to please Emily, to give her as much pleasure as she was receiving. Hayden wanted her as hot and out of control as she was, and she desperately needed to touch her. She slid her hand further. Her fingers were immediately coated with warm wetness.

Emily's center was soft and smooth and Hayden moaned at the sensation. She parted the wet lips with her fingers, and a rush of Emily's desire flowed into her hand. She ran her fingers through the liquid and slid them slowly over Emily's clit several times. She memorized every smell, every whimper, every twitch of flesh around her fingers. When Emily moaned she increased her pace.

Hayden sensed how close to orgasm Emily was and backed off just enough to stay poised in the moment for as long as she could. She wanted to go slow and explore every inch of Emily. She wanted to remember this moment for as long as she lived. But their passion was as carnal as the nature that had thrown them together. Her senses were magnified by the raw hunger of the woman in her arms and their desperate circumstances. It was as if the combination of the two were coming together in the affirmation of life.

Emily lifted her hips higher and grabbed Hayden tightly. She could feel the beginnings of her orgasm rise again. She wanted to wait so this intensity would last longer, but there was nothing she could do to stop it. She grasped Hayden as first one, then a second orgasm tore through her. Stars as bright as those sparkling down on them beat her eyelids, accompanied by a kaleidoscope of colors. She was soaring, her body as high as the clouds, Hayden the solid earth beneath her.

This was the most powerful orgasm she'd ever experienced, a force that swept through her, washing away all that had led up to this extraordinary moment. She felt reborn, new and tender in Hayden's arms. When she slowly emerged from the fog of orgasm, her blood still raced and her body still quivered.

Hayden watched in amazement as Emily's breathing slowed. A cloak of contentment draped over her. A strong, beautiful woman lay in her arms and Hayden wanted, no, she needed for her to come again. Slowly she moved her hand, and Emily's body twitched in response. It took very little to push her over the edge once more. Hayden held her close as wave after wave of pleasure racked her body. She was beautiful. Her little moans and soft whispers only heightened Hayden's arousal. She felt strong and powerful but soft and tender at the same time.

Making love with Emily was more than she had imagined it would be. It was intense, then sweet and gentle. One minute she wanted to own her, the next to treasure her. Emily's body was like a sheet of music. Every place was a different note, a different beat all coming together in a beautiful song she played over and over again. She wanted to give her everything she had.

A light sheen of sweat covered Emily's body as Hayden set out to explore as much of her as she could. She glanced at the children who, true to Emily's word, were sleeping soundly. Hayden felt slightly self-conscious making love to Emily so close to the kids, but she couldn't help herself. The passion had been released from the bottle, and it was not going back in until she had her fill. If she ever had her fill.

Emily felt as if she were floating in a sea of pleasure. Hayden's lips and hands and tongue were everywhere. One after another, her senses exploded in ways she never thought imaginable. She arched her neck as Hayden's tongue sensuously licked the lone bead of sweat that slid down her collarbone. Quick kisses and soft nips followed as Hayden explored first her left breast, then her right. She grasped the back of Hayden's neck, encouraging her wandering mouth to settle on her nipple, and a loud moan of pleasure escaped her lips. She had a direct nerve from her nipple to her clit, and Hayden quickly discovered this when she came again. Of course, it helped that her fingers were doing magical things between Emily's legs. She had never been loved so thoroughly. Every nerve was touched, aroused, soothed, and aroused again. The world around her was crystal clear, her senses heightened by their life-threatening situation, the stars overhead, and Hayden's skillful lovemaking.

It was when exhaustion threatened to overwhelm her that Emily finally grabbed Hayden's wrist and softly whispered for her to stop. Her legs felt like lead and her arms like rubber. She barely had enough strength to keep her eyes open. Calmness settled on her, replacing stormy passion, and she smiled.

Despite the post-orgasmic lassitude that swept over her, she wanted to touch Hayden, to return the pleasure she had received. The thought gave her the energy she desperately needed, and she rolled Hayden onto her back. Lazy eyes as black as the night sky stared up at her, and Emily looked deep into the soul of the woman who had saved her life. Hayden's heart beat solidly beneath hers, a staccato of rhythm matching her own. The intensity of her feelings momentarily frightened her, and Hayden must have sensed it as she started to speak. Emily didn't give her the chance. She covered Hayden's lips in a deep kiss and made a silent promise to herself. Whatever happened, she would never forget this night.

Hayden let Emily take the lead as their tongues jousted back and forth, teasing and exploring. Emily's body on top of hers was as light as a feather, yet more than capable of providing the right amount of pressure to all the right places. Hayden basked in her attention, focusing on the sensations created by her touch. Once she had the presence of mind to glance at the children, she relaxed when they hadn't moved.

Time after time Hayden came, each climax stronger than the last. Emily teased her, bringing her to the brink of climax, then backing off just enough to make her moan with frustration. Her body screamed with the sensations Emily brought out in her. Some were coaxed and others exploded of their own free will. Finally, when exhaustion claimed them both, they collapsed into each other's arms, unable to resist as sleep closed in.

Not a word had been spoken between them.

CHAPTER SIX

"There's people alive over here."

A voice woke Hayden and she struggled to climb out of the fog of slumber. Her left side was warmer than her right and something tickled her nose. She felt lethargic, her limbs heavy like they always were after a night of sex. Her eyes shot open. *After a night of sex.* Emily lay in her arms, her uninjured leg thrown across Hayden's, a tan hand resting lightly over her breast. Just before dawn she and Emily had somehow managed to put their clothes back on before falling back into the sleep of exhaustion.

Any other time, Hayden would have savored the moment, lying here with a stunning woman knowing they'd made love all night. But she didn't get the opportunity. She heard the familiar sound of boots on the ground and a movement to her right caught her eye. A man and a woman dressed in khaki shorts and white shirts stood looking down at her. For an instant Hayden flashed back to the two men who had attempted to assault Emily the day before, but the bright red cross on their shirts registered like a beacon.

"Oh, thank God," she whispered, almost ready to weep.

"Are you two okay?" the woman asked. "We're from the Red Cross."

Hayden could hardly find words. "For the most part, we're

okay. I'm Hayden Caldwell, U.S. Army Joint Readiness Training Center."

She felt slightly ridiculous, lying on the ground in filthy clothes, cuddling a woman but sounding like she was reporting for duty. The Red Cross pair seemed thrilled.

"U.S. Army. Excellent," said the man. "We need all the help we can get. Are you healthy?"

"You want to enlist me?" With a dazed laugh, Hayden began to sit up, sorry to have to force Emily out of her deep sleep.

"If you can walk in a straight line, we can use you," the women said. "The situation is…unimaginable."

"I'm okay. A few scrapes here and there, but I was lucky." She indicated Emily's cut. "This woman has a pretty deep gash on her leg that's gotten infected, but some medical attention will take care of it. The children aren't hurt but they are hungry and thirsty."

"Come on, let's get you into the truck," the man said. "We're heading back to the hotel."

"What hotel?" Hayden stood and extended her hand to Emily, who was now fully awake.

"The Lam Koh. It was the least damaged and it's been set up as a temporary hospital."

Emily stumbled as she got up. She moaned and fell into Hayden's arms. "Fuck," she murmured under her breath. The pain in her leg was excruciating. It had only hurt a little last night but, then again, all she'd felt was orgasm after orgasm in Hayden's arms. Now she could hardly put any weight on it.

"What was the extent of the tsunami?" Hayden asked. "Were other places affected?"

"Everything was destroyed up and down the coastline," the man replied. "There's not much left standing near the beach, but the buildings farther inland are okay. Some of the survivors are saying the wave was at least fifty feet tall."

"Jesus." Hayden lifted Emily into her arms as the other Red Cross worker crouched down by the children.

She followed the man to a flatbed truck, bothered that she hadn't had an opportunity to talk to Emily. There was no time now, and she'd have an audience of aid workers and survivors if she tried to have a serious conversation on the way to the hotel. The truck was filled with people with injuries, some serious. She lifted Emily up into the helping arms of another Red Cross volunteer, then the children were handed up.

"Aren't you coming with us?" Emily asked when Hayden didn't immediately climb into the truck.

"I'm not hurt, and there isn't enough room for me."

Emily instantly lifted Victoria onto her lap. "Yes, there is. Please."

Hayden almost gave in to the frightened look on her face, but if the truck had to stop for a seriously injured person between here and the hotel, she would only have to give up her place anyway. She took Emily's hand. "I'm fine. I'll help out, searching around here until the next truck comes along. Don't worry, I'll find you. It's not a big island."

She was not going to abandon her. They had gone through too much together, and after last night—well, after last night, Hayden never wanted to let her go. She gave Emily a reassuring smile and signaled the driver to leave.

As Emily released her hand, the truck jerked into gear and started to move. Complete panic pinched her face. "Come as soon as you can," she urged. "I don't want to…lose you."

"Don't worry," Hayden called after her. "That can't happen."

❖

The next thirty minutes were a blur for Emily. The increasing pain in her leg pushed any other thought from her mind. The ride was not a smooth one, the truck lurching and weaving in every direction as it made its way back to the beach. Several times they stopped and picked up more survivors, and both children sat on her lap to make room. She hated that she hadn't had a chance to say anything to Hayden before they were swept away by the rescue team. There was so much she wanted to say to her. For God's sake, she hadn't even given Hayden her last name.

Emily blushed. She wasn't the type who slept with women before a proper introduction, at least not since her early twenties. In college she'd had more than her share of sexual interludes. She'd had lots of friends and spent most weekends getting drunk and getting laid. How she managed to pull out a solid A average and stay ahead in her accelerated classes was still a mystery to her. It wasn't until one specific spring break in Mazatlan that she'd finally realized that her sexual adventures might someday get her in serious trouble.

One morning, she woke with a terrible headache and what she could have sworn was an entire box of Kleenex in her mouth. When she pulled herself together enough to look around, she had no idea where she was and even less of an idea who was lying beside her. The woman was pretty enough, with dark hair tumbling across her bare shoulders, but then there was the other woman, lying on her side, also sharing the bed. She said something in Spanish that Emily did not understand, but the tangled sheets and the lustful look in her eyes told her they were not strangers. Maybe last night they were, but definitely not that morning.

Ever since she'd awakened with two women and a white powdery substance on the bedside table, Emily had vowed she would never go to bed with a woman that she didn't know at least fairly well. But making love with Hayden was different. Sure, they hadn't shared life histories. She could have been a criminal, a con artist, or one of the high-class call girls that frequented the resorts on Khao Lak. But Emily doubted Hayden was any of those. She knew nothing about her, yet they had an almost immediate connection. She'd read numerous accounts of people thrown into life-or-death situations who had come together sexually. It was as if the only thing that mattered was feeling alive, sharing the bond of life with another human being.

Her senses had been on high alert since the tsunami, and she knew Hayden felt the same. Their heightened reactions to each other were not surprising. Natural chemistry and the horrific conditions around them were as combustible as gasoline and fire. A flicker of disappointment burned in the back of her throat. Was that all? Had they simply come together in the night due to circumstances, or was something more profound at work? She sighed and held Victoria tightly. She was too tired to make any sense of her own emotions. All she could do was get through the next few days, and then she and Hayden would talk.

When they finally arrived at their destination, she handed the children down and slid off the back of the truck, falling in a heap on the ground. She was unable to walk and was finally helped by a pair of strong, dark hands. She passed the children over to a Red Cross organizer after giving their names and explaining what little she knew about them. She felt hot and weak, almost nauseous. Hunger was taking its toll, she supposed, and shock. Now that she was safe, she could almost feel the adrenaline draining out of her. The stranger practically carried her into the hotel as gently as he could and deposited her on a chair in a hall. People milled about, some covered in blood, others wrapped in bandages, and some with no visible sign of injury at all. But regardless of their physical condition, they all had the same dazed expression in their eyes. They had all witnessed more than anyone should and probably wondered, as she did, why they had lived when so many were taken.

Tears rolled down her cheeks, blending with beads of sweat. There was no electricity, of course, so no air-conditioning. The hotel lobby was like a sauna. She mopped moisture off her forehead and daydreamed about taking a cold shower. She wondered if there was some drinking water somewhere. Her leg burned, sharp pierces of pain up and down her leg. The pressure near the wound was so intense Emily thought her skin would explode if touched. Dark streaks radiated in every direction from the cut. Thick yellowish fluid oozed from the wound unchecked.

Her throat hurt when she swallowed and her vision was getting fuzzy. Her head throbbed and she reached out a hand to steady herself, but there was nothing for her to grab onto to stop from sliding out of the chair onto the floor.

A man floated toward her, out of focus. Emily blinked several times, a hard, cool surface pressing against her face.

"Are you all right?"

Emily felt like she was emerging from a deep dive and could see the surface but wasn't quite there yet.

"Ma'am, are you all right?"

It took a moment for her to be able to respond. The stranger helped her sit up and it was then Emily realized she must have fainted. Her cheek hurt and she winced when she touched it.

"Everything will be okay." The man helped her sit up and put a plastic bottle in her hand. "Have a drink."

"I need a doctor," Emily said croaking out the words from her parched lips.

"You'll see one. There are a lot of patients."

Emily looked around, slowly, so as not to pass out again. Every breath she took was an effort, and even minor movements caused her head to roll. She fought off the blackness that threatened to swallow her again. She was so tired she wanted to simply give in to sleep, but she knew she had to remain conscious for as long as possible.

"Okay." She wrenched the cap off and drank in great, thankful gulps, the liquid spilling down her chin and onto her tattered clothes.

"You'll be fine," the man assured her.

"I need to lie down." The people around her were starting to float through the thick air.

If the man hadn't held on to Emily, she would have slid onto the floor again. She moaned as a wave of pain shot from her leg and she started to shake. She wondered where the children were. She should have asked where she could find them after the paperwork was done. The next time she saw an aid worker she would find out. Closing her eyes, she reminded herself that they were someone else's children and not her responsibility. But she had a feeling Hayden would be angry with her for not taking better care of them.

The thought agitated her and she started crying again, but this time she couldn't stop. She wanted Hayden to come and find her. Surely the next truck couldn't be far away. Hayden would save her again. She would come to her rescue, get her the treatment she needed and the children back to their family. Hayden was her hero, and Emily knew she would never let her down.

Hayden followed the trail left by the aid workers and an hour later began to see more and more evidence of the destruction. There was barely enough room for the severely injured on the next truck she saw, so she chose instead to walk. The workers gave her two bottles of water and said it was about a mile to the beach. A mile? Was that as far as they'd needed to go? Hayden had originally estimated they were only a few miles from the beach where they were swept away, but since they'd walked for almost two days it was much farther than that. How could she have been so wrong? Surely they hadn't walked in circles the entire time? She was well trained and knew they had been walking in a consistent direction, at least as much as they could. Nothing had looked familiar, but then again, nothing could. The tsunami had obliterated everything in its path, and what it didn't destroy it made almost unrecognizable. They must have been carried miles inland by the force of the water. Either that or they had to walk so far around the destruction that time and distance increased their journey.

Without the children in tow she made good time, but the walk was the worst of her life. Bloated corpses littered the ground. Many of the dead were clad in swimming suits or shorts and T-shirts, their flesh burnt by the sun. Bodies hung from the trees where rising waters deposited them in branches like debris. Palm trees lay flat on the ground, broken furniture littered the landscape. A railroad track was twisted like a corkscrew as far as she could see. The stench of decay was strong, and the scene only got worse as she approached the beachfront hotels, or what was left of them. Roads that were not blocked with debris were jammed with homemade stretchers made out of bed sheets and people sporting cuts, bruises, bloodied bandages, and broken limbs. All wore the mask of shock. Grieving families sobbed over dead and dying family members. Some vehicles were wrapped around the few trees that remained, while others were smashed and stacked on top of each other like Matchbox cars.

Only the shells remained of buildings that once stood tall and proud in the tropical paradise. Support beams reached into the air like lone pillars in a war zone. A boat teetered precariously in what remained of a third-floor hotel room, its rear end protruding over the balcony. Hayden walked slowly by a pool filled with brackish green water. A small tourist bus floated in the deep end, a torn beach umbrella blocked the steps. She shuddered to think what was in the dark water that couldn't be seen.

Farther and farther down the beach Hayden walked, sidestepping blocks of cement, piles of wood, an assortment of shoes, a schoolbook, a tourist guide, and of course, bodies. Looters rifled through the pockets of the dead searching for anything valuable they could sell or barter for much-needed supplies. As far as she could see, the façade of every building had been shorn off by the force of the water, leaving only the shells of what once was.

A soft breeze ruffled her hair. The sea to her left was calm, giving no indication of its anger and destruction two days earlier. Determined more than ever to help in any way she could, she headed for the village square but was unprepared for what she saw there. Row after row of bodies covered in white sheets lay neatly side by side. Men were spraying what smelled like disinfectant on the bodies. Their only protection was gloves and masks. The treatment was necessary to contain the spread of disease, but the mechanical way the bodies were sprayed made it all seem surreal.

Inside the hotels that were still standing, cots lined every available space, leaving only a maze of narrow isles to walk. Dozens of people stood patiently in line a pay phone wearing the same dazed expressions she had seen all morning. Another line was for water, with people holding buckets, bottles, and anything that would hold fresh water. A motor scooter almost ran her over in its haste to get somewhere.

The devastation and destruction was unlike anything Hayden could ever imagine. She would forever be changed by this experience. The everyday trials of life that she and her friends knew were trivial compared to this. Life was short, everything you owned and dreamed of could be ripped away in a heartbeat. Life was precious, and as she walked through the crowded streets, Hayden vowed never to take it for granted again.

CHAPTER SEVEN

"Colonel? Colonel Caldwell?"

She spun in the direction of the voice calling her by her rank. Someone here knew who she was. She didn't immediately recognize the man approaching her, but his regulation haircut and confident walk told her he was military.

"Jeffers, ma'am. Lieutenant Bruce Jeffers. Are you all right, ma'am?"

"Yes I am, Lieutenant." Hayden had no idea where or when she had encountered the guy, but she had a good memory for faces, and his square jaw and intense gray eyes were familiar.

"You gave a talk to a bunch of us guys a few years ago at Fort Huachuca in Arizona, ma'am."

Hayden didn't even bother to pretend she knew the young officer from that event. After twenty-three years in the Army she had met thousands of people, and there was no way she could remember them all. Instinctively, she slipped into officer mode. "Were you deployed here? Where is your CO?"

"No, ma'am. I wasn't deployed here. My wife and I came for our honeymoon. We were supposed to fly home today. I guess we won't be going anywhere for a while."

A badly injured woman passed in front of them, bleeding profusely from her head. Returning her attention to the chaos,

Hayden asked, "Where are they taking the injured?" She had no idea where Emily was and desperately wanted to find her.

"Everywhere, ma'am. The hospital was badly damaged, so the aid workers have been situating them at the hotels that weren't hit. A lot of folks have headed up into the hills in case of aftershocks and another tidal wave."

Aftershocks were common after a major earthquake. Hayden wondered if another tsunami was possible. The prospect was terrifying, and how would anyone know? There had been no warning for the wave that struck. "Do you know if any have been recorded?"

"None that caused the motherfucker that made this mess."

Hayden ignored the man's profanity because she could hardly disagree. "Is the American embassy in Bangkok in operation?" The embassy would be coordinating relief workers and emergency supplies.

"Yes, ma'am, the ambassador has set up in one of the hotels. Land lines are down, as you can imagine, and only a few cell phones are working. It's been nothing but chaos since it hit. Nobody seems to be in charge. Christ, where's the National Guard when you need them."

"Show me where the ambassador is," Hayden ordered.

"This way, ma'am," Lieutenant Jeffers replied without hesitation.

They stepped around a man and woman holding hands seated on the ground, and Jeffers's initial words came back to her. "Is your wife all right?"

"Scared shitless like the rest of us, but yes, ma'am, she is, thank you. She's an officer's wife. She knows what that means."

Hayden immediately thought of Emily and how she would make an outstanding officer's wife. A snapshot of Emily on her arm clad in a stunning black dress and herself in full dress uniform walking into the officer's ball flashed in her mind. Emily would be the most beautiful woman in the room.

The crowds grew as they walked, and a sense of desperation

hung in the air. It was almost impossible for them to get any closer to the hotel where the ambassador had established a satellite embassy. People were in various states of dress, some with shoes, most without. She heard snippets of conversation as they weaved their way through the throngs of people. Most were talking about how they had lost everything in the flood. No one had any money, passports, or any other form of identification. They had no way of proving who they were or calling their loved ones back home to tell them they had survived.

It took some convincing, but Hayden was finally allowed to see the ambassador. Ralph Boyce was in his early fifties with more hair on his face than on his head. Sweat beaded on the top of his bald pate and his face was flushed from the heat. He looked annoyed when his assistant escorted her in.

"Ambassador Boyce, I'm Lieutenant Colonel Hayden Caldwell, Army." Hayden extended her hand. Boyce gave her the once-over from head to toe before tentatively shaking her hand. "I know it's difficult to believe, Ambassador, but like everybody else, I was here on vacation. I was swept away by the water and just now made it back into town. How can I help you, what do you need?"

Boyce looked at her skeptically as if she was an angel sent from heaven with mortal powers. "Colonel, if you have any clout with our government, I wish you'd get them on the stick and get us some goddamned help down here. Tens of thousands of people are dead, hundreds more in danger of disease, there is limited fresh water, and where there is, the lines are over a mile long. Four people have been stabbed when people tried to steal their water buckets."

Hayden had seen signs of unrest as she came into the city, but what surprised her the most was what she hadn't seen. Nowhere was there evidence of the American military, or any military assistance, for that matter. The locals were doing their best to control the crowds and deal with the dead, but the situation was a powder keg ready to explode.

Boyce rubbed eyes bloodshot with fatigue. "Sorry for that. I haven't slept in two days. "What I need you to do, Colonel, is muster up some able-bodied citizens with strong stomachs and get a search party to the beaches from here north." He pointed to a spot on a well-worn map spread out on the top of the table. "Bodies are everywhere, floating in the water, and starting to wash up on the beaches. We've got to get them rounded up and buried before typhoid or cholera or some other devastating disease takes over. The Thais have focused on locating survivors, but we've got to control the spread of disease."

"I'll take care of it, Ambassador. One other thing." For the first time in her life, Hayden's personal interest took precedence over her professional duty. "Was the airport damaged? Are medical flights making it in and out?"

"Yes, they're starting to evacuate the most seriously injured the day after tomorrow."

Hayden was relieved. Infection had started in the cut on Emily's leg, and she didn't want to think what would happen if she didn't get treatment soon. If it got too bad, she would be sent back to the States for further treatment. "That's good news, sir. I'll report back to you as soon as I know something concrete."

A wave of relief crossed Boyce's face as she shook his hand. Hayden didn't know exactly how she was going to do it, but she did know that she had a duty and an obligation to fulfill.

Nothing was easy about this. The recovery of bodies and body parts was something Hayden hoped she would never have to do again. She and Jeffers rounded up thirty-five volunteers, including twelve fellow military personnel also on Phuket for vacation, and set about the gruesome detail.

The bodies that had been washed into the ocean when the water receded had been submerged for two days, subjected to the forces of Mother Nature. Bodies that looked perfectly intact as they floated on the surface were often missing eyes, lips, and fingertips where fish had eaten them away. Hayden was not prepared, and when she turned the first corpse over she staggered backward and heaved what little was left in her stomach into the salt water.

Bloated arms and legs exploded in the recovery team's hands when they pulled the bodies onto the shore. Those already onshore were dragged further inland, so they would not be carried out in high tide. In a feeble attempt to keep the smell and bodily fluids from getting on their skin, Hayden had ordered everyone to wear masks or something over their faces. Several times she saw a dead woman or child that reminded her of Emily or Jake, and her heart broke for the victims and their families. But at least those who claimed the bodies would know the disposition of their loved one and would be able to bury their family member and have closure. Thousands of others had been pulled out to sea or buried under yards of mud. There would never be a way to know how many people were lost, without a trace. Everywhere she looked, bodies were floating in the water, lying lifeless in the sand, trapped in debris, or wrapped around the trees that remained. Staring at the horizon, Hayden said a silent prayer for each one of them.

The sky glowed red and orange, its colors trickling into the water on the horizon. She sat in the sand, exhausted, as she watched the sun slowly set. The waves were calm, gently breaking and sliding over the top of the sand like silk over the thigh of a beautiful woman. She could not imagine a scene so peaceful was capable of such destruction.

The next morning Hayden woke before dawn. She had told Ambassador Boyce the previous night that her team would resume the recovery at 9:00 a.m., giving her a little time to search the aid stations for Emily and the children. She had refused the ambassador's invitation to have one of the few available rooms in the hotel, preferring to sleep with the other volunteers. She admired her team for their dedication and self-sacrifice when most had family members on the island and were trying to get home themselves. She had everyone's names and would be sending letters of commendation to their commanding officers.

She approached the first aid station confident she would find Emily. If not here, at one of the others. According to the ambassador, the first medical flights weren't scheduled to depart until tomorrow, and she would find Emily before then.

Dozens of sheets of paper with name after name were pinned up on large boards at every aid station. Pictures were identified with numbers of the dead or unconscious and those children too young to say their name. Wall after wall was covered with photographs of the missing.

Hayden didn't spend any time looking at the pictures. Emily was conscious when she'd put her on the truck, and there was no indication she would not be able to tell the medical staff who she was. The names were listed in alphabetical order, and she ran her finger down the list searching for Emily's.

After visiting eight aid stations and temporary hospitals, Hayden was frantic with worry. There was no trace of Emily, and no sign of recognition on the weary faces of the volunteers who listened to her description. Her steps were more hurried and desperate with each room she entered, and she scoured the rows of injured with increasing despair. She felt like a mouse in a maze, searching for the right tunnel to get to the cheese she knew must be somewhere. With every dead end, she grew more despondent.

She felt a connection with Emily that she'd never known with another woman. In part it was due to the heightened emotions of their ordeal, but Hayden refused to dismiss her feelings on that basis alone. Emily meant something to her. They had made love that was mixed with passion, desire, lust, fear, and joy at being alive. Hayden couldn't leave without saying good-bye. With a heavy heart, she pushed open the door to the hospital and stepped outside. Her sharp mind was uncharacteristically muddied and she couldn't think clearly. Emily was not here and she had to keep looking until she was forced to abandon her search for the day.

A blast of hot, muggy air hit her face and she immediately started to sweat. People were milling about and the unmistakable stench of death still hung in the air. The rows of bodies grew as more victims of the tsunami were discovered. Hayden's step faltered as she approached several rows of bodies smaller than the ones she had just passed. She hoped that Jake and Victoria had been located by their family, and said a quiet prayer for those in front of her who had not.

Emily lay drenched in sweat on the hard cot. By the time the doctor had been able to see her, her leg was horribly infected. She fought through the fog of consciousness and opened her eyes. The ceiling was cracked and the paint had started to chip along the jagged line. If she stared at it too long, the line would start to spin and disappear as she lost consciousness.

Finally, she was awake when one of the nurses was taking her vital signs. "Where am I?" Her voice cracked and her throat burned.

"You're in Phuket, in one of the hospitals." The nurse shined a light in her eyes. "Do you remember what happened?"

"There was a tsunami. I was washed…" Emily started to cough. Her head pounded.

"Okay, that's enough. Relax and take a few deep breaths. You got a pretty bad cut on your leg. It got infected and you're a pretty sick lady."

"My leg?"

"You're going to be fine. You'll have a nasty scar, but we caught the infection in time. It's going to take a while for you to fully recover, but you'll be up and about before you know it."

"How long have I been here?" Emily asked, having no sense of time. She couldn't remember being put in this bed.

"Well, you were here when I arrived, and that was two days ago."

Two days or longer. What happened? Suddenly it all came back to her. The water, the rescue, Jake and little Victoria, Hayden, the night they spent together. Did Hayden make it back? Had she been looking for her? She needed to know.

"Is anybody looking for me?" she managed to croak out before another coughing fit took over.

"Not that I'm aware of. Have you been separated from someone?"

Emily wasn't sure how to answer the nurse's cautious question. Obviously she was probing carefully, suspecting someone close to her might have been swept away. "Not exactly. I mean, yes. I was rescued by a woman. We were separated when the Red Cross picked us up."

"Well, I'm sure she'll reconnect," the nurse said. "You were able to give us your name before you passed out, and according to your chart your parents were contacted. You're going home on tomorrow's flight."

Emily's head spun. Hayden hadn't come looking for her. She'd said she would. Her parents were coming? No, she was going home. Home? To Michelle? She didn't want to go home to Michelle. Michelle was not home anymore. Hayden was home. Hayden was safe and warm and strong. Thought after thought swam in her head, and she tried to get up but collapsed back onto the pillow and fell into exhausted sleep again.

All the trucks looked alike. Hayden could not remember which truck had picked up Emily and the children. Hell, she was so relieved they had been rescued she barely remembered what the driver looked like. She had to find the truck. She had to talk to the driver. He would know where he took Emily.

Everywhere she went the stench of death and decay permeated the air. The grocery stores had no electricity to keep food fresh, and water-damaged meat and produce were a haven for flies. For God's sake, it had been three days since they had been rescued and five days since the actual tsunami, and some people still didn't have fresh water. Ambassador Boyce told her that relief supplies were making their way inland, but progress was slow due to the broken terrain and lack of undamaged vehicles. Those trucks that could get through were still searching for survivors.

Her recovery team had been disbanded, the volunteers able to go home eager to begin the new year with the devastation behind them. The only one who remained was Lieutenant Jeffers, and that was partly because his wife Susan was a nurse and had volunteered to help in one of the clinics. Hayden had described Emily to her, even down to the birthmark on the left side of her lower back. She was desperate to find Emily, and at this point she didn't care who knew what.

She hitched a ride with one of the aid workers who headed back to his base camp for more supplies. She must have asked eight or nine people if they had knew which truck she was looking for or who the driver might have been. She ignored the looks she received from people as she went from driver to driver asking questions. The more places she looked, the more places there were to look. The more people she asked, the more despondent she became. Finally, after scouring what felt like the entire country for several more days, Hayden admitted to herself that Emily was gone.

She had never met a woman like her and suspected she never would again.

Chapter Eight

Four Months Later
Fort Tanner Army Base
Braxton, Alabama, April 2005

"Get your fucking hands off me!"

Hayden heard the expletive before she saw the speaker. Her head started to pound. She had left standing orders to be called if and when the protesters arrived, and when the notification came she was up to her elbows in dirt. Military bases up and down the coast were the target of a band of activists protesting President Bush's decision to send more troops into Iraq. The protesters were generally peaceful, but lately they'd started crossing over into the bases, where they were arrested for trespassing. Hayden had a suspicion her base was next.

"I said let me go."

Hayden quickly checked that the military police under her command were not mishandling the protestor, then turned her attention to the crowd. A group of men and women, mostly in their thirties, were milling around the guard shack carrying signs and placards. So far only one had stepped over the white line onto the base, and she was the one currently swearing at the officer.

Hayden tipped her head slightly, the brim of her hat shielding her eyes from the glaring sun. The protester was sitting on a metal folding chair under the awning that was being used as a temporary holding area. Her hands were handcuffed behind her back, the position confirming, without a doubt, her gender. Hayden's hands didn't tingle and her crotch didn't throb at the sight of the perfectly formed breasts like they would have before Khao Lak. Before Emily.

Four months had passed since Hayden had returned from Thailand, and she had not once looked at another woman. The other lesbians on the base were pissed, and Hayden knew her friends worried over her change in behavior. They made vague references to trauma and dropped hints about long-term therapy, but Hayden reassured them that she was just not interested.

When she'd first returned, Emily had occupied her thoughts most of her days and all of her nights. Hayden often dreamed there would be a knock at her door and Emily would be waiting on the other side. But that could never happen. Emily only knew her first name, and with all the places to live in the world, Hayden doubted they were neighbors.

She tuned in with half an ear as the officer began to question the woman. The rest of the protesters had lost their verbal punch when their friend was arrested. She was obviously the leader, and her flock was left wandering aimlessly around, faced with the decision to follow their leader in solidarity or to leave before they, too, were arrested. From the diminishing numbers, most were choosing the latter. Their leader was brimming with attitude. Hayden caught a few fragments of the conversation with the arresting MP.

"Yeah, yeah. I know the drill. Anything I say can and will be used against me… Just finish the paperwork, Einstein."

Hayden froze, her full attention centered on the voice. It sounded familiar, but she couldn't quite place where she knew it. The noise of the passing traffic kept overriding the voice of the woman. She thought she detected a slight Southern twang but couldn't be sure. It held more than a hint of sarcasm, that she could be sure of.

"Oh, come on, Marshall Dillon. Stop being a hard-ass and unlock these cuffs. I'm not a terrorist sent to blow up your stupid little base. I'll sign your stupid little summons and promise to show up in court."

Hayden's heart started to race. It almost sounded like…no, it couldn't be possible. Feeling foolish for even entertaining the idea, she stepped around a couple of her colleagues to get a look at the woman causing the commotion. She almost doubled over from a blow in her gut. Everything around her disappeared. The hair was slightly longer, the skin a little paler, but the body was unmistakable and the face even more beautiful than the one she couldn't forget. *Emily.*

Emily was furious. She didn't know if she was more angry at her fellow protesters who had suddenly gone quiet or herself for getting caught up in the protest and stepping onto the base. She didn't need this hassle, another in a long line of events that had somehow spiraled out of her control. First Michelle. Then the falling out with parents, and the media attention that had dogged her return from the nightmare of Khao Lak. Nothing was simple anymore.

Her breakup with Michelle had dragged on for months. She'd left Thailand committed to ending their relationship and thought Michelle would be grateful that she was taking the lead to end what should have ended years ago. One of them had to.

But Michelle had other ideas. She refused to accept that their relationship was over and hovered over Emily as though afraid to let her out of her sight. She told her constantly how terrified she'd been that Emily might have died and that she wanted to give their love a second chance. Attentive to the point of smothering, she insisted that she was simply trying to make their relationship work.

Emily didn't know if guilt or love was motivating Michelle,

and found it hard to care. She had taken two weeks off work to allow her leg to heal and to recover from the ordeal. She didn't have the energy to deal with her ex-partner's neediness as well. Finally she had to move out of the house. She'd been living at her friend Julia's place.

At first, Michelle had called several times a day begging her to come home, but Emily remained firm. Her trip to Khao Lak had confirmed that she was no longer in love with Michelle, and the subsequent months only solidified her feelings. Emily knew her choices had nothing to do with the woman who'd rescued her. Even if she'd never met Hayden, she would have come back home and ended her relationship. But that fact didn't stop her thinking of Hayden constantly.

She'd tried to find her. She had contacted the American Embassy, the Red Cross, and various other aid agencies that had swarmed the island to assist the Thais in recovering from the disaster. Without Hayden's last name, she could find no record that she was either dead or alive. But she felt strangely defeated, dealing with bureaucrats and rehashing events she wanted to erase from her mind. The more she thought about Khao Lak Beach, the more stuck she became.

Lately she felt as if she didn't know who she was anymore. Ridiculously minor things irritated her. She had trouble concentrating and was always looking over her shoulder. For what, she didn't know, but her eyes were never still. Her friends had noticed and suggested she see a therapist, someone who specialized in post-traumatic stress disorder. They loved her and they were probably right. But Emily wasn't ready for that and hadn't made the call. Julia was the only person she really talked to about the terror, and those conversations were strange. Emily always felt distant, reciting sanitized facts and leaving out the images that kept her awake at night.

Her life seemed out of control, yet nothing terrible was happening. She knew she should be thankful. So many people had lost so much, and here she was. Alive. Healthy. Getting back to life as usual. And, of course, she was at a military base sitting on a hard metal folding chair with her hands cuffed behind her back like a criminal.

Even her mouth sounded delinquent. Normally, she would never have talked to a peace officer like she had just spoken to this one. Her reference to Marshall Matt Dillon on the old TV western *Gunsmoke* was totally uncalled for. Emily lowered her head. She wasn't the type to have outbursts and lose control. Was this what her life had come to?

She wasn't sure why she was so outraged when the president announced additional troops were being sent to Iraq. She hadn't waved signs when the war began. Why now? Emily frowned. She'd never been seriously involved in political activism. Sure, she had opinions and had donated to causes like Planned Parenthood and the Human Rights Campaign. But she was disconcerted by the fury that simmered below the calm surface she presented to the world.

The last straw for her had been a news item about a soldier who gave his life trying to save his buddies. She must have cried for hours that day, thinking about his parents and the dreams they'd lost along with their only son, and for what? It made no sense and she couldn't sit idly by, so she'd started organizing rallies and protests. And now here she was, being treated like *she* was the enemy.

Emily had a strong dislike for the military or anything remotely related to it, and her experiences during protests had sharpened her views. It seemed obvious that members of the armed services were so brainwashed into following orders that they were incapable of independent thought. They were blindly accepting orders to march off to places like Afghanistan and Iraq and willingly placing their lives in jeopardy. She couldn't understand what motivated such unquestioning obedience. Patriotism and national security? That was the rationale she kept hearing from politicians and the media. But she loved her country, too, and she didn't think the U.S. had any business invading other nations. Why did the government ignore people like her?

Emily shifted in her seat and tried to focus on answering the questions being thrown at her. But a prickling sensation crawled up the back of her neck and a sense of unease settled in her stomach. Someone was watching her. Angry at being gawked at by someone who probably didn't have the guts to sit where she was sitting, she lifted her head and surveyed her surroundings. She quickly zeroed in on the only person looking at her, an officer standing across the street. Emily smirked at the blinding shine on the shoes, the razor-sharp crease in the perfectly cut tan trousers, the flawlessly centered buckle, the slight rise under the breast pockets of the fitted shirt, and the cornucopia of ribbons on her chest on display like a shield of importance. The only thing out of place on this soldier was the expression on her face.

Emily frowned, puzzled by the conflicting messages. The piercing eyes were telling her one thing, but the image in front of her was telling her something altogether different. One was heart-stoppingly familiar, the other completely foreign. Something was definitely out of place here. She tried to draw a breath, but her chest was frozen and she was suddenly falling down a tightly wound spiral. The world spun and the roar in her ears was deafening. She was looking down a funnel, one that got smaller and smaller as the image at the end rushed into sharp focus. The eyes that haunted her dreams stared back at her, barely visible beneath the brim of the army hat. The nose and the high cheekbones were achingly familiar to her trembling hands, and she knew those lips from their tender kisses in the early morning hours before the world took another strange turn and Hayden was lost to her.

Shocked, Emily averted her stinging eyes. For a split second she wondered if she was imagining that the woman standing tall and official was Hayden. It had taken several months, but she had finally stopped looking for her everywhere she went. Still, she could not escape the blistering look of desire, or the softness of Hayden's touch. She returned to the safety of Hayden's arms almost every night, in dreams that felt so real she often woke feeling Hayden's lips and responding wetly to her caresses.

Forcing herself to breathe, she dared another look. She had given up hope of ever seeing Hayden again, and none of her dwindling daydreams about reunion included *this*.

A woman in uniform.

Hayden reached a hand out instinctively to steady herself. The wall of the guard shack was the only steady thing in her life at this minute, and she clung to it like she had clung to that tree those long months ago. Her heart pounded so hard, she thought it might beat a path right out of her chest. Her senses were flooded with memories of those few days in Thailand. The sea air filled her nostrils, the warm sun caressed her back, and her arms ached to hold Emily once again.

She took a tentative step toward the woman who had miraculously materialized from her memory but stopped herself, frozen with uncertainty. Should she interfere with the officer arresting Emily? Should she refuse to press charges? Or should she simply walk away? She was an officer of the United States Army. As such, she had certain responsibilities, one of which was protecting her military installation from threat wherever it might originate. But this was different.

No amount of training could have prepared her for the feelings crashing through her body and the range of emotions filling her heart. She and Emily shared a connection born of their harrowing experiences in the tsunami. They would always be linked together as survivors, two women thrown together by fate and a bizarre set of circumstances. But there was something else. It had been there from the first moment Hayden laid eyes on Emily floating in the water. The connection she felt wasn't a matter of ego, as the one who saved her life, but a sense of calm excitement and challenge. No other woman had evoked such feelings in her. And certainly not one as beautiful as the woman staring at her now.

Hayden watched the myriad of emotions cascade over Emily's face as she finally recognized her. Hayden knew the same shock and disbelief was all over hers as well. Her breathing was ragged and her body was damp with perspiration that had nothing to do with the April sunshine and the frustration of dealing with the protest.

"God, I hate these so-called do-gooders." A booming voice startled her. General Foreman had taken a peculiar interest in Hayden when she first arrived on the base, and he was now literally breathing down her neck. "They don't have any idea what we're doing over there and how much it hurts troop morale to see this. Christ, it reminds me of Vietnam."

"Over there" was Afghanistan and Iraq, and the speaker had served in the post currently occupied by Hayden during the Vietnam War some thirty years ago. "I understand, General," She watched helplessly as Emily was led away by the officer and placed in the back of a patrol car.

Their eyes met. Hayden's gut wrenched at the look of confusion and despair on Emily's face, but there was nothing she could do about it. At least not right now.

Chapter Nine

Hayden put her sunglasses on, pulled the ball cap low on her head, and stepped out into the sun. Her tennis shoes squeaked on the cement, wet from a light drizzle that had sprung up after lunch. She had changed out of her uniform into jeans and a polo shirt, and as she walked rapidly to her car, she prayed no one had recognized her. She would be hard-pressed to explain why she was coming out of a police station.

She tried not to think about the ramifications for her career if anyone found out she'd posted bail for one of the trespassers on her base. There would be hell to pay from her commander, and if word got back to her father she would never hear the end of it. Without a doubt Hayden knew that if she were asked to explain herself, she would have a hard time hiding her feelings. That rattled her. So did the fact that her careful reserve, mastered over years of self-discipline, had crumbled at the shock of seeing Emily again. But she couldn't let Emily stay in lockup. Her hands shook as she opened the car door and fastened her seat belt. She gripped the steering wheel to steady them. Emily Bradshaw. She said the name out loud a second time and the butterflies in her stomach increased. Finally she had a name and address, but no clue as to what she was going to do with the information. She had agonized for months, chasing dead ends in a desperate attempt to find Emily. Finally she had accepted that she would never see her again and now here she was, practically in her lap. Hayden should be thrilled, but she was petrified with uncertainty.

Indecision was not a state Hayden was familiar with. She had been trained at an early age by her father, and later fine-tuned by the Army, that hesitancy could get her or those under her command killed. This episode with Emily was certainly not a matter of life or death, but Hayden knew her next move could change her life forever. How would her life be different if she saw Emily again, spoke with her, touched her? What would her life be like if she didn't?

No closer to an answer than she was a few hours ago, she focused on the front door of the police station.

Emily ignored the loud clanging of the jail doors. They had opened and closed every few minutes since she was dumped unceremoniously into the cell several hours ago. A lone window high on the stark wall provided the only natural lighting, and the bare toilet bolted to the floor in the corner was the crowning jewel in her temporary abode. She was not alone; two other women occupied the benches on the other side of the small, bleak room. One seemed to be a seasoned inmate and proud of it. She'd been after Emily since the door slammed shut, making it clear that she would be the queen bitch in this cell even if it meant beating the shit out of her to prove it. Emily had managed to avoid any direct confrontation but was fully prepared to defend herself if necessary. The other occupant had just violated parole.

Sleep was impossible. Her companions were embroiled in a sordid conversation about their criminal pasts and low-rent lawyers who made them take pleas. They paused only when the door swung open and her name was called.

"Your bail's been posted," the guard said. "Let's go."

It took a few moments for his words to sink in, then she scrambled up and headed for the door as fast as she could.

"See ya, sweet thing." The sticky voice behind her belonged to her would-be "friend," the Queen Bitch of holding cell number 8.

Emily called, "Have a nice life," and marched down the sterile corridor, wondering how Julia had heard that she was here and posted her bail. Despite the fact that she'd typed the "What to Do If You Are Arrested" handout herself, she hadn't called anyone when she was booked. She'd been in a fog, giving her name and address on autopilot. Seeing Hayden again at the base had shaken her so deeply she didn't react the way seasoned protesters were supposed to.

She had thought of nothing else but Hayden since. She was breathtaking in her uniform, everything a military officer was expected to be. Tall, imposing, and intimidating. The clusters on her collar sparkled in the midday sun, explaining her command over their situation in the aftermath of the tsunami. Emily had been amazed at Hayden's levelheadedness. That she'd known exactly what to do, where to go, and how to get there. In fact, she'd been trained to handle chaos and crises like the nightmare they found themselves in. *Thank God.*

"Sign here." A large manila envelope was thrust at her from a hole in the thick glass window that separated her from the jail matron on the other side.

Emily hastily signed her name on the envelope, and the guard beside her ripped it open and dumped the contents on the counter. Emily gathered up her watch, wallet, car keys, cell phone, and her grandmother's pocket knife that she always carried with her, and put everything in her pockets. The guard pointed to a large exit sign in multiple languages and Emily escaped through it, grateful for her freedom.

The outer room was crowded and she scanned the people waiting there, expecting to see Julia. The absence of a friendly face made her want to cry. She recognized her disappointment with a bitter little smile. It wasn't Julia she was really hoping for. Irrationally she had hoped Hayden would be there. She was looking for her the way she always did. Just in case.

The sun blinded her as she exited the building, and she shielded her eyes until they adjusted to the bright light. She looked around but didn't recognize any vehicle parked nearby. Sighing, she flipped open her phone and dialed Julia's number. Maybe they had told her the process would take hours after the bail was paid. She was probably at home watching TV, waiting for a call.

"Emily? Oh, thank God." Julia greeted her with audible relief. "I was horrified when your friends called. I'm in the car now, on my way."

"I'll be waiting out front," Emily said. "There's a bench."

"Those jerks," Julia muttered. "Strange set of priorities, that's all I can say."

Emily smiled, knowing Julia hadn't even started. They would be talking about this for days, and one thing was certain, she was not going to mention Hayden's name.

For the second time in twelve hours, Hayden didn't know what to do. Her gut was telling her to step out of the car but her mind prevented her from moving. She needed to talk to Emily and see for herself that she had fully recovered from her injury on the beach, but under the circumstances that didn't seem like a good idea. Emily was probably angry that Hayden hadn't intervened back at the base. And shocked. She'd just been arrested, for God's sake.

Hayden watched her pace slowly back and forth as she talked on her cell phone. She wasn't limping, so her leg must have healed well. Her heart beat wildly and a pang of loss tugged at her stomach. Emily pushed a strand of hair out of her eyes and

Hayden ached at the memory of sliding her fingers through the soft brown tresses.

She could so easily step out of her car. All she needed to do was open the door. Her hand shook as she reached for the handle. Emily would immediately see her. They could walk down the street to a quiet coffee shop and talk. Hayden could say the things she hadn't had a chance to say that morning, after their lovemaking. Their time together had been left hanging, with no resolution and no way to tie up loose ends. Hayden had felt lost and adrift since she returned home, unable to return to life as she'd known it. Now, standing just across the street, was the reason for her turmoil…and the solution.

Surely Hayden owed it to both of them to act. She would invite Emily back to her place. They could take some time to catch up on each other's lives and discover more about each other. Then what? Talk about their major philosophical differences, the American military in Iraq, debate the funding of the war on terror like two rational, mature women with differing opinions? Or would they simply fall into each other's arms to reexperience the connection they had in Thailand?

Hayden realized she was gripping the door handle like a lifeline. She relaxed her fingers. This wasn't the time for a tender reunion. Emily would probably hit her over the head with her cell phone. Hayden watched her look up and down the street, then settle on a bench. She put the phone away and remained watchful, obviously waiting for someone. Hayden deliberated once more, framing what she would say. An apology over the arrest would be necessary, to break the ice. The thought made her uneasy. She was proud to serve and had no intention of making excuses. Emily and her friends had broken the law by trespassing on the base. They might have even wanted to be arrested, to prove a point and get media attention.

She slumped back into her seat despondently, struck by the no-win situation. At Khao Lak, she and Emily were united by their shared determination to survive and to save the two children who depended on them. Their differences were irrelevant. They had neither the time nor the luxury to get to know each other enough to find out what those differences were. Magic had been able to happen between them in part because they occupied their own tiny, intense universe, completely severed from the world outside. That was not the case now.

Her stomach sank as she saw Emily stand. A tall, lanky woman with fiery red hair rushed toward her and they fell into a tight hug.

"Is that your girlfriend?" Hayden asked into the quiet of her car. "Do you have a girlfriend, Emily?"

Of course she did. A woman as beautiful as Emily could have anyone she wanted. But if she had a girlfriend, then why make love with a stranger? Hayden wanted to believe they had something special, and for a moment in time she thought they did. But fate and circumstance had thrown them together, and in the carnage there were no rules. Hayden wondered if Emily had told the redhead in the short shorts and fashion sandals about that night. Probably not, and perhaps Hayden should back off now and let her get on with her life. She knew without having to hear it that picking up the pieces must have been hard for Emily, too.

She slid down in her seat when Emily and the other woman crossed the road and passed in front of her, several cars away. They were obviously close. Hayden could tell from the way they touched and the protective arm the woman kept around Emily's waist as they walked.

Jealousy flared, then was quickly quenched by an overwhelming sense of regret. What she had envisioned and dreamed about was not to be. The evidence was right before her eyes. Never again would she touch Emily's skin or feel her soft breath caressing her cheek. The whisper of her name in the night would come from another woman, and would never sound as it did coming from Emily's lips. Would they have been able to build on their similarities or would the divide between them be too deep to overcome?

Sadness gripped her like a vise and she started the ignition and pulled away from the curb. Some questions would always be unanswered, and if she was going to move on, it was time she accepted that.

❖

"I think you should see a doctor," Julia said. "You were a bit unsteady on your feet back there."

"Because I haven't eaten all day," Emily said as she settled into the passenger seat. "Really, I'm fine, Julia. It was no big deal." She knew enough to keep the full details to herself or Julia would question her for hours. "Thanks for posting my bail."

"What bail?" Julia asked blankly.

Emily hesitated. "You did post my bail, didn't you?"

"No, I just got here. One of your friends phoned to see if you were back home yet and told me what happened."

A tingling sensation crept up Emily's spine. Other than her fellow protesters, no one else knew she had been arrested. Only Hayden. She immediately dismissed the possibility that her rescuer had bailed her out of jail. No matter what she might have felt, Hayden had made it obvious that she couldn't get involved. She had walked away with the other officer, everyone saluting them.

Emily looked around, this time with a more observant eye. No one was on the sidewalk, and the cars parked along the street were unoccupied.

"Emily, what is it?" Julia asked. "Is something wrong?"

Her eyes searched Emily's face with concern. Emily knew that worried expression well. Julia could always sense when something was bothering her. In recent months, when Emily had behaved irrationally, Julia was the one who calmed her and helped her see that she was being overly sensitive. Like an older sister, she could see the signs and anticipate trouble almost before it happened.

Emily was tempted to tell her everything. Julia knew about the rescue and how upset Emily was that she and Hayden had never gotten the chance to swap addresses or even say good-bye. If she guessed that something else had happened between them, she didn't press for information. She would probably make a case for "closure" if Emily mentioned seeing Hayden at the base, and perhaps that was exactly what was required. Maybe if she stood face-to-face with Hayden, Emily could thank her and wish her well, and walk away with some kind of resolution.

Maybe she was strong enough to do that. Emily wasn't sure. "Nothing's wrong," she told Julia. "Let's go, I'm ready to go home."

CHAPTER TEN

Hayden tapped the pen impatiently on the desk while she was on hold. She was in her office with the door closed so she could have this conversation in private. It had been a week since she bailed Emily out, and she'd barely slept. Food tasted like cardboard and she snapped at everyone no matter how minor the infraction. She sat upright when she heard the click of the line.

"Okay, I've got it," said the desk sergeant of the Braxton Police Department.

Hayden fumbled with the pen in her haste to write down everything she was told. "Go ahead." Her voice sounded strange to her ears.

She heard papers shuffle. "Emily Elizabeth Bradshaw, DOB eight, twenty-two, sixty-nine. Five feet four inches, brown and brown. Address…"

She listened intently to the rest of the arrest information, jotting down the vital particulars. She thanked the sergeant for his time, hung up the phone, and stared at the information scribbled on the personalized tablet. Her name and rank was emblazoned at the top and her strong, bold handwriting filled up the remainder of the page. As the garrison commander of Fort Tanner, she had the authority to request and receive the information just provided to her by the local PD.

Now that she had what she wanted, what was she going to do? Officially she would use the information to ensure that Emily was prosecuted to the fullest extent of the law, but what about personally? She wanted to bolt out of her chair, drop into the front seat of her Acura and drive to Emily's house. She shook her head in disbelief over the address. Emily lived only a few miles from the base. Incredibly, their paths had never crossed, but then again, they most likely didn't frequent the same establishments. Hayden did most of her shopping on the base, and those times when she needed to grab something in one of the off-base stores, she was usually in and out in less than ten minutes.

Emily lived in one the better neighborhoods in Braxton. Hayden had even toyed with the idea of buying a home in that location, but decided it would raise too many questions as to how she could afford it even on her officer's salary. She had a nest egg of what some would refer to as "old money," inherited from a great aunt widely rumored in her family to be a lesbian. She'd passed away when Hayden was twenty-six, and in the intervening years the inheritance had grown, through investment, to a sum anyone would be proud of.

There was a tentative knock on her door, and her assistant, Corporal Stone, asked if she needed anything before he left for the day.

"No, thank you. Have a good weekend. I'll see you on Monday."

The door closed behind the young enlistee from Macon, Georgia. The words on the page danced in front of her and the sky was dark when Hayden tore the page from the tablet and slid it into the pocket of her pants.

"You're awfully quiet."

"Just thinking about last week," Emily replied truthfully.

"Wanna talk about it?" Julia turned off the TV.

"Hayden was there. At the base."

Julia's brow creased in a puzzled frown. "She was protesting?"

"No," Emily replied dryly. "She was standing on the other side of the guard gate, in uniform."

Comprehension dawned on Julia's face. "Oh, my God."

"Yes, exactly."

"Holy shit." Julia knew of her friend's distaste for the military.

"Yeah, holy shit." Emily sighed. "And from the look of all the medals and the way everybody buzzed around her, she was in charge."

"You're kidding me."

"I wish I were."

"Did she recognize you?"

Emily nodded. "Not only that, but she bailed me out of jail. I phoned the cops a few days ago to find out who I should be thanking, since it wasn't you."

Julia was silent for several long seconds. "Double holy shit. What are you going to do?"

"I don't know. She didn't even acknowledge me at the base. And she didn't wait for me at the police station. Obviously she doesn't want anything to do with me."

Saying the words out loud made them hurt even more. Hayden had rescued her again, but her actions had sent a signal. Over the past few days Emily had figured out a few things. Hayden felt a responsibility for her. Supposedly that was normal when a person saved someone's life. So she'd done what she could to get Emily out of trouble. But that didn't mean she wanted them to reconnect. If she did, she would have done something about it. A week had passed. Her silence could only mean one thing. Posting bail was her version of good-bye.

"What did you expect her to do?" Julia said impatiently.

"Run over and sweep you into her arms and make love to you right there? For heaven's sake, if she's the commander of the base or something, do you really think she could do that?"

Julia's point of view made sense, but Emily didn't feel any better. She'd been through all the rationalizations, time after time. She could understand why Hayden didn't come and talk to her then and there. But why not wait at the jail if she wanted to see her?

"I was just so shocked to see her," she murmured. "And at the base, of all places. I'm still in shock. Ever since I got back from Khao Lak, I've been imagining what I would say or do if I saw her. Nothing turned out the way it was supposed to."

"Life isn't that well scripted," Julia said. "Or you two would never have met in the first place. What were the odds? You're both in Thailand on the same beach when a tsunami hits, and it turns out you're virtually neighbors back home. That kind of coincidence is too bizarre to be anything but fate."

Emily smiled sadly. She had been tempted to believe that herself, except that fate seemed to be playing a cruel trick on them. "Whatever the cosmic explanation, in real life she's a bigwig in the Army and I was handcuffed to a chair and mouthing off to a law enforcement officer when 'fate' brought us back together. What an impression that must have made. No wonder she doesn't want anything to do with me."

"You can't assume that," Julia said.

Emily closed her eyes and leaned back against the headrest. "I read it in her face. I've seen enough military types, and showing emotion is explicitly frowned upon. But I saw it. She was just as surprised to see me. She was still wearing that look when they hauled me away."

"What are you going to do?"

"I have no idea."

"Well, at least now you know where she works, so you can find her and have that talk you've been telling me you wanted."

Emily didn't know weather to rejoice or bury her head and

cry. She had everything she needed to contact Hayden again, but was she brave enough to do it? Or would it be schoolgirl stupidity? They were from completely different worlds with different values and beliefs. What if Hayden had a girlfriend? What if she'd had a girlfriend when they were in Thailand? She didn't mention one, and she'd acted like a single woman. Emily still remembered her answer when they discussed why she chose Khao Lak for her vacation: *Pretty girls. Lots of them. I come here when I need to fuck myself silly for a week. Then I go home.*

Hayden didn't seem the type to escape to a foreign country so she could cheat on a partner, but Emily wouldn't have guessed she was an army officer either. They knew nothing about each other, not even last names, and technically, Emily was still in a relationship when they'd made love. She hadn't mentioned Michelle, other than in vague references. She'd chosen to ignore that small detail so she could grab the moment, and she had no regrets about her choice, only about the consequences. Hayden had touched a place in her that no one had ever touched, and she couldn't pretend that counted for nothing. She still felt raw, and that was why Hayden's silence hurt so much.

Theirs was a one-time thing brought on by perilous circumstances. They'd taken refuge in each other out of fear, adrenaline, and survival instinct. Being in the military, Hayden probably understood how to separate herself from those events better than Emily did. She was trained to deal with decisions made in the heat of a situation. A relationship based on what they'd shared in those moments was doomed. It could never survive the pressures of daily life.

A relationship? Jesus, where did that come from? What the fuck was she thinking about?

"I'm not going to do anything," she told Julia.

"Nothing?" Julia looked incredulous. "You've got to be kidding me. I don't know what happened between the two of you out there in paradise, but I can guess. And the way you've been acting, you have some unfinished business with that woman."

"Julia." Emily didn't want to discuss this anymore.

"Don't 'Julia' me. You know I'm right, and as your friend it's my job to tell you these things. And to kick your butt if necessary. And from where I'm sitting, it needs kicking."

"We're too different." Emily didn't know if she was trying to convince Julia or herself. "It's just not meant to be."

"Oh, please. Since when are you a quitter?"

The question stung, but it also hit home. Emily had survived a terrible disaster, against all odds. She had fought for her life and reached for Hayden's hand when it seemed hopeless and the force of the water was more than she could resist. Sheer willpower had kept her from giving in. She wasn't sure what had happened to her since she got home. She should be proud of herself and confident, but she felt vulnerable and afraid, just a pathetic shadow of the woman Hayden thought she was, the woman she'd desired.

Was that why she was hiding away, feeling sorry for herself? Was she afraid that Hayden would see a different person and the heat would leave her eyes? Emily had just spent several years seeing nothing but neutral familiarity in a partner's face. She knew she couldn't cope with that in Hayden. It would break her heart.

Every stop light en route was green. Long before she was ready, Hayden was across the street from the house the police had listed as Emily's residence. It was still early evening, and except for the occasional dog barking, the street was quiet. A green Toyota Tacoma was parked in the driveway adjacent to the lush yard. Flowers edged a winding walkway with three steps leading to the front door.

Hayden sat in her car deciding whether to knock or drive away. For the umpteenth time she weighed the pros and cons of each, which was a waste of time because she had methodically listed them on a yellow legal pad several nights ago. The list was long and dead even in both columns.

The drapes opened and a figure crossed in front of the window. Hayden's heart jumped into her throat and her hands began to shake. She wanted to see Emily. No, check that, she needed to see Emily. If for no other reason than to lose herself in the dark brown eyes that had captured hers so often in the few precious days they'd shared together. Who was she kidding? One look would never be enough.

Gathering her resolve, she pulled the key out of the ignition and got out of the car. Her legs almost buckled when she stood, but she forced herself to maintain a steady stride up the sidewalk. A woman she didn't recognize opened the door. It wasn't the auburn-haired woman who'd picked Emily up at the police station.

"I'm looking for Emily Bradshaw." A bad feeling came over Hayden.

The woman stared at her more closely, with a hint of distrust. "Who's asking?"

"Hayden Caldwell. I met Emily during the tsunami in Thailand." Hayden couldn't miss the possessive look that flashed in the woman's eyes and the way she stood taller inside the house. She was staking her claim in no uncertain terms.

"She's not here." The woman didn't offer any additional information.

"Would you tell her I stopped by? I was in the neighborhood and just wanted to see how she was doing. She had a pretty nasty cut when I last saw her." The words tumbled out of Hayden's mouth.

"She's fine. She had to stay in bed for a few days, but with a little TLC and some antibiotics she's okay now. Just a little scar."

Hayden didn't miss the inflection in the woman's voice, implying that it was *their* bed she stayed in and *she* was the one administering the TLC.

"Okay, thanks." Hayden hesitated. "Er…"

"Michelle," the unfriendly woman supplied. "I'm Emily's partner. This is our home. We've been together for eight years."

The door closed in Hayden's face and her heart plummeted to her feet. With her remaining pride coupled with years of training, Hayden walked calmly down the sidewalk to her car. She should have known. It was odd that "Michelle" hadn't bailed her partner out of jail a week ago, or that she wasn't in Thailand, but who could guess at why couples behaved as they did?

Chapter Eleven

"What are you doing here?" Emily kept a grip on the front door handle, refusing to step back politely so Michelle could enter the house. She'd been coming around all of a sudden and Emily was tired of finding her waiting on the doorstep when she came home from work.

"I've been looking for the key to the treadmill. Do you have it with you?"

Emily rolled her eyes at the feeble excuse. "Did you try looking on the hook inside the hall closet? You know, the one that says 'treadmill key'?"

"Oh, right." Michelle was characteristically vague, and her self-effacing laughter sounded fake. "Silly me. Listen, do you want to come over for dinner? I left some potatoes baking and I have a couple of good steaks I could put on the barbecue."

"Michelle," Emily said angrily. "It's over. We are not going to make dinner, make amends, make up, or make love. We are done. I don't love you, I'm not in love with you, and I'm not going to fall back in love with you. Now please stop trying."

They'd had this conversation many times and she was sick of it.

"Come on, Em, I love you. I'm not willing to throw everything away just because we're having a rough patch. Be reasonable. I have the name of a good couples counselor, or you could just go by yourself. Obviously you need—"

"No!" Emily didn't let her finish. "I do not need a counselor to tell me I have suffered a trauma. And for the record, I did not end our relationship because I am nuts. Okay? It's the sanest thing I've done in a long while."

"All I'm trying to say is that I love you."

"And why didn't you love me enough to make this kind of effort before I went to Thailand? Why did it take me almost dying for you to realize it?" Before Michelle could reply, Emily said, "Don't answer. We are done. Through. Finished. How much clearer do I have to make it?"

"All right, all right, I get it." Michelle started to walk away but turned around, flashing Emily a look she'd never seen before. It was almost as if she were gloating. "Just remember. We had eight good years, not just a vacation fling. I know more about you than any other woman does. I know what you like, what pushes your buttons, and what makes you cry out with pleasure. Remember that when you think there's something better out there."

And with that parting shot, she left.

Emily marched into Julia's kitchen, took a beer out of the refrigerator, pushed the Play button on the answering machine, and dropped into the La-Z-Boy chair, exhausted. A reporter had left his number, wanting to talk to her about the protest. Emily couldn't imagine what was left to say about an event that was old news. Ten days had passed, and all she wanted to do was put the whole thing out of her mind.

She had not been sleeping well, and being ambushed by Michelle again was the crowning touch to an already stressful day. She sipped the cool liquid until she felt her muscles begin to relax. Michelle's persistence was one of the qualities that had originally drawn Emily to her, but now it was a just a royal pain in the ass.

Something Michelle said nagged at her, but she couldn't quite put her finger on it. Michelle had a knack for word games and subtleties, and Emily was often in the dark about what she was hinting at. It was as if there was some underlying message in her words and their definition was just out of her reach. More than once she'd asked Michelle to be direct with her, but she had a feeling Michelle preferred to wield power by getting under her skin.

Emily went into the kitchen to make dinner. She felt restless and frustrated. As she chopped tomatoes for a salad, she sliced one of her fingers open and cursed loudly. Blood ran all over her wet hands and the white plastic chopping board spilled with pink fluid. Infuriated, she hurled the knife into the sink and ran water over the cut.

She was sobbing when Julia walked in. The white-faced panic on her friend's face made her fall abruptly silent.

Julia's eyes fell instantly to the hand she was clutching. Her dread was palpable. "What did you do?"

"Christ," Emily shouted. "I'm not trying to cut my wrists. Jeez. What are you thinking?"

Julia was silent. They stared at each other.

"I'll get a Band-Aid," Julia said.

Emily laughed. She couldn't help herself. A Band-Aid. The idea was hilarious. Aware of Julia looking at her strangely, she pulled herself together and said quietly, "Yes, that'll fix everything."

Hayden woke to the chiming of the grandfather clock and tried to sit up. A sharp pain shot down the left side of her neck, reminding her that she had fallen asleep in the chair and not her king-size bed. She turned off the TV mounted in the middle of the wall above the fireplace. The screen was as dark as her mood and as blank as her state of mind. She had no idea how she'd managed to work for the past three days. Her mind was a fog. Emily had a partner, and a long-term partner at that. Eight years.

A myriad of emotions flared once more, with anger and hurt leading the way. It didn't take a math genius to figure out that Emily was in a relationship when she was in Thailand. Hayden wasn't proud that she'd set aside her suspicions and allowed her instincts to rule. Never before had she been an accomplice to infidelity, at least not knowingly, and she felt soiled by the knowledge. She'd always refused to be the other woman in any relationship, and she'd had to make that choice plenty of times over the years.

It had taken courage to go to Emily's house and walk up those few front steps. She hadn't known what she was going to say or how Emily might react, but she certainly hadn't expected to be put in her place by a jealous girlfriend. The woman who answered the door *knew*, Hayden could see that right away. She doubted Emily had told her the details, but partners weren't stupid. Michelle could very easily have tossed her on her ass, and rightly so for messing with her woman. Hayden was grateful that their terse interaction hadn't come to that, but she was left with no doubt that Emily was off-limits.

She pushed the light on her watch and checked the time. It was one thirty in the morning and she had to be up in about five hours. She stumbled down the hall into her bed knowing a repeat of her nightly dream awaited her. The dream always started out the same. The beach, the sun, and the sand. Then came the water. Millions of gallons carrying her away like a twig. She fought the current, coughing and choking on the salt water until she grabbed on to the tree that had saved her life. Only in her dream, she was not able to save Emily or the children. She tried. She reached as far as she could. But her fingertips barely grazed their outstretched hands.

Every night they floated by, screaming at her to help them, knowing they were going to die. Every night she woke up panting, drenched in sweat. It took her a long time to fall back asleep. Some nights she never did.

❖

Emily didn't want to open her eyes. She dozed, dwelling on the dream she was barely awakening from. Two tall, strong women vied for her attention. One was demanding, manipulative, and forceful, the other considerate and strong, but also gentle. Sparks consumed both pairs of eyes but one glinted with rage, the other with desire. Hands reached out to touch her. One pair grasped her firmly, taking what they wanted. The other softly caressed her, asking her to give. Both women wanted her, but only one desired her. Neither had a face.

When the chiming of the alarm clock dragged her out of bed, she stumbled into the kitchen and made coffee. She could never remember to make it the night before and cursed as she spilled coffee grounds on the counter. Her bandaged finger was tender, which didn't help her dexterity or her mood. She was in a foul temper and hoped the coffee would soften her before she had to be patient with a room full of children.

She thought of her students as she soaped herself in the shower. They were a motley crew. Some with unkempt hair, others with worn-out clothes and always hungry. They were all wonderful, bright, inquisitive kids with big smiles and the innocent eternal hope only children can have. She loved them, every single ragtag one of them, and she believed she made a difference in their lives every day. They would still have a school, teachers, and a hot breakfast without her, but she wasn't sure if every teacher would care about them as she did. Not everyone would give each child a hug every morning when they stepped into the room or a nod of encouragement when they struggled to pronounce a new word and a high five when they succeeded. These children needed so little but gave so much back in return.

She'd been thankful to get back to work. In her two weeks

off after she returned from Thailand, her days were unspeakably empty. Since then she'd made sure the children filled them completely, often working late and planning extra activities to keep herself busy. Driving the twenty-eight miles from her house, she tried to focus on some new ideas for a class project, but her mind strayed to the dream. The meaning seemed fairly obvious. One of the women was Michelle and the other Hayden. What troubled her was that she couldn't connect the names to the faceless women in the dream.

Her relationship with Michelle had been filled with kindness in the beginning. They shared a kiss first thing in the morning and last thing before sleep. They were together in every sense of the word. They had the same hopes and dreams and would often talk late into the night about what their future together would bring. Emily wasn't sure when everything changed. The process had been so gradual she couldn't pinpoint a key event or issue. But long before she left for Thailand in December, they were practically strangers living under the same roof. They rarely talked, shared even less, and were more interested in the morning news than a morning quickie. Emily didn't know if the cold, manipulative woman she'd seen over the past few months was simply the Michelle she could not see while she was in love, or if her ex had changed. The other day, when Michelle accosted her on the doorstep, Emily was a little afraid of her.

She wished they could make some progress on selling the house, but Michelle was taking her time, claiming that none of the realtors she'd spoken with so far were the right kind of people, whatever that meant. Emily tried not to show her impatience. She didn't want Michelle to know how aggravated she felt about not being in her own home, now of all times.

Then there was Hayden. She too had been strong yet soft. She tended to Emily and the children with a strong dedication to their safety that defined her character. At least it did to Emily. She was tough when she needed to be and instinctively knew when a kind word would do more than a command. But there was another side to Hayden that Emily didn't know about until the day of the protest; that was the cold, hard eyes of power and control. The Hayden who was used to giving orders and having them obeyed without question. Everything about her screamed that she was in charge.

Emily pulled into the lot and parked her car in the first row. It was early and the hustle and bustle of downtown was just beginning. Businesswomen and men scurried down the sidewalk balancing their lattes in one hand, their briefcases in the other, and the morning paper somewhere in the middle. She used to be one of them, a nameless hopeful on her way to the top in a burgeoning workforce where her qualifications were stellar.

She had the usual dreams. Youngest Nobel Prize winner. A woman after whom science buildings were named. Her destination had seemed clear. She was blessed with good genes, was doing revolutionary work in the top think tank in the world, and had parents with influence in the technical community. There was nowhere to go but up. Her research work had been the center of her universe until Julia introduced her to the children who changed her life, inspiring her to become a teacher.

Her destination today was quite different. Barcelona Elementary School was on the third floor of a building so old it was a blight in the city skyline filled with ornate glass and chrome towers. The floors creaked, the plumbing groaned, the heat worked sporadically, the paint was peeling off the walls, and staff rode the elevator at their own risk. The building was a wreck. Emily had traded in her state-of-the-art laboratory, high-priced equipment, alligator briefcase, and Bruno Magli shoes for recycled paper, rickety desks, and sneakers. She couldn't imagine doing anything other than this.

Her footsteps echoed on the staircase worn from years of shoes clacking up and down from one classroom to the next. Her cadence up the steps almost sounded like a children's rhyme; *Michelle, Hayden, Michelle, Hayden.* When she reached her floor, Emily was no closer to certainty than she was when she woke up. The hard, rough hands and cold eyes could belong to either woman. And Emily would not be ruled over. First it had been her parents, then Michelle, and then Hayden as they struggled to survive.

She stopped on the third-floor landing. Hayden had not ruled over her, she had let her take charge because she was obviously well trained to do so. What troubled her now was that Hayden was probably used to giving orders and having them obeyed without question. Emily was no longer a pushover, and they were no longer in a life-or-death crisis.

CHAPTER TWELVE

Hayden stood quickly when General Foreman entered her office unannounced. He had a habit of dropping in as though trying to catch her doing something she shouldn't be. She had an uneasy feeling about the general, one that had nagged at her ever since she arrived on post fifteen months ago. He was old school in his mannerisms, his leadership, and the opinions he seldom kept to himself. He didn't know what was happening on his base, or with the men and women under his command, and he rarely added any value to the meetings he elected to attend. He believed that respect was due to rank and he used the single star on his shoulders as an angry man would use a choke collar on a puppy. If you didn't jump at his command, your life was his.

In Hayden's opinion, he should have retired years ago. But then again, General Foreman would never ask her opinion. If he did, he always let her know first what he expected to hear.

"Good morning, General." Ever since Foreman had showed what an ass he was, Hayden always referred to his rank rather than using the customary "sir" befitting a superior officer. This wasn't her usual practice, but the three-letter word got stuck in her throat every time she struggled to offer it.

"Caldwell," Foremost said as a return greeting. "Got any

coffee around here?" He plopped into the chair adjacent to her desk.

Hayden hid her annoyance. Regardless of her rank, Foreman believed that she, and women in general, had a place, and that place was not in the military and certainly not wearing bronze clusters on their collar. She noticed that he never addressed her by her rank. He simply used her last name.

"I believe so, General." She bit her cheek and walked around her desk and into the anteroom where Corporal Alex Stone was waiting.

Stone was her right-hand man, the Johnny-on-the-spot who could make her look good or make her fail miserably, and she knew it. He had his nose just far enough in everything to keep her informed, not far enough that he was a snitch and nowhere near enough to her butt to be considered a brownnose. She liked the young enlistee and his soft Southern drawl was calming.

"Coffee?"

Even though he never said as much, Hayden knew Corporal Stone was aware of her dislike of their commanding officer. As a matter of fact, it was difficult to find anyone on the base who admired the general. Hayden thanked him, appreciating that he put her in a position where she didn't have to wait on Foreman. She returned to her office and sat stiffly behind her desk.

"Corporal Stone will bring your coffee right in. What can I do for you this morning, General?"

The old man blatantly eyed the various medals, awards, and commendations Hayden had scattered around the room. He repeated this perusal every time he came into her office, looking for something that might have arrived without his knowing. His face betrayed his thoughts, and he scowled at the display of Hayden's accomplishments.

"What's up with those protesters from the other day?"

"General?" Hayden took small pleasure in making him be more specific.

"The namby-pamby protestors that were at the south gate last week. What's happening with them? Are they in jail or what?" He practically snatched the coffee when Stone brought it in.

Hayden immediately thought of Emily. Actually, no matter how hard she tried not to, after the not-so-subtle message from the girlfriend, she had done nothing but think of Emily.

"I doubt it, General. Only one of them was arrested, and I'm sure her bail was probably posted pretty quick." *And if you had any idea it was posted by me, my ass would be in a station in Greenland watching the ice caps melt.*

"Only one. That's ridiculous," he bellowed. "Those damn hippies were determined to come onto my base and disrupt operations and God only knows what else, and they only charge one of them. Go down and talk to the chief of police. I want the book thrown at her. Make an example of the bitch or we'll be dealing with plenty more like her, mark my words." Foreman was practically salivating.

"I'll speak to him, General." Hayden made her voice calm and not condescending. "But I think it's the district attorney who determines the charges."

"I don't care who does what. I want that woman put away for a long time." Foreman stood and Hayden quickly followed suit. "No one fucks with my base and gets away with it."

Her training kicked in and she automatically snapped to attention as Foreman left the room. She had grown tired of this aspect of military life, the respect compelled for rank even when none was earned.

Corporal Stone stuck his head in the door and she sat back down in her leather chair and motioned him in. "While you were at lunch a reporter called wanting to talk to you, ma'am. I have his number if you want to call him back."

Hayden sighed. Just what she needed, another reporter asking questions. She took the pink message slip and tossed it on her desk.

"Is there anything you need me to do, ma'am?"

Hayden only hesitated for a few seconds, weighing the

situation. "Yes. Get the district attorney on the phone regarding the protestor that was arrested last week. Emily Bradshaw. I need to know what charges will be filed against her."

It was an hour before Hayden was able to talk with the DA, and Foreman was not going to be happy with what the civil authorities planned to do about the incident. As she suspected, the only charge against Emily was simple trespassing. She'd been given a court date and the DA expected her to pay the fine and walk away. Case closed. If she didn't, and wanted to be a hero for her cause, then a trial date would be set. He had no plans to waste the court's time by filing additional charges that would only be thrown out. Hayden was relieved but apprehensive. She was going to have to manage the general carefully.

It was a beautiful day and she decided to postpone making her report. Instead, she drove to Grant Park in the center of the city. The park was located on seven acres of prime real estate and was often the topic of debate. The city wanted to maintain the green space, developers wanted to buy the land, and hungry taxpayers wanted the land sold and the money put in the local coffers to lower their taxes.

Hayden chose a spot not far from the playground and sat under a tall ficus tree. The sun was warm and her mind drifted. She hadn't been sleeping much lately and in a matter of minutes she was lulled into half-wakefulness. The sounds of children laughing and playing tickled the edges of her consciousness and she smiled, remembering Jake and Victoria and how bravely they'd faced the days after the tsunami. She wondered if they were reunited with their parents or orphaned by the disaster.

A shadow crossed in front of her, blocking the sun's warm rays. After a few moments when it didn't move, Hayden looked up, directly into a pair of familiar brown eyes and her heart seemed to spasm in her chest. She drew an uneven breath. Emily was more beautiful than she remembered. But she looked pale and uncertain. Hayden's stomach knotted.

"I never thought I'd see you again." Emily's voice shook.

"Neither did I." Hayden's mouth was so dry, she had trouble forcing out the words.

She blinked several times and resisted the urge to jump up and grab the woman standing over her. She almost expected her to disintegrate like she did in every dream. But this was reality, even if Hayden doubted it.

"We've never been properly introduced. I'm Emily Bradshaw."

Emily's hand shook when she held it out in greeting. She still couldn't believe Hayden was sitting right in front of her. She'd brought the kids to the park after lunch and was stunned to see her on the bench across from the playground. At first she'd started to pack the kids up, determined to escape before she was noticed. But then she realized that she simply couldn't walk away without saying a word.

Hayden stood and removed her hat. Grasping Emily's hand, she said, "Hayden Caldwell."

Hayden practically jumped at the contact. The electricity between them sparked where their palms connected. Heat coursed through her body, from her hand to her heart. It responded by racing crazily.

"Don't you mean 'Lieutenant Colonel'?" Emily's gaze fastened onto the insignia on her collar.

"No." Hayden was in uniform, but this was not official business where she would use her rank in her introductions. This was personal. Very personal. She smiled faintly. "You know my rank."

"The police told me when I asked who bailed me out of jail. How do your bosses feel about your generosity?"

"I don't discuss my personal life at work."

"No, I'm sure it would be a problem if you did." Emily didn't wait for a reply, but asked, "What are you doing here?"

Hayden hesitated. "I like walking here. It clears my head."

She was still holding Emily's hand, but Emily wasn't resisting. Her gaze lifted to the scar above Hayden's left eye, and the concern in the depths of her eyes seemed to caress the mark. Her lips parted and her voice was almost wistful when she spoke.

"How have you been, Hayden?"

Distracted, Hayden said, "Fine."

She was transported back to their one night together. To the deep, endless kisses and the warm wetness that enfolded her. She tightened her grip on Emily's hand, unable to let go. She wanted to ask why Emily hadn't tried to find her. And why she'd slept with her when she had a girlfriend. Why fidelity and honesty didn't matter to her. Why she'd captured Hayden's thoughts and subconscious like she had. Did she ever think of her, or was Hayden simply a fling, explained away as a natural reaction to surviving a tragedy?

Emily watched a myriad of emotions and questions dance on Hayden's face. She had many of her own. Why did she leave without saying good-bye? Did she think about all that had passed between them? Was it as special for her as it was for Emily? Did she want them to see each other again? She finally spoke.

"I never got the chance to properly thank you. For saving my life."

"You don't have to. It was what anyone would have done."

Emily squeezed Hayden's hand gently. "Didn't we already have this conversation?"

She was rewarded with a small smile. "We talked about a lot of things." Hayden's eyes were deep and searching, as though probing her soul for answers. She started to say something else, then stopped and cleared her throat. Releasing Emily's hand, she asked, "Is your leg all right?"

Bereft of Hayden's warm, safe grasp, Emily felt like she was drifting, losing the lifeline that had saved her so many months ago.

"It's fine," she said automatically. She'd answered the same question a hundred times since January. "Just a few stitches. You can hardly see the scar."

"I looked for you," Hayden said. "But I didn't know your last name and there were dozens of places to check. You weren't on any of the lists."

"Oh." Emily didn't know what to say. She took another quick look at the kids, automatically counting heads.

"I found out later that they didn't include people whose families had already been notified," Hayden said.

"They flew me back home pretty quick." Emily wanted to say more, needed to say more, but her mind and mouth were not in sync. Her heart was thudding so loudly in her ears that she was afraid Hayden could hear it. Butterflies danced in her stomach and tickled her arms and legs. She wanted to feel Hayden's strong arms hold her and her lips caress her mouth. She felt herself swaying into Hayden. "I tried to find you, too. After I got home. But…"

"I'm sure you had enough distractions." There was a faint edge in Hayden's reply, and a flash of cynicism tightened her mouth.

Puzzled by the distance she sensed all of a sudden, Emily reverted to a more general topic. "The media hounded me for a week or two, then the novelty wore off. How about you? How was it when you came back? I mean, did everybody want to ask you questions?"

"I don't know too many people here. I'd only been at Fort Tanner for a few months before the trip."

There was plenty Hayden could add, but why get into it? Nobody had given a damn when she came back. There was no one at the airport, no parents or siblings to grab hold of her and bust into tears. She'd seen those welcomes for a few of the other survivors in her flight. Emily probably had a similar reception—thankful parents and an ecstatic partner. *Michelle.*

She met Emily's eyes and waited for her to say something

about the people waiting for her. Here was the perfect opportunity to mention her relationship, by way of signaling that she wasn't free to date, just in case Hayden was planning to ask. Which she would have been, under different circumstances.

Instead Emily's eyes pooled and she said, "We never got to say good-bye."

"No, we didn't." Hayden waited. She could sense something rising up in Emily, but just as her lips began to form a word, a squeaky voice dragged them both back to reality.

"Miss Bradshaw, I have to go to the bathroom." A child shifted from foot to foot in front of them.

Emily shook herself, as though to regain her bearings. "This is one of the children I teach. We come here after lunch. I have to go."

"Of course."

Hayden didn't know if she felt relieved or disappointed, but she definitely felt something. She didn't want Emily to go, but she couldn't ask her to stay. Emily had responsibilities. And a home to return to at the end of the day. Tonight she would get into bed with another woman. Hayden was trained to keep her emotions off her face, and did so now.

"It was good seeing you again, Emily," she said in a friendly, but impersonal tone. "I'm glad you're doing well."

Emily's heart jumped at the sound of her name coming from Hayden. The last time she'd heard it was in the heat of passion, just before Hayden came in her mouth. She would never forget what she heard and felt that night. It sounded like Hayden didn't intend on seeing her again, but the message in her eyes was saying something different. Hope rolled through her like a warm tide and she smiled.

"It was good to see you too, Hayden." After a brief hesitation, she turned and headed back to the playground.

As Emily walked away, Hayden felt as though the midday sun had slipped behind a dark cloud. Her hand was still warm from holding Emily's, and her blood boiled from the long look Emily had just given her. She followed Emily's progress toward the restrooms. The sight of her holding the little girl's hand reminded her of Thailand, of watching Emily with Victoria.

Hayden was still stunned by the turn of events today. She wondered how many times Emily had been in this park while she was also taking a walk here. It was incredible that they lived in the same town, yet they had only met on the other side of the world when they both happened to be in Khao Lak at the same time.

What kept bringing them together? Mother Nature was responsible the first time, and they'd needed each other to survive. Then Emily was protesting at the base, and now their paths had crossed once more in this park. Was it fate that kept bringing them together, or simply sheer coincidence? They were strangers when they met, connected by a moment in time. What were they now? Neighbors? Adversaries? Survivors? Lovers?

She put her hat back on and watched until Emily stepped into the restroom. As she returned to her vehicle, she was in such a trance she almost walked into a man snapping photos of the park. Apologizing, she continued on her way. She was thankful they'd had a chance to say good-bye. Maybe now she could look forward to some peace of mind.

"Are you going to eat that or just push it around your plate?"

Emily looked up. She and Julia were having their weekly dinner at Sombrero's, a little hole in the wall with the best Mexican food Emily had ever tasted. Tonight, she hardly ate anything. "I saw Hayden today," she said simply.

"You did?" Julia's voice rose an octave.

Emily nodded. "She was at the park by the school."

"What was she doing *there*?"

Emily gave up pretending to be hungry and put her fork down. "She said she likes walking there to clear her head."

"Do you believe her?"

Emily looked hard at her friend. They'd known each other since they were in college, and Julia still had the same skeptical attitude almost fifteen years later. "Why wouldn't I?"

"Come on, Em. Don't you find it kind of odd that she just happened to be sitting where you take your kids to play every day?" Julia sipped her margarita.

"Let's not assume a conspiracy theory, for heaven's sake. It was a beautiful day and she stopped at the park. Just a bizarre coincidence."

"Uh-huh." Julia rolled her eyes.

Emily's patience with the topic was already running thin. Seeing Hayden again, and saying the good-bye they owed each other, hadn't left her feeling resolved. If anything, she was even more unsettled.

"Don't you think it's little more than coincidence that you keep seeing her?" Julia continued. "That's what now, twice in two weeks? Don't you think that's a bit more than fate?"

Emily did, but she flatly refused to consider the word that kept jumping into her mind: Destiny. She folded her arms across her chest. Were some things meant to be? After finding herself hauled from certain death, one of the few on that Khao Lak beach who survived, she didn't know what to think. Fate, on that day, seemed completely random and cruel. Mothers died and their children somehow lived. Fine, decent people were killed and would-be rapists and robbers survived to troll the disaster area for victims afterward. She would make herself crazy if she tried to find any special meaning in events that were, by definition, insane.

"I didn't give her the third degree, Julia. We talked, that's all. Don't even start thinking she's stalking me."

Julia wasn't ready to let it drop. "What did you talk about?"

"Nothing much. The usual stuff. What happened back then and how we're both doing now." Emily kept her emotional reaction to herself. At least for the time being. Even now her body still tingled.

"Sounds like a deep, meaningful conversation," Julia responded sarcastically.

"Stop it, Julia." Emily couldn't hide her frustration. "What did you expect? Neither one of us expected to ever see the other again. It wasn't as though we'd rehearsed what we were going to say to each other, when and if we happened to meet."

"Baloney. I know damn good and well you've thought about what you would say to her." Julia didn't buckle under Emily's withering look. "I'm your friend. I know you better than you know yourself. Didn't I tell you Michelle was not the one for you? Wasn't I right about you getting out from under the thumb of your parents? I could go on, you know."

"Trust me, I know."

"Something happened between the two of you out there on that beach," Julia said emphatically. "So you can stop pretending it didn't."

Emily gave up trying to hide the obvious. "We made love. The last night before we were found." Julia didn't say anything, so she continued. "It just happened. It was building almost from the first moment I saw her. And not having any clothes on didn't help matters. Here I was, in a life-or-death situation, struggling to get back to civilization, and I couldn't keep my hands off her."

Emily caught her breath as an image of Hayden's fabulous body flashed in her mind.

"So she's hot," Julia said.

"It wasn't just physical." The words were out before she fully registered their meaning. Trying to avoid explaining herself, she presented Julia with a glowing account of Hayden's heroism and admirable qualities. "She was unbelievable. She really cared about me and the children. We always came first. We had most of the food and drink. She had to be thirsty, I certainly was. But she never complained. I know we slowed her down. She could have just left us for the Red Cross to find, but she stuck by us. She was…incredible."

Emily stopped, self-conscious that she could easily keep gushing about Hayden now that the floodgates were open.

"Do you think you're suffering from a case of hero worship?" Julia asked quietly.

Emily thought before replying. The possibility had occurred to her. After all, who wouldn't sing the praises of someone who saved her life? "I don't know. Jesus, Julia, I hardly know her but I can't stop thinking about her. And she's a colonel in the U.S. Army, for God's sake." Emily put her face in her hands. "Maybe I am just so grateful to be alive that I can't figure out what I really feel."

Julia searched her face. "Girl, you've got yourself one big mess."

"Yes, and what am I going to do about it?"

"Sleep on it," Julia recommended.

CHAPTER THIRTEEN

Hayden waited nervously outside General Foreman's office, having been summoned to provide an update. She had no good news to give him about the case against Emily, and she was furious that she'd allowed Emily to affect her yesterday when they met at the park. She wasn't thinking clearly. She needed to pull it together before Foreman started grilling her.

She'd had the opportunity to practice with her father at dinner last night. He was a lot like Foreman. They shared the same derogatory opinion of people who protested over things they knew nothing about. He had pontificated for several minutes before her mother calmed him down and served coffee. What would he think if he knew everything that had happened on Khao Lak Beach?

He had told her how proud he was of her actions. They'd talked about her trek back to civilization with Emily and the Hight children. She had served the Army well, he kept repeating. The more Hayden thought about it, the more she realized that he never said he was proud of *her*. Just that she had made him and the Army proud.

Foreman's door snapped open and he motioned her in and plopped into the chair behind his massive desk. Hayden often wondered where the big desk came from. It certainly wasn't standard military issue.

"What've you got for me?" He didn't even try to be civil.

Hayden braced herself. "Nothing yet, General."

"Nothing? What in the fuck have you been doing all this time? Knitting?" His face reddened. "I want you to find out everything you can about that woman. I want to know who she is, where she works, and what she had for breakfast. I want to know who she's sleeping with and how often she fucks him. I want to know everything." Foreman had broken out in a sweat, he was so agitated.

"General, I don't think that's a wise course of action to take," Hayden replied cautiously.

"If I want your opinion, Caldwell, I'll give it to you. Now get on it."

"It's going to take some time to get this information. Unless you want the entire department of military justice breathing down your neck." It was a stretch, but Hayden knew Foreman would buy it. He wasn't smart enough to know otherwise.

"God damn."

Hayden stood patiently while Foreman ranted and raved about the inadequacies of civilian laws. She didn't understand why he was so wound up over the protest and dared not ask. When it was clear that he was showing no signs of letting up, her mind began to wander. The images were all of Emily. Emily reaching for her from the water. Emily's firm, round breasts moving rhythmically up and down while she dozed in the tree. The way she looked bathed in moonlight the night they made love.

"Caldwell!" Foreman barked.

"Yes, General?" Hayden replied far more calmly than she felt.

"I said I see your point. I want something we can use to discredit that woman. But I don't want my balls busted because of it." He swiveled in his chair turning his back on Hayden, effectively dismissing her. "Carry on."

Hayden winced at his choice of words. She could file sexual

harassment charges against him for his language, but then again, she could pack her bags and go to no-man's land for the same result. *God, I'm tired of this shit.*

She retreated from the office, stunned by the order. There was no reason for Foreman to know about Emily. There was no justification for him to ask for that kind of information. She stopped in the middle of the hall, the answers coming to her in a flash. Emily had insulted the old man by having the nerve to protest at his base. The protest was all over the news and was the talk of the base. Emily had embarrassed him in front of his cronies. He was out to get her no matter what, and he was going to use Hayden to do his dirty work.

She was grateful for the cup of coffee Corporal Stone brought in after she'd stalked to her office. She was reading a report and had pored over the same page three times, losing concentration.

The young corporal hesitated. "Emily Bradshaw is on the phone for you. The protester."

Hayden's stomach shot to her throat. "Did she say what she wanted?"

"No, ma'am."

Hayden took a deep breath. "Okay, thanks, Corporal. Would you close the door behind you?"

She knew what her request might signal, but she didn't know where the conversation would go and might be overheard by anyone passing the door. She felt she could trust Stone, and suspected he knew she was a lesbian, but she didn't want to test her theory. So far, he'd never said anything to her, fishing for information, but there were other personnel who had speculated. A couple of officers had dropped hints, implying she could speak freely with them. Hayden resisted the urge. What she didn't disclose couldn't be used against her, and no one had ever asked directly. She was grateful for that.

Her hand trembled when she picked up the receiver. Typically she answered the phone by saying "Colonel Caldwell," but this was Emily, the woman who'd held her, who touched her in the dark under the stars, the woman who'd caused her to cry out in ecstasy. She still couldn't stop thinking about her. Despite the girlfriend. *Michelle.* Despite the fact that Emily protested her very existence as an Army officer.

She spoke the name she whispered at night. "Emily?" It flowed off her lips.

"I hope I'm not disturbing you." Emily's formality sounded forced. She was probably wishing she had hung up instead of waiting for her call to be transferred.

"No, not at all." *Liar.*

"How are you?"

"I'm well." *Lie number two.*

"I'd like to talk to you. Can we meet for lunch?"

Hayden was almost speechless. This was the last thing she had expected. Lunch? Dinner was too intimate, she supposed, and Emily was probably thinking ahead. An evening date was always more awkward to end, if things weren't going well. Lunch was brief and casual. Even so, what was the point? Did Emily think they could be "friends"?

"I don't know if that's wise." Hayden's inner voice screamed, *Yes! Make it happen.*

There was a long pause at the other end.

"Why?"

Hayden scowled at the cryptic reply. "Why? Well, for a start, it's obvious that we can't talk like casual acquaintances. Apart from our history, and your personal situation, you trespassed on my base. We have some major philosophical differences." *That and the fact that if Foreman ever found out, I'd be slinging hash for the remainder of my enlistment.*

"Hayden, it's just lunch. Good God, I'm not asking you to marry me."

For an instant Hayden pictured Emily in a white dress walking down the isle toward her. Sweat made her hand slip on the receiver. She should have nothing to do with this woman. Emily would only be trouble for her career, if it ever got out that they'd shared a meal. Could she have a normal social conversation with a woman who was the total opposite of her? Hayden hesitated. Of course she could. They'd talked about a lot of things in Thailand. *Things I would never have told anyone, let alone a total stranger. Maybe that's why I did. It was safe. And there was that time when we didn't need any words...* Memories of their passionate encounter on the beach instantly trampled over Hayden's good judgment. She wanted to see Emily. Now.

"All right," she said before she could change her mind. "How about Roscoe's? It's a little Italian place on the corner of Gillcrest and Hecker." Roscoe's was warm and friendly and offered privacy without overt intimacy.

"Yes, I know it."

Hayden scanned her brain, looking for something else to say.

As though Emily sensed her ambivalence, she said, "Hayden, you don't have to come. Forget I even asked. I'm sorry I bothered you."

Her despondency was tangible. Hayden didn't get the chance to reply before she heard the click on the other end of the line. She stared at the receiver as if willing the voice to continue. She was a mess. Her heart was racing. Her blood pounded in her ears, and she couldn't think straight. Recent history had shown that she couldn't even form a complete sentence where Emily was concerned.

She dropped the receiver back into the cradle and stared at the opposite wall for several seconds. Then she got up and stuck her head around the door. Corporal Stone appeared to be deep in his work. No one else was hovering.

Relieved, Hayden said, "Corporal, please have my car brought around. I'll be out for a couple of hours."

❖

Why was she even here? Hayden had not a clue. It was two blocks to the school where Emily worked. What would she say to Emily? How could she make her understand? Would she even be at the school? She sat still for several minutes contemplating her next move. As she'd circled the block trying to find a parking spot, she'd convinced herself that she wanted to see Emily to challenge her. Emily had a partner, so why was she trying to see Hayden socially?

Hayden wasn't going to judge her, but she needed to make her own position clear. She wasn't going to be the "other woman" in a love triangle, or a stud on the side for a woman discontent in her relationship, if that's what Emily had in mind. Feeling self-righteous, she got out of the car and started walking. The sidewalk was littered with trash and it had a strange odor she didn't want to even try to identify. She rounded the corner and saw the brightly painted green door of the school. There was still time to change her mind, she reflected as she stepped inside and turned automatically toward the small lobby. The reception window was empty. No one had seen her.

"Can I help you find someone?" a woman asked, and a head bobbed up at the window.

Hayden wavered. The reception clerk was ogling her like she'd never seen a woman before. She had changed into a pair of jeans and a polo shirt and thought she looked less imposing than if she were wearing her uniform. Hayden kept a dignified demeanor, giving no indication of her nervousness. "I'm here to see Emily Bradshaw."

"In connection with which student?"

"I'm not a parent. This is a personal matter." Hayden hoped she sounded calmer than she felt.

The receptionist checked her computer and said, "She's not teaching this morning, but she's here doing paperwork. I'll get her for you. Have a seat."

Hayden fed some coins into the beverage dispenser in the

corner of the room and pulled out a Coke. She soothed her dry throat with a long sip. As she lowered the can, she felt Emily's presence before she even came into view. It was obvious when Emily emerged from the adjoining hallway that she was taken aback. Joy was the first expression on her face, followed quickly by apprehension. Hayden felt responsible for the swift shift in her emotions. She stepped forward, not giving Emily the chance to speak first.

"I'd love to have lunch with you." She was relieved to say the words. The truth was she wanted to see Emily again. Wanted to talk with her about anything, nothing, and everything. She wanted to know her favorite color, her favorite beer, and the name of her pet hamster. She wanted to know all there was to know about her.

"What made you change your mind?" Emily did not understand this woman. She'd thought Hayden felt the same way she did, that there was something there more than just a survivor connection between them. But Hayden's cool response to her phone call had crushed her hopes and caught her off guard.

"You hung up on me, remember?" Hayden said. "You withdrew your invitation before I had a chance to refute your assumptions, and my phone line doesn't have that star sixty-nine feature."

Appropriately chastised, Emily lowered her eyes to the threadbare carpet. "Yeah, I guess I did."

"I didn't know your number but I did know you worked here. At least this time I knew where to go to find you." Hayden knew she was probably rambling but didn't care. She tilted her head to make eye contact with Emily. "So, are you free now?"

Emily broke into a smile. "Yes. I'll go freshen up."

"Okay, I'll wait for you here."

Hayden felt like she was floating over glass as she waited for Emily to return. She couldn't control the bounce in her step as she paced from one side of the room to the other. When she became aware of the receptionist's quizzical stare, she sat down, feeling like an eager teen waiting for her high school sweetheart. She wasn't sure she cared.

❖

"Get a grip, Emily. It's lunch."

Emily's hands shook as she studied her reflection in the mirror at Roscoe's. She was wearing a pair of plaid shorts she knew she looked fabulous in, and a sleeveless solid-color tank top, brown sandals, and a leather rope bracelet. Goose bumps had erupted on her arms from the cool air inside the restaurant and her nipples had hardened as well.

Hayden had chosen a table by the window, and as Emily slowly walked across the room returning from the ladies' room, she knew from the look on Hayden's face that she'd noticed the tight peaks pressing against the fabric of her tank. Hayden's mouth dropped open, sending a rush of desire surging through Emily. *She wants me, too.*

Hayden stood where she was, silhouetted by the rays of the afternoon sun. Her short blond hair was spiked and her long legs were covered by faded jeans. A pressed polo shirt and worn boat shoes completed an ensemble that screamed "lesbian." Her green eyes sparkled and danced. Emily resisted the impulse to kiss her cheek, sitting down instead.

No one spoke until the waitress had taken their drink order. The butterflies in Emily's stomach would certainly inhibit any attempt she made to eat, so she didn't reach for her menu but continued to study Hayden instead.

"You look great." Her voice was a little breathy. She couldn't make herself sound normal.

"Thanks, so do you."

"Thanks for agreeing to see me."

"Well, it's only lunch, and I do have to eat." Hayden inwardly rolled her eyes. Who was she kidding? It was more than lunch and she knew it.

"So what are you in the mood for?" Emily asked, finally picking up her menu.

Hayden wanted to explain exactly what she was in the mood for but let the comment slide. Even with the glaring issues of Michelle, Emily's politics, and her career, she couldn't deny her attraction to Emily. "I think I'll have a pizza. Wanna share?"

The thought of sharing food suddenly became as intimate as sharing a bed. Hayden's body reacted to the idea with a tug of tension at her groin.

"I'd love to," Emily said.

The waitress returned and took their order. Hayden had a thousand questions but bit her tongue. This was Emily's invitation, and she said she wanted to talk. She sipped her Coke and waited patiently.

"I bet you're wondering why I called this meeting," Emily joked, trying to loosen the tension that threatened to strangle her. She knew Hayden desired her; that had been obvious months ago, and nothing had changed. She still stared at her as though she wanted to drag her away somewhere and make love.

"Well, free food is one way to get people to come." Hayden chuckled.

"I know several other ways to get *you* to come."

Emily gasped at her comment and Hayden choked on her drink. She reached for the extra napkins on the table. Emily wanted to slide under the tile. She flushed, remembering the many times Hayden had come that night they were together.

"Well," Hayden managed to say, still coughing. "I can't argue that point." She took a deep breath and wiped her mouth. "Nothing like getting right to it."

"My God, Hayden, I have no idea why I said that." Emily felt her face flush again. "I…"

She looked cute when she was embarrassed. Hayden

interrupted her. "Yes, Emily. You do. And I'm certainly glad you said it." She hesitated a second, then decided to cut Emily a break. "Look, we shared something incredible, something most people never will experience in their lifetime. We were in the middle of a life-or-death situation."

"Yes, the adrenaline was certainly racing." Emily sounded strained.

"Exactly, and in those circumstances people behave differently than they might normally. It doesn't have to mean anything, and it usually doesn't. It's just what happens."

Emily was relived that Hayden was looking at her hands when she spoke. Averting her eyes, she saw her own incredulous expression of pain in the decorative wall mirror hanging near their table. Hayden still reacted to her physically, but she didn't *want* her. She was giving her the brush-off. Hayden thought she was after her like a new puppy. Emily had never chased after anyone who didn't want to be caught. Her anger rose to the surface.

"Let me get this straight," she said. "Our sleeping together was environmental? Our *circumstances* caused some kind of aberrant behavior that means nothing. Did I understand it correctly?"

"Emily." Hayden didn't like the way she'd been paraphrased. She was trying to give Emily an out, a way to put their encounter in its proper place: in the past. No matter how much she wanted to see Emily again, to touch her, make love to her, she was not going to risk her career for what she knew would not work. Besides, Emily had a partner, even if she seemed to forget that fact when it suited her.

Emily held her hand up. "Don't 'Emily' me. I'm not one of your little soldiers to be spoken to like I can't think for myself. I have a brain in my head, a very smart brain, as a matter of fact, and I don't appreciate having you tell me *your opinion* of why I did what I did."

"Are you trying to deny that we were caught up in the

moment? I think we both know that in everyday life, it's pretty unlikely that we'd have slept together."

"Really? Well, let me tell you something. I don't get 'caught up in the moment.' I'm a trained scientist and a grown woman. I make my own decisions. I'm not some helpless female."

Hayden started to say something but Emily didn't let her.

"Don't even think of barking some kind of order to me, *Colonel*," she continued, determined to make her point. "I had sex with you because I wanted to and not because of something I had no control over. I was attracted to you. You have a fantastic body and I wanted to know what it felt like to make love with you. That's it."

Emily was surprised at the words that came out of her mouth. Where they came from she had no idea, but she was angry, and when she was angry, she spoke first and thought second. It was one of her major flaws. She stood and gathered her purse and keys. She knew her ears were red from anger.

"Silly me, thinking that we had some unfinished business to discuss. Obviously our *interlude* doesn't fit into your perfectly crafted, orderly, military-issued life. Well, that's fine with me because I don't need the complication of *you* in my life, either."

Hayden was blindsided by Emily's speech but spoke very calmly, as she always did when she needed to control her reactions. "I'm sure Michelle will appreciate that."

"What?" Emily looked stunned.

"Michelle. Your partner. You do remember her, don't you? Or have you conveniently forgotten about her like you did when you were fucking me?" The burn of humiliation she'd endured from Michelle still simmered just below the surface.

Emily's mind raced. She didn't remember ever mentioning Michelle. How had Hayden found out? Had she spied on her, as Julia suspected? Was she afraid that Emily would blab to someone in exchange for the Army dropping charges? Had she decided to preempt a potential problem by digging some dirt? *Unbelievable.*

"About five-six, red hair cut kinda like Reba McEntyre? That Michelle? You'd better hurry home before she gets suspicious. Or is she used to you going on vacation to exotic places without her?" Hayden's comments were ugly and she knew it, but she couldn't help herself. She was hurting and she wanted Emily to hurt as well. "I guess you're pretty good at inventing excuses, or does she believe every word you tell her?"

"When did you see Michelle?" Emily asked weakly.

"When she opened your front door. Actually I think she said it was, quote, *our* house. But don't worry, I didn't give anything away. I have a feeling she knows your little secret. She made it very clear that you belonged to her." Hayden sat back waiting for what Emily would say next. This was not how she expected their lunch to go, but she was glad that now all the cards were on the table.

Emily shook her head. "Well, she's mistaken." She stared down at Hayden, unable to hide her disappointment and anger. "So this is what you think of me? A liar who cheats on her partner?"

"Emily, sit down. I didn't come here to fight with you."

"And I didn't come here to be insulted. Good-bye, Hayden." Emily turned on her heel and walked past the waitress delivering their pizza without a second glance.

Hayden didn't try to stop her. She watched her walk out the door and stand on the sidewalk waiting for the traffic to clear. From her vantage point at the window Hayden could see Emily's chest heaving up and down, a sure sign that she was still fuming. Her jaw was clenched tighter than her fists.

Hayden wondered if she was pissed because she'd been called on her infidelity or because she got caught.

❖

Emily shoved past a man with a zoom lens on his camera, almost knocking him sideways as she stormed away. She didn't know what to do with herself. She couldn't face returning to work, and she had no classes, so she called in and said she intended to work from home for the rest of the day. Somehow she managed to drive without smashing into another motorist. When she reached the tranquility of her temporary home, she took a cold shower and left a whiny message on Julia's voicemail.

Her friend understood her well enough to finish work early and arrive with Chinese food. They ate and watched CNN for a while before Julia could contain her curiosity no longer.

"It's *her*, I suppose. Just a wild guess."

"Of all the arrogant, self-centered, condescending jerks."

"So you saw her again, then?"

"To even think that I'm not capable of making my own decisions. She needs to think again. She has *no idea* what I can do for myself." Emily got up and paced back and forth while Julia sat calmly on the couch, wisely saying nothing. "Do you believe she actually implied that my libido is stronger than my brain? Does she really believe those things? How chauvinistic is that? My God, she thinks like a man. She is everything I despise about the military." She finally fell back into the chair across from Julia.

"Why are you so tanked up about it? Let it go."

Emily glared at her friend, amazed at her cavalier attitude. "You weren't there. You didn't see her face. She actually believes all the crap she spewed."

"So what? It's not like you two run in the same social circles. You're never going to see her again. Forget about her. You survived an experience that makes for damn good cocktail conversation, and you had some great sex doing it. Not many people can claim either one, let alone both. Move on." Julia accentuated her last two words to make her point.

"That's exactly what I'm going to do. I'll show her high libido and loss of self-control. Let's go." Emily grabbed Julia's hand and dragged her toward the front door.

"Where are we going?"

“To get laid.”

“I’m driving,” Julia replied, leading the way.

Even though it was Emily’s idea, it looked like Julia was the one who was going to get laid almost immediately. At the first club they walked into, she hooked up with a tall brunette. Emily set her sights on a petite blonde on the other side of the room, and in no time they were dancing, closer and closer as each song played, until not an inch of space separated them. The constant drumming of the music mimicked the pulse in her veins. The blonde’s seductive moves didn’t hurt either. Names were not important but when the stranger kissed Emily, there was a problem.

Emily wanted to pull away. She didn’t part her lips but the blonde sucked and licked while she reached for Emily’s butt. Emily tried to relax, but she hated feeling the small hands squeezing as if they had a right. The woman gave up trying to get her tongue into Emily’s mouth and swooped down on her throat instead, nibbling like she got plenty of practice. Her ponytail tickled Emily’s chin and a stray strand of pale hair slithered unpleasantly across her lips.

There was nothing wrong with the woman, Emily reasoned, she had some moves. What more did she want? She put her arms around the eager woman’s waist and tried to get interested.

The blonde instantly ground against her. She whispered in Emily’s ear, “I’m wet. Let’s get out of here.”

Emily pictured the platinum ponytail bobbing between her thighs and felt repelled. Fighting an urge to jerk her body out of range, she gave in to more intimate caresses. One of her breasts was squeezed. Her nipple responded with a brief, feeble tightening. Her body was letting her down, refusing to become aroused. If she got any drier, her jeans would chafe. She glanced swiftly around, looking for someone who was more her type.

Tall. Powerful. With a commanding presence and incredible green eyes she could lose herself in.

"Hello?" The blonde's query was accompanied by a pout.

Emily mumbled an apology to the miffed woman, found Julia and said she would grab a cab, then almost ran out the door. She stopped on the sidewalk and instantly started shivering. She didn't know if her reaction was due to the cool night air rushing over her heated body or the realization of what she'd almost done. She had not picked up a woman in a bar since college and here she was, allowing a stranger she didn't find attractive to practically fuck her on the dance floor. What was she thinking?

It was still early and the sidewalks were crowded, so Emily decided to walk the five blocks home instead of fighting for a cab. The evening stroll would give her a chance to clear her head. Whether or not she wanted to admit it, Hayden had gotten under her skin. She was humiliated and upset that Hayden could think so poorly of her. It would have been easy to correct her mistaken assumptions about Michelle, but Emily had been too hurt. It was as if Hayden wanted an excuse to discard her, to trivialize all that had happened between them.

But their connection was more than adrenaline and hormones, as Hayden had tried to explain it away. Emily refused to accept that Hayden really believed her own dismissive statements. No one else had been around to pull her from the water. No one else had come out of nowhere to save her from the two ugly men. Of all the possible venues, Emily had chosen to protest at the Fort Tanner base. She took her students to the same park every day and one day there Hayden was, sitting on a bench. It was almost as if something was steering them in the same direction. Could it be fate? With her technical mind, she generally didn't believe in such things. But what else could it be?

Every time she turned around, Hayden was there.

CHAPTER FOURTEEN

Emily heard the phone ringing as she pulled the door closed behind her. She glanced at her watch. She was already late and if the call was important, whoever it was would leave a message. She was groggy from only a few hours of sleep again for the third time this week. She knew it wasn't a case of insomnia, it was a case of Lieutenant Colonel Hayden Caldwell. She had tried everything to get Hayden out of her head, including her disastrous attempt to sleep with someone else, but the minute she laid her head on the pillow at the end of the day her thoughts returned to Khao Lak Beach. Oftentimes, she woke in the middle of the night with her hand where Hayden's mouth had so skillfully caressed her. Her only relief came when she let her fantasies take her away.

Yawning, Emily hit the garage door button, slid into her car, and backed out of the drive. She managed to reach the school without falling asleep at the wheel or driving into a parked car. Mobile television trucks crowded the front of the school as she drove by on her way to the parking lot reserved for the teachers. The trucks, bearing logos of *Live at 5* and *Eyewitness Now,* had been here before doing stories on the school itself or incidents involving parents of the students. Emily didn't think twice about their presence as she parked and locked the car.

Molly Riverson, the school secretary, met her at the staff

entrance. Molly was normally well put together, so Emily immediately noticed her frazzled appearance and excited look in her eyes.

"Molly, what is it? What's happening?"

"You are what's happening, Emily. You're in the paper and the news people want to interview you."

Molly's words came out in such a rush, Emily wasn't sure she heard her correctly. "What?"

"You're in the paper. Right here on page eight. Didn't you see it?"

Molly thrust the morning newspaper at her. Emily opened it casually. Her parents had been in the paper many times, and she'd been interviewed occasionally before she left the Ashley Institute. After her remarkable tsunami survival story, the media had swarmed all over her for a week, but the fuss had died down since. So why the TV vans? In a split second, she knew the answer.

MAKE LOVE NOT WAR

TSUNAMI SURVIVORS ON OPPOSITE SIDES?

The headline was centered over two pictures of her and Hayden. The one on the left showed them shaking hands in the park. In the other they were sitting close at Roscoe's.

"Oh my God." Her knees began to shake and she steadied herself against the cool brick building. She felt Molly's prying eyes on her as she read:

> Our very own Emily Bradshaw and Lt. Colonel Hayden Caldwell both survived the deadly tsunami that struck Thailand the day after Christmas. In fact, Ms. Bradshaw was rescued by Lt. Colonel Caldwell just before she would have been swept away to her death in the wave. The women traversed death, destruction and

> savage conditions for two days until they were rescued by aid workers sent to the devastated country.

Emily skimmed the next few paragraphs that provided the readers of the *Braxton Daily Bugle* a detailed, if not exactly accurate, account of their experience together on the beach. The *Bugle,* as it was known by the locals was, in Emily's opinion, not much more that a gossip rag, spewing innuendo and half-truths to anyone stupid enough to pay the seventy-five cents to buy it. What caught her eye was the reporter's account of her arrest at the Army base.

> Ms. Bradshaw was arrested for trespassing on the military base famous for its rigorous pre-deployment training. Lt. Colonel Caldwell, the woman who saved Ms. Bradshaw's life, happens to be the garrison commander for the Fort Tanner base and ordered her arrest. When contacted for comment, Ms. Bradshaw did not return this reporter's calls. Lt. Colonel Caldwell was unreachable as well.
>
> But are they on opposite sides? This reporter has seen Ms. Bradshaw and the Lt. Colonel several times looking far chummier than Army regulations would allow. You tell me…do they look like adversaries?

"Emily, I had no idea. Are you—" Molly was stopped in mid sentence by Emily's scalding look.

"Get a substitute for me today, Molly. I don't think it's in the best interests of the children if I'm here. It'll be too distracting."

The principal of the school was the most liberal person Emily knew, so she didn't expect there to be an issue about the article and accompanying pictures. But others might not be so understanding. Leaving the building, Emily quickly walked back to her car and pulled out of the parking lot.

The streets in downtown Braxton were one-way, but thankfully the way Emily needed to go took her in the opposite direction of the television crews. She slowly merged into the morning rush-hour traffic, fighting the urge to race around every car in front of her. Finally she was moving at a pace that still didn't come close to the racing of her heart. She turned onto her street and immediately hung a U-turn at the sight of a news van parked in the vicinity of Julia's house.

Emily took refuge near the municipal park a few blocks away and shut off the engine. Tightly gripping the steering wheel, she rested her forehead on the back of her hands. What was going on? Who was this reporter and where did he get his story? How had he connected her to Hayden? She took several calming, deep breaths and sat back in her seat. She was a scientist, trained to think analytically, to consider all the evidence before drawing a conclusion that could be validated and substantiated.

There was only one thing she could be certain of: Hayden would never have risked her Army career by leaking information. Emily could imagine exactly what she was thinking right now.

As Hayden waited for the ax to fall, a grim suspicion crossed her mind. Had Emily sold their story? Was this some form of carefully orchestrated payback for the arrest? Had Emily and her anti-war friends dreamed up the perfect way to poke fun at the military, at Hayden's expense? She'd tried calling, but Emily's phone rang and rang with no answer, and when she called the school they simply said she was not in today.

Hayden's office was small and she paced the six steps back and forth, her eyes never straying far from the newspaper. The photographer must have taken them with a long-range lens because she would have seen him otherwise. An unlikely assumption, when each time she was with Emily the only thing she saw was Emily. The color of her hair, the smoldering darkness of her eyes, and the way her lips moved when she talked. Hayden wouldn't notice a bomb going off next to her if she had Emily to look at. She wouldn't have seen a man with a camera.

Corporal Stone was speaking to someone just outside her door, and Hayden knew from his tone it was not Foreman. Her phone had rung constantly since she got in, and the corporal had done an excellent job of deflecting any unwanted calls. After a quick knock, he stepped into her office.

"Captain Caldwell is on the line." His face looked pale.

Her father. Just who she didn't want to talk to. "Thank you, Corporal. I appreciate everything you're doing. I'll take it."

Hayden had been concerned when her rank surpassed her father's. She suspected he was bitter because he was never able to move past captain, but he never let on. Hayden detected more than a touch of sarcasm when he joked that he should be calling her ma'am instead of using her name.

She walked around her desk and picked up the receiver. "Hello?"

There was no point in pleasantries, she knew why he was calling. Even though he'd retired several years ago, Frank Caldwell was still closely connected to the inner circle of the Army. She knew her father well and held the receiver several inches away from her ear.

"Hayden, what in the fuck is going on?"

"Nothing, sir."

Her mother said that her first word was not "mama" or "dada" like most kids said, but "sir." Of course it was. Her father was an officer in the Army and she was his child. There was no other option than to refer to him as "sir," especially when she was in trouble. And she was in big trouble.

"What do you mean, 'nothing'? This shit is all over the paper," he bellowed.

Hayden was eerily calm. She was a grown woman, but her father still had the ability to rattle her nerves with his military voice. "First of all, Dad, I wouldn't call the *Braxton Daily Bugle* a credible source of journalism. Secondly, the piece is filled with speculation. There is nothing going on between me and Emily Bradshaw."

She had rehearsed this speech several times and was fully prepared to repeat it to General Foreman when he decided to summon her to his office for a browbeating.

"Well, it doesn't look that way to me," her father said. "Who is this woman, anyway?"

"I met her when I was in Thailand, during the tsunami. She's the one I rescued." Hayden filled him in on the details of their recent meetings, from the protest to their disastrous meal at the restaurant. "I don't know how this guy connected us, but what he's implying is simply not true."

"Then you need to issue a statement. Demand a retraction."

"I'm not going to do that." She'd anticipated this suggestion.

"Why the hell not?"

"Because giving this story air will lend it credibility. I won't dignify this kind of smut reporting with a response. The media has been here all morning and I refuse to speak to them. In a few days this will blow over and the *Bugle* will be on the bottom of the neighbor's bird cage."

Hayden hoped this would be the case, but knew deep down that the story would get legs, as they said in the news business. It was filled with excitement, intrigue, sex, and conflict. A news producer's dream.

"Do you know how many calls I've received this morning?" Her father was relentless.

Hayden softened her tone but remained firm. "I'm sorry, sir, but this has nothing to do with you." As soon as the words were out of her mouth, she knew they were the wrong ones.

"Nothing to do with me? You're my daughter and an officer of the United States Army. You're supposed to set the example of what an officer should be. You keep your nose clean and your head down and do your job, for Christ sake."

Hayden let him continue without interruption. She read between the lines and knew he was more concerned with his reputation than hers. His buddies would drop subtle comments or snide jokes about his daughter the dyke. She'd heard them all before.

Hayden hadn't officially come out to her parents, but her lack of boyfriends when other girls were sporting hickies and going to the prom might have been their first clue. That and the fact that she was forty-three and never married or talked about getting married. That should have been their second clue. And if they took a good look at her, especially in the last few years, they would see that her "lesbian" neon sign was glowing brightly. Her normally short hair was cut shorter, her edge was a bit edgier, and her attitude was *You don't have to ask, here I am.*

Hayden felt remarkably calm. She let her father finish and then said, "I'm sorry that you're upset and I'm sorry for any embarrassment this may cause you. But it's not true, and that's all I'm going to say about the matter." She didn't apologize for seeing Emily because she wasn't sorry. She waited a few seconds, expecting him to start in again, then said, "I've got to go, sir. I'll call you later this evening." She hung up without saying good-bye.

Corporal Stone must have been waiting for the light on his phone to show that her line was no longer in use because he knocked on the door as soon as she replaced the receiver. "Excuse me, ma'am, but Ms. Bradshaw called when you were on the phone with the captain. She left her cell phone number and asked if you would please call her."

His face had regained some of its color and his eyes were filled with understanding.

Her face softened as well. It was good to have an ally.

"May I say something, ma'am?" the young man asked hesitantly.

"Of course you can, Corporal. You know that."

Hayden was more relaxed with her staff than other officers,

who preferred to pull rank and demand proper protocol. She typically called them by name and not rank, and never issued what she termed as "orders" to them. In addition to treating people respectfully, she'd learned long ago that her staff had the power to make her look good or very, very bad.

"I'm sorry that you're going though this," Corporal Stone said. "That paper is a rag and nobody believes what's written in it anyway. I don't care who you—" He stopped, his face flushing red.

Hayden smiled for the first time that day. "Thank you, that means a lot to me. Unfortunately, from the number of calls you've fielded and the reporters at the gate, I'm afraid everybody isn't as enlightened as you. I *do* appreciate your support."

The relieved young man retreated and Hayden picked up her cell phone. All incoming and outgoing calls were taped, and her next one was not for public disclosure.

"Thanks for calling," Emily said. Hayden hadn't started the conversation by shouting. That was a good sign. "We're having quite a day, aren't we?" She was only partially successful in keeping her greeting light.

"That's one way to describe it, I suppose."

Emily could hear a smile in Hayden's voice and she relaxed. "I have no idea where this came from," she said. "I'm not the source."

It was important to her that Hayden didn't think this embarrassment had originated with her, that it was a political ploy, reflecting her distaste of the military and Fort Tanner. She was relieved when she heard a soft sigh at the other end.

"I wondered about that for five seconds, but I never believed you were responsible."

"I wouldn't do that."

"I never saw the guy," Hayden said. "But then again, I

can't take my eyes off you when we're together, so that's not surprising."

Emily's stomach jumped at the compliment. "I could definitely say the same thing." She lightly tested the waters and was rewarded with Hayden's laugh.

"Well, let's keep that to ourselves, at least for now. It's nobody's business, especially the *Bugle*'s."

The inference was not lost on Emily. She wanted to pursue that train of thought thoroughly, but more important things were happening. First, she had to correct a wrong. "I'm sorry about lunch that day. I way overreacted. I was upset that you would assume I cheated on a partner." But what had hurt most was that Hayden had taken their interlude so lightly, and seemed to be giving her the brush-off.

"I'm sorry too," Hayden said. "I blindsided you about Michelle, and that wasn't fair."

Emily realized that Hayden wasn't going to ask her about Michelle directly. It was something she needed to clear up, so she said simply, "Michelle was lying to you that day, in case you haven't figured that out yet."

After a short silence, Hayden asked, "What do you mean?"

"My relationship with Michelle is over. I don't live with her. I've been staying with my friend Julia for months." She heard the sound of a breath being released. "We'd been together about eight years when I went to Khao Lak. We'd been having problems… no, that's not right. We were getting along fine, and that was the problem. We were roommates more than anything else. She had her life and I had mine, and they rarely crossed."

Especially in bed, but Emily spared Hayden those details.

"I'd planned the vacation as a kind of second honeymoon, to try to rekindle what we had. But she came up with some lame excuse the day before we were to leave. So I went without her."

"What did she think about that?" Hayden sounded tense, perhaps embarrassed.

"She tried to guilt me into staying home. But I needed to

leave. It was as if the trip would separate us, then I could finally let go."

"Was that how it happened?" Hayden asked quietly.

"More or less. It had been over between us for a long time, but we were both just cruising along day to day. No conflict, no problems, no passion, nothing. I knew it but just didn't do anything about it. Her refusal to go to Khao Lak was the final straw. Actually, there weren't any straws. We didn't fight. Or fuck," she added sarcastically.

"When did you decide to…let go?"

Emily knew what she was asking. "It wasn't about you, Hayden. I didn't cheat on Michelle when we were together. I'd already made up my mind before we met. On the flight over, I decided I would tell her as soon as I got back. So when I landed in Thailand, I was free and single."

Hayden didn't say anything. "Infidelity is not an option for me, no matter what the circumstances. But once I made the decision it was over, it was over."

"She didn't seem to think so when I saw her," Hayden said. "She certainly gave the impression it was your house together."

"Technically it is still our house. Michelle refuses to discuss selling it, and since both our names are on the deed…" Emily left the statement open for Hayden to make her own conclusion.

"Did you ever say anything about us?"

"No, but she guessed something had happened other than surviving the tsunami. She would toss out innuendos and leave comments hanging in the air hoping I'd say something. But I never did."

"Why not?"

"It had nothing to do with her. I wish I'd been able to speak with her before we met, but I have no regrets."

"Have you considered trying again with her?"

"There's no point. She's asked me. She said that my almost dying made her realize how much she loved me. But our relationship has been dead for a long time. I just had to bury it." Emily recalled the numerous discussions she and Michelle had when she returned. Some were calm, others filled with rivers of tears and angry, hurtful words. "Actually, it was almost dying that made me realize even more how unhappy I was. I decided I was going to live the rest of my life very differently. It sounds corny, but it's true."

After a long pause, Hayden said, "Thank you for telling me. I owe you an apology."

"Okay, we're square. What are we going to do about this *Bugle* piece? More importantly, what is going to happen to *you*?" Emily wasn't concerned about herself; she was a big girl. Hayden was the one who had everything to loose.

"I'll be fine. We've done nothing wrong. No one knows what happened in Khao Lak, and everything in that article is conjecture. There are very few facts. As for the photos, they simply show two survivors of a terrible tragedy reuniting. Why wouldn't we stay in touch?"

"You make it sound so…what is the word…plausible," Emily said.

"You don't sound convinced."

"No, no, that's not it. It's just that you're going to be eaten alive over this, and I'm sorry."

The Army would abide by their "Don't ask, don't tell" policy, but they would take care of this little embarrassment in their own subtle way. Emily was afraid for Hayden. The military was her career, and it could very well be ripped away from her in an instant.

"Don't worry about me, Emily. I'll be fine. This will blow over in a few days and we'll go back to anonymity. Our fifteen minutes of fame will expire in twelve."

"You think so?"

"There's no story," Hayden said. "You and I are the only two people in the world who know the truth."

"The truth," Emily murmured, wondering what Hayden's "truth" was. Wanting to find out, face-to-face, she asked, "When can I see you?"

She heard some muffled sounds. Hayden had placed her hand over the receiver. Her voice was strained when she spoke again.

"I have to go. I'll call you."

Emily didn't have time to reply before the line went dead.

CHAPTER FIFTEEN

After a thirty-minute tongue-lashing by General Foreman, Hayden had one hour to pack a bag and be on a plane to Washington DC. She wanted to call Emily and tell her, or warn her, but she didn't want her to worry. She could take care of herself, but she had a bad feeling about this. Eventually, she couldn't resist hearing Emily's voice and called her from the airport. They spoke for less than a minute. Hayden explained where she was and that she would probably be under orders not to speak to Emily. Emily reacted with a concern for her welfare that was the total opposite of her scathing comments the other day. Her gentle words made Hayden cautiously optimistic.

In Washington, three men grilled her for hours about what she'd done before, during, and after the tsunami struck. They didn't wear uniforms, but their haircuts and stiff demeanor told Hayden they were Army and on a witch hunt. They wanted details, absolutely every detail. They didn't get any from her.

On her third day she knew her fate. The Army was going to put their spin on the story and use her as a poster child for effective military training. Her physical training had saved three lives, and her mental toughness got them back safe. The Army would drop all charges against Emily and parade Hayden around the country as though on a USO tour. The Army needed a boost. A boost in morale and image, and in enlistment. They knew it and Hayden knew it. She was sick to her stomach.

Her cell phone rang as soon as her return flight landed and she knew instinctively that it was her father. Much to the chagrin of her fellow passengers, she ignored the ring tone and let the call roll into voicemail. He was not the person she needed to talk to. However, a conversation with Emily would have to wait. The people surrounding her had big ears and even bigger mouths.

She waited impatiently for her luggage and forced herself not to run to her car. The familiar chirp of the alarm echoed in the parking garage. She tossed her bag into the trunk. It wasn't until she'd closed the driver's door firmly behind her that she reached for her phone. She'd been ordered to stay away from Emily until the Army's public relations people spoke to her first and she had taken that command literally. She would not see Emily, but even by calling her, Hayden was consciously disobeying a direct order. The phone clicked into voicemail and she left a message.

Traffic was light and it only took her fifteen minutes to get home. She tossed her mail on the counter and closed the door behind her. Dropping her suitcase at her feet, she kicked off her shoes and unbuttoned her cuffs. She glanced at her answering machine, and the rapid blinking of the red light told her there were several messages waiting. Emily didn't know her home number, so Hayden walked right by the little black box, sidestepped the pile of uniforms waiting to go the laundry, and headed for the shower.

No amount of scalding water or scrubbing could wash off the disgust she felt. For the first time in her career, she was ashamed of the Army, of what they were capable of doing. First they were after her hide, and when they didn't get what they were looking for, they decided to use her to their advantage regardless of what she or Emily wanted. She was used to this, but with her rank, she'd mistakenly thought she deserved better.

Hayden cocked her head, certain she had heard her cell phone ringing. Opening the shower door, she heard the distinctive ring again and jumped out of the shower. She snatched the phone from the counter, leaving droplets of water scattered across the floor.

"Emily?"

"Hayden, I was worried about you."

There was something in Emily's voice that Hayden didn't understand. She took it for irritation and replied a little too sharply, "I'm sorry you were worried. I told you not to."

"Well, I was, and I don't take orders from you. Look, Hayden, I'm sorry. I've been a bit on edge since this whole thing started as you can imagine. I'm not used to this kind of scrutiny." She paused. On a puzzled note, she asked, "Where are you?"

"In the shower. Actually, getting out of the shower." Hayden turned off the faucet and reached for the towel. "Emily?"

"Yes, I'm here. Look, I've called at a bad time, why don't you call me back when you—"

"No, I'm okay. Just give me a minute to dry off. Shit." Hayden dropped the phone. Hastily picking it up, she asked, "Emily, you still there?"

She'd caught snippets of the news and could only imagine what a circus Emily must be going through. Her soft voice was music to Hayden's ears.

"Yes, I'm here."

Hayden wrapped a thick blue terrycloth robe around her and turned off the bathroom light. Belting the robe, she walked down the short hall to the kitchen. "How are you?"

"I'm fine, now that you've called. What happened in Washington?"

"I've been reassigned."

"To where?" Emily sounded panicked.

"PR." Even saying the acronym gave her heartburn.

"Puerto Rico?"

Hayden chuckled. "No, public relations. They're going to parade me around the country as a symbol of the Army. You know, 'we can make you a hero' kind of stuff." She still had the bad taste in her mouth, hours after being told by the military brass.

"I take it you're not too happy." There was a trace of humor. "You don't seem the type who revels in the spotlight."

"Neither do you. And I have bad news. You'll be hearing from someone soon about your role in this patriotic endeavor." Hayden had rebuked the idea of Emily's involvement, to no avail.

"Me? Why me?" Emily sighed. "Never mind. That was a dumb question. I know why they want me."

"They're going to drop the trespassing charges against you, and I have to do any interview they arrange. They've already got me lined up for the morning news shows next week in New York."

Hayden had been furious when they told her she would be on the national morning talk shows. They were also working on something with Larry King. Even though she didn't want to be their poster child, she could handle it, but she didn't want Emily to have to face the intrusive questions and constant scrutiny. Hayden was an officer, and it was her job to represent the Army. Emily was just a bystander, and it infuriated Hayden that she was going to be used and there was nothing either of them could do to stop it.

"I'm sorry, Emily."

"There's nothing for you to be sorry about. You didn't do anything. Other than save my life and those two kids. You know, typical stuff in the life of an Army officer."

"Is that why you despise me so much?" The question came out of the blue, but Hayden knew it had been festering ever since their lunch. She grabbed a beer out of the nearly empty fridge and sat on the couch.

Emily dropped her head in her hands. "I don't despise you, Hayden."

"Could have fooled me."

"Hayden, I don't. How could I? It's not you, it's the whole

idea of the military. Their outdated ideas and methods and heavy-handedness in places where we don't belong."

Hayden's beer suddenly tasted flat and unappealing. "They're one and the same," she countered, holding her breath, waiting for another caustic remark about her life.

There was a long pause before Emily finally spoke. "Am I going to be doing some of these appearances with you?"

Hayden grimaced as she explained the deal. "Yes, they want you for a kind of point-counterpoint thing. You know, you have a right to voice your opinion, and the military is in existence to preserve that right."

"My God, Hayden. I'm sorry." Emily didn't sound angry.

"You have nothing to be sorry about. You were just floating by, minding your own business, when I decided to snatch you up. If they could find the kids, I'm sure they'd have them on as well. Oh, by the way, I'm not supposed to talk to you about this. As a matter of fact, I was given strict orders not to see you."

"Then why are we having this conversation?"

"They said I couldn't *see* you. They didn't say anything about not *talking* to you." Hayden had used this same argument in her mind many times and it still sounded weak. She knew what the order really meant.

"That's stretching it a bit, don't you think?" Emily's tone was warm and tender.

"Maybe, but who's going to tell them? You?"

"No, ma'am, not me. So when can I expect to hear from your bosses?"

"Probably sooner rather than later. They want to get some serious mileage out of this and the story is going to fade fast if they don't jump on it." Hayden heard the click of Emily's call waiting. "That's probably them now," she said jokingly.

"They can wait," Emily said. "Hayden, we have to talk."

Her voice was different, more serious and Hayden knew what she wanted to talk about. "We shouldn't have this conversation on the phone." So far no one knew about what happened at Khao

Lak, and Hayden wanted to keep it that way. For both their sakes.

"You're right, I didn't think about that. Can we meet somewhere? I promise I won't bite your head off this time. Or at least I'll try not to," Emily added lightly.

Hayden smiled. She wanted to see Emily again, if only to gaze into her dark brown eyes, listen to her voice, and watch her hands move. But she'd already gone too far and they both knew it. "I can't."

"When can I see you? I need to see you again."

Hayden felt frustrated and helpless. "I don't know. I'll have to play it by ear until they're comfortable with us together. The protest and the pictures have made them nervous. When the time is right, I'll ask, but until then…"

"All right, but can we at least call each other?"

"I'd like that," Hayden said firmly.

She'd had plenty of time to think about Emily on her flights to and from Washington. Emily was unlike any woman she had known before. She was strong and impulsive, and even though Emily disagreed with everything Hayden stood for, she still showed her respect. Emily was not afraid to voice her opinion and she accepted the consequences even when they were as unpleasant as going to jail. In some ways, Hayden respected her more than she respected herself. She was tired of taking orders.

"Worried" was not a strong enough word to describe what Emily had gone through over the past few days. She felt anxious and at odds with herself the entire time Hayden was gone. She couldn't step out of the house without having to muscle her way through the media that had practically cordoned off the street. She closed the curtains and jumped every time her phone rang, hoping it was Hayden calling. But ever since the story had broken, the phone had rung constantly. The local news stations were clamoring for an interview, and *Good Morning America* and *The Today Show* wanted to fly her to New York to be on their morning programs. Everyone wanted to talk to her, but the only one she wanted to talk to was not responding to her voice messages.

Emily sighed in relief that she was back on firm ground at last. All it had taken was the sound of Hayden's voice and a short conversation. While Hayden was gone, she'd practically relived their time together on Khao Lak. Hayden had been strong without being overpowering, resourceful without being a know-it-all, and most of all, kind and gentle to her and the children.

Emily now knew where her instincts came from, what made her the woman who'd saved their lives. She was a soldier, plain and simple, U.S. government trained, and Emily thanked Uncle Sam for every minute. Regardless of her distaste for the military, she could see that Hayden had used her training and ingenuity to keep them alive. She'd sacrificed her well-being several times, getting get them to safety.

The image of Hayden standing naked and wet flashed in Emily's mind and her hands started to tremble. She was suddenly thirsty to lick the droplets from hard, tan skin, all the while caressing the exposed flesh. She needed to sit down before she fell down. Hayden had no idea what effect she had. During their phone call, erotic images danced around in Emily's head. The tone of Hayden's voice was the same one she remembered from that night on the beach. It had a slight whisper of longing and awe, but also an edge of concern. She wanted to hear it again. Very soon. And not at the other end of a telephone.

Hayden stood ramrod straight looking out the window onto Times Square. Why they called it the green room she didn't know. It was decorated in hues of blue and tans that reminded her of her parents' bedroom. Emily was on the other side of the room sitting in one of the wing chairs, and they had barely said anything to each other since she entered the room ten minutes ago. The chief protocol officer, or CPO, had done most of the talking, coaching them in what to say and how to say it. Brad Tillman was a civilian hired by the military to act in an advisory role, similar to that of a public relations firm. He had several meetings with them leading up to this trip to New York. Hayden had nicknamed him "The Handler" minutes after he opened his mouth.

She was still recovering from the effects of seeing Emily first thing this morning. She'd exited the hotel elevator wearing a royal blue suit with brass buttons down the front of the jacket. Her hair was up in a French knot and her makeup was impeccable. Her legs were longer than Hayden remembered and were covered in what looked like silk stockings. Black pumps tapped out a solid beat across the marble floor. She looked elegant and beautiful, and Hayden stared at her as she walked across the lobby toward them. The CPO murmured something that sounded an awful lot like "Holy shit, she's hot" but Hayden was too spellbound to notice. She had no idea how she had managed to do her first interview with Emily looking like that.

"Colonel, are you listening?" Tillman asked.

Hayden turned away from the view of the city and fought to keep her eyes from drifting to Emily. Her short skirt was even shorter when she crossed her legs. "Yes, I'm listening."

"Good. Now, do either of you have any questions about the rest of the schedule?"

They shook their heads.

Tillman said, "I'm sure I don't need to remind you that you're here representing the U.S. Army and should behave accordingly, even in private. You never know whose eyes could be on you."

"I understand," Emily said.

The interview went about as Hayden expected. Their host was an African American with a British accent who kept referring to the teleprompter for every question. The makeup itched, the questions were boring and the seats uncomfortable.

Hayden did not relax until they were out of the building. The cool New York morning air was refreshing after the hot lights in the studio. They walked the three blocks to their hotel, Tillman continuing his lecture the entire way. The bellman held the door and they stepped into the bustling lobby.

Hayden was too on edge to return to her room. She needed to walk off some of her energy. Having Emily sitting beside her for the past few hours, looking absolutely fabulous, had raised her temperature.

"I'm going to take a walk."

Their handler glanced at her, surprised. Hayden suspected his job was to keep an eye on them as well as get them from appearance to appearance. "I can accompany you."

"I'll be fine, Mr. Tillman. I promise I won't get lost and I don't think I'll get mugged. I'll see you all tomorrow morning." Hayden spun on her heel, not giving the CPO the chance to reply.

She darted out the door and fell into the morning crowd crossing the street like a swarm of bees. She kept walking until she rounded the next corner, then stepped into the doorway of a shop not yet opened for business and looked around to get her bearings. Spotting a coffee shop a few doors down, she melted in with the crowd again.

She ordered a plain black coffee when those around her were ordering drinks with words like latte, non-fat, mocha, venti, Frappuccino, and chai. She felt a little out of place. Everyone in the store wore uniforms of one type or another, including thousand-dollar business suits, Dockers, or jeans and flip-flops. Hers just stood out more prominently than the others. She was surprised when it was her turn at the cash register to hear that beverages were free for members of the military in uniform.

She mumbled a polite thank-you and found a table by the window.

A woman who looked like Emily walked by and Hayden jumped from her chair intending to go after her. After an instant, she realized the woman was a stranger and returned to her seat, deflated. Emily's face danced in front of her. Her eyes sparkled and she had a smile that could light up the night. This morning she was intelligent and poised. It was a side of her that Hayden hadn't seen, and she'd been enthralled. She could picture her on a podium accepting the Nobel Prize, cameras flashing from every direction.

During the interview, it had been difficult to maintain her concentration. When Emily spoke, the words sounded like a melody flowing from her lips. On those rare occasions when she looked at Emily, Hayden had completely lost track of what was being said, and at one point she had to ask the host to repeat the question. She couldn't keep making that mistake, so she needed to concentrate. Now that she knew what to expect, she would be better prepared.

Dropping her empty cup in the garbage can by the door, she headed back to the hotel. She had all day to kill and needed to burn off some more excess energy, but she didn't want to do it in her uniform. She was fairly confident that she would not run into the CPO or Emily when she strode through the lobby.

Chapter Sixteen

"Hayden?"

The way her name was called, it could have been either a question or a statement. She recognized the voice and turned around to meet the eyes that rattled her each time she looked into them.

"I've been waiting for you," Emily said.

Hayden couldn't help but smile. "Then I'm glad I came back to change clothes."

"Me too. These chairs aren't the most comfortable."

Emily had changed into a pair of faded jeans, a long-sleeve dark red T-shirt, and a pair of sneakers. Her hair was down and her faced scrubbed free of the pancake makeup so skillfully applied at the studio. She looked young, fresh, and beautiful.

The silence stretched and even though the lobby was noisy, Hayden could hear her heart pound. A series of questions ran through her head as to why Emily was waiting. Did she want to talk about the show tomorrow or something entirely different? Did she want to take Hayden upstairs to her room and make love in a comfortable bed this time, or were they going to pretend their one time together didn't happen? Hayden waited.

Emily's gaze darted around the lobby. "Can we talk?"

They were still under the thumb of Tillman and she had strict orders not to be alone with Emily. Hayden knew the military was off their rocker to think that people didn't fraternize up just because they said so. And she really wanted to fraternize with Emily again.

"I was going to spend the day sightseeing. Would you like to come along?" she asked hopefully. If they were seen together, it would simply be a case of two out-of-towners playing tourist.

"I'd love to," Emily replied excitedly.

Hayden couldn't help but respond to the joy in Emily's expression. "I'm going to change clothes. I'll be down in a few minutes. There's a coffee shop down the street about a block or so," She pointed in the direction she had just come. "Why don't you wait for me there? I won't be long."

She knew that it would be less than five minutes before she was standing in front of Emily again, this time in a totally different uniform.

"Okay, I'll see you there. Would you like me to order you some coffee or something?"

"No, thanks, I've had my fill for the day. But you go ahead if you'd like."

When Emily nodded, Hayden stepped away and headed for the elevators, her original destination when she entered into the lobby a few minutes ago. She was an imposing figure in her uniform, and every eye in the lobby watched her.

One of the spectators, Emily was transfixed. Her heart raced as she remembered how it felt to be held in Hayden's arms, safe and warm and absolutely adored. She wanted to be held by her again. She ached to make love with her once more. With her pulse racing, she stepped out of the revolving door and was almost run over by a pedestrian who muttered something about "fucking tourists." She quickly fell into step with the other walkers headed in the same direction she was. She wondered what the street looked like from the roof of the tall buildings on Park Avenue that towered above her. She imagined the passersby were all ants scurrying to and fro, their eyes straight ahead in concentration like good little workers.

Emily found the coffee shop, and when she stepped inside, the smell of fresh ground coffee, cinnamon, and warm bread assailed her nostrils. The only empty table was in the back, and she stirred the sugar into her decaf on the way. She had barely sat down when Hayden walked in. Emily had a moment to observe her and grabbed the opportunity. Hayden had changed into a pair of Doc Martens, khaki pants, and a dark blue button-down shirt. Her hair was mussed. Many times in Khao Lak Emily had seen Hayden run her fingers through her hair. She thought it was more out of habit than the need to push any wayward strands from her eyes.

The expression on Hayden's face was not one she had seen today. Before and during the show this morning, Hayden wore a serious look, almost a scowl, as if she were trying to hold something in. Now she looked optimistic. Either way, Emily was glad to see her, and she was especially happy to see her alone.

"That didn't take long," she said and at once wanted to kick herself. She didn't want Hayden to know that she was actually aware of the time they were apart. How sappy.

"Years of practice," Hayden replied, making fun of herself. "You know, I can be packed and ready for a twelve-month deployment in thirty minutes." She explained this as if it were the most important thing on the face of the earth.

"Wow." Emily played along. She feigned being awestruck. "That's a skill every girl should have."

She was rewarded with a bright smile that practically lit up Hayden's entire face. "Yep, and if you play your cards right, I just might show you how I roll my clothes to save space in my bag."

"Promise?" Emily asked in her best child's voice. She felt anything but childlike sitting across from Hayden. She felt like a woman, a woman who wanted to spend the day getting to know her knight. "I don't want to intrude on your plans for the day," she said, suddenly feeling nervous.

"You're not. I don't really have any. I was going to see the typical tourist sights, and maybe even a few that aren't. That's all." Hayden hesitated and then looked into Emily's eyes. "I was also going to try to not think about how you looked in that suit this morning."

Emily's heart jumped. "Really?" Emily held Hayden's gaze.

"Really. Like to damn near killed me when you stepped out of the elevator," Hayden responded, her eyes raking over Emily's body.

"Well, I'm glad to see that you're okay."

"It was touch and go there for a minute, but I managed to pull it together."

Emily shook her head. "Very admirable." She suspected Hayden had several admirers. Why wouldn't she? She was good looking and smart, and had a job. All the important things.

She'd had a difficult time keeping her eyes off Hayden during the interview, too. Forget about in the green room, she hadn't even tried. Hayden was stunning in her uniform; she oozed confidence and control. She was everything the Army wanted her to be. There were times when Emily didn't think she could string more than two words together to form a coherent response to a question, but Hayden was totally in control. She listened attentively, thought for a moment, and then replied clearly and concisely. She didn't embellish her reply, nor did she give one-word answers. She was calm, cool and very professional.

Emily, on the other hand, was a nervous wreck. What she really wanted to say was that she'd been plucked from danger by a strong, debonair, witty, charming, drop-dead gorgeous knight in shining armor. It was the perfect plot for a Harlequin romance. What made this story different was that Emily's knight just so happened to be the most amazing woman she had ever met.

The bantering stopped and Emily could not think of anything else to say.

Hayden helped her by extending her hand across the table. "Are you ready? I think the Statue of Liberty is calling our name."

❖

The day passed and they had only seen a few of the sights identified as "must see" in the tourist guide Hayden bought at a newsstand. They rode the subway to Yankee Stadium, bought souvenirs on Ellis Beach, and prayed at Ground Zero. They were walking through Central Park just before sunset and stopped to allow a horse-drawn carriage to cross the street in front of them when Hayden finally brought up the subject that had hung in the thick air.

"You said you wanted to talk."

It took a moment for Emily to grasp the question and even longer to formulate a response. "Um, yes, I did, didn't I? We've never really had a chance to talk about Khao Lak. About what happened."

Hayden knew what she was getting at. Sure, they had talked, but they had skirted around what had happened between them. She took Emily's elbow and crossed the street to a bench in a quiet spot.

Even though she was the one who'd brought the subject up in the first place, Emily didn't know where to begin. The sun was just beginning to set and the remaining rays streaked through the trees, leaving fingerlike traces of light on the dirt path. "I don't know what to say."

Hayden had prepared herself for "I hate you" or "I want to do it again," but not the uncertainty she saw in Emily's expression. "What do you want to say?" she asked.

Hayden knew what *she* would say if things were different. If they were different people. *I'd like to see you again.*

Emily decided to be as honest as she knew how. "Well, before I knew anything about you other than your name, I suppose I would have said that that night was fabulous and I want to see you again."

"But?"

"Then I saw you at the base. I was shocked, to say the least, and I probably would have said something ugly and hateful. But now, after spending the day with you, I have absolutely no idea." Emily turned her palms up, signifying her confusion.

"Why do you hate me?" Hayden asked, wondering if she'd get a straight answer this time. She wasn't even sure she wanted to know.

"I don't hate you, Hayden."

"All right, then, let me rephrase the question. Why do you hate everything that I am?" She knew she was rehashing questions she had asked earlier, but she had not yet gotten a straight answer. Hayden was tired of people looking at her as if she were stupid for choosing the military as her career. Some even went so far as to make comments to her in the checkout line or the gas pump that she should get out before she got sent "over there." That attitude coming from Emily was the last straw.

"At the risk of repeating myself, I don't hate you."

"Let's not quibble over a few words. You know what I'm talking about. You hate anything that has to do with the military. You hate the fact that I'm an Army officer and everything that means. You hate that I serve my country without question. You think I'm some kind of tyrant when I issue orders and you absolutely can't stand the fact that I follow them. What more is it than that?" Hayden looked straight ahead.

"Hayden, my best friend Kim was lured into the Marines by all the pomp and pride, snappy uniforms, and that *The Few, the Proud, the Marines* bullshit. She blindly left her job, her husband, and her two-year-old daughter to *be all she could be*. And you know what? She died. She was gunned down by a sniper in the middle of the street in some fucking God-only-knows dirt little town in Iraq."

Hayden didn't think it wise to correct Emily that the *be all she could be* was the Army tag line, not the Marines. She watched a range of emotions play across her face.

Emily remembered when Kim's husband Phil had called to

break the news. She was stunned by his precise, clipped words. "She's dead." That was all he said. No prelude, no "I'm sorry for calling so late." Just two simple words that changed her life forever.

She and Kim had been friends since the third grade when the tall, gangly girl from Oklahoma sat next to Emily in the lunch room. From that point on they were inseparable, spending almost every waking hour with each other. They were in the same homeroom class the following year and several other years as well. Their lockers were next to each other in high school, they were both on the debate team, the chess club, and the yearbook committee. They'd even double-dated a few times—until one tear-filled night when Emily finally told Kim she thought she might be a lesbian.

She was terrified that she would lose Kim's friendship, but Kim had told her there were only a few things that could end their friendship, and Emily's sexual orientation was not one of them. After talking for several more hours, they fell asleep next to each other, exhausted and closer than ever before.

Emily was the maid of honor when Kim married Phil and had waited nervously in the waiting room when their daughter was born. They spoke on the phone at least three or four times a week and saw each other several times a month. Kim was the sister Emily never had, and she was petrified when she enlisted. She had a wonderful husband, a beautiful little girl, and great friends. Emily had not understood when Kim said she needed a purpose in her life.

"Emily, if Kim was your friend, then she had to have a mind of her own. I doubt if she was coerced or persuaded into doing anything she didn't want to. After September eleventh, a lot of people simply felt the need to do something. They wanted to defend our country. Defend the rights the terrorists were trying to take away from us."

"But how could she leave her baby and just go?"

"I doubt it was that simple."

"You don't know shit about it." Emily was angry again. The heads of a few pedestrians turned their way.

"You're right, I don't know anything about your friend or her circumstances. But I do know about the people who voluntarily serve their country. They are strong and proud and believe it's an honor to serve. Do they gladly go to war and die? Of course not. No one in their right mind wants to die, especially so far away from their loved ones. But it's their job, the one they signed up for. So don't blame the military for what happened to Kim. Blame the Iraqi that shot her. Blame her squad that didn't have her back. Blame the little kid she was handing a candy bar to. Blame her for volunteering in the first place. To tar and feather me by association is no better than thinking I pulled the trigger."

Hayden stood up from the bench, angry and wanting to simply walk away. Away from Emily, her opinions, and the confusion she felt every time she thought of her. Where was her simple, ordered life? Where had it gone? And did she really want it back?

She felt the sting of Emily's words as they walked silently back to the hotel. She didn't look at Emily but felt her presence beside her. She nodded to the doorman, entered the cool lobby, and headed straight for the bar. She needed a drink to calm her nerves—several, as a matter of fact. And maybe even a few hours in the arms of a beautiful New Yorker. She groaned when she saw her handler, and by the look on his face, knew she would probably not get either.

"Where have you been? I've been calling your room all afternoon."

Hayden was in no mood to be bullied by this twerp. "I wasn't aware we had any commitments this afternoon," she replied, not answering his question. It was none of his business where she'd been and he certainly wouldn't like it if he knew.

"I wanted to discuss tomorrow's interview, Colonel."

Hayden didn't rise to the invitation. If he was going to

critique her performance, he should have said so and done it immediately after the interview when her answers were fresh in her mind. "What about it?"

He shifted his weight from foot to foot and Hayden knew he was uncomfortable with the setting of their conversation. Her tone and her "don't fuck with me right now" stance probably didn't help. When he didn't answer quickly enough for her short fuse she said, "I've read the briefing several times, Tillman. I think I know what to say. I was there, remember?"

She knew her comment was snippy, but she was not in the mood to have this conversation. She was angry. Angry at Emily for dumping her and every other serviceman and woman into a category that most didn't deserve. Yes, there were soldiers who blindly followed orders and those who got off on issuing them, but those people were rare in the Army, she knew. Emily's assumptions and preconceived ideas were prejudiced and just flat-out wrong.

Hayden was angry at herself as well. This was not the first time she'd been exposed to someone who believed as Emily did. She didn't give any of these opinions a second thought. But coming from Emily, the stereotypes hurt. They had shared something, and Hayden realized that she expected them to be bound effortlessly together by it. Obviously Emily had missed that memo.

"I wasn't implying that you're not prepared." Tillman all but stumbled over his apology.

"I'll be fine. Your briefing packet was very thorough. I know who's going to ask the questions and what I'm going to say. It will be even easier the second time around. Now, if you'll excuse me, I have to go."

She left him with an exasperated look on his face and disappeared into the elevator.

❖

Emily sat on the couch in the lobby, not yet ready to go up to her room and stung by the severity of Hayden's words. They'd had a wonderful day, or at least she thought they had. She was hoping to have a quiet dinner with Hayden and continue the easy conversation they shared during their tour of the city. Her hopes were dashed when one minute they were talking and the next they were in each other's faces, arguing.

She hadn't meant to start in with the story of Kim. Her nerves were still raw and she had not yet finished grieving for her friend, but she knew that if she didn't get a hold of this anger, someday it would get her in trouble.

"Like getting arrested for trespassing on a military base isn't trouble," she said to herself.

Emily stretched out her legs and leaned her head back against the soft cushions. Her anger toward Hayden had cooled and in its place was a sense of melancholy. She replayed Hayden's words in her mind. It was unfair for her to paint Hayden with the same brush she applied to the military. Hayden was as much an individual as she was a military officer. The two were interrelated like the individual threads of a rope, the strands wrapped together to create something stronger than the single pieces.

Emily gave up trying to sort out which threads made sense to her and headed for the elevator. Her stomach was growling and all she wanted was to order room service and take a hot bath. Tomorrow morning would come early, and she had a nagging feeling that she would not sleep much again tonight. She hesitated when she saw Tillman standing in the lobby, and he chose that moment to turn around. Emily cursed that she was not quick enough to escape without being seen and pasted a smile on her face as he approached.

Tillman was in his mid thirties and quite attractive in a Cary Grant sort of way. Unfortunately for Emily, he knew it. He smiled when he saw her, and she could almost feel the charm ratcheting up.

"Ms. Bradshaw, there you are."

For a moment, Emily thought he was going to give her a peck on the cheek like she was a long-lost friend.

"Mr. Tillman," she replied coolly.

"Brad, please. We're going to be spending too much time together to bother with formalities. May I call you Emily?"

She would have loved to say no, but her parents had taught her to be more polite. Still, she couldn't bring herself to actually give him permission. His forwardness was something new, and Emily had a bad feeling about it. He reminded her of a pompous fraternity boy she'd known in grad school.

"I was wondering if you'd like to have a drink? I'd like to talk to you about the show tomorrow. There is a cozy piano bar in the penthouse with a fabulous view of the city."

"I'm hardly dressed for it," Emily replied, hoping he'd jump at the excuse.

What her reluctance did, however, was give him reason to leer, no doubt imagining what she looked like underneath the layers.

"Nonsense, you look lovely," he said. "It's nothing formal. Come on, let's grab this elevator."

He took her elbow and shepherded her into the elevator she was hoping would take her to her room. It passed her floor and kept climbing. Tillman chatted nonstop, and five long minutes later they were seated at a table, waiting for their waitress to bring their drink order. The lounge was dark with a smattering of light reflecting off candles at each table. Indirect lighting on the walls gave the room a soft, seductive atmosphere.

"So, Emily, how do you think it went this morning?" Tillman's palms were together, his fingers steepled under his chin. He looked like he was about to pray.

"I think it went well. Colonel Caldwell is a good spokesman. She didn't appear to be nervous at all." Emily thought back to how calm and self-assured Hayden had been under the bright lights.

"Yes, the Army's done a very good job with her."

Something in Tillman's voice made her ask, "What do you mean?"

"Why, your conflict, of course."

Their waitress arrived with their drinks and Emily waited until she'd left before asking, "Our conflict?" She knew what he was talking about but wanted to hear from him just how big a conflict he thought it was.

"Yes. She was calm and never gave one indication how angry she is that you dared to trespass on her base." Tillman sipped his drink.

"I didn't know who she was when we selected Fort Tanner," Emily said. She didn't know why she was defending herself, and even less why she was defending Hayden.

"Yes, but still." He chose to elaborate. "She risked her life to save you, not once but twice, I may add. And you aren't falling all over yourself saying what a hero she is."

Emily took two swallows of her scotch, letting the hot liquid calm her. "Mr. Tillman." She couldn't bring herself to call him by his first name. "I've thanked the colonel in person, in print, and this morning on national television. I don't know her well at all, but I seriously doubt her nose is bent out of shape because I'm not, what did you call it, falling all over myself. What more am I supposed to do? Pledge my unending love and give her my firstborn?"

Tillman held his hands up. "Okay, okay. Look, I know you don't like the military and she doesn't like people like you…" He didn't get a chance to finish.

"What do you mean people like me?"

Tillman seemed a bit uncomfortable. "Well, you did protest at her base."

"So? It's my right to protest and speak my mind, and Colonel Caldwell would say it's her job to protect those rights." Emily surprised herself at her staunch defense of Hayden.

"Do you know she's a lesbian?"

Emily pulled out all of her experience to mask her reaction to Tillman's question. "What does that have to do with anything?"

"Did she hit on you?"

The leer in his eyes made Emily's stomach turn. "What are you talking about?"

"On the beach, under the stars, when you two were naked in the tree." His gestures indicated he could give many more examples.

Emily met his gaze head-on. She knew he was fishing for something and doing a terrible job of being subtle. He was looking for dirt, something to hang over their heads or to jerk off to if nothing else.

"Mr. Tillman, Colonel Caldwell was nothing but an officer the entire time, and she has continued to act in a way that the Army would be proud of. If you're looking for dirt, you need to dig it up somewhere else."

"Emily, please, I didn't mean to upset you. It's just that a woman like you needs to watch out for women like Caldwell. They'll come after you and won't take no for an answer, if you know what I mean."

He winked, and it was all Emily could do not to pour her drink in his lap. Where did the Army get this guy? He was a Neanderthal, or better yet, an idiot. He had to have seen the picture in the *Bugle* and the caption below it. Was he so dense that he couldn't see that she was a lesbian too? The sheer absurdity made her laugh.

"Let me assure you I can take care of myself around all kinds of people. Including you," she added, but he missed the inference. "Colonel Caldwell made no unwanted advances." Emily reminded herself to keep that exact phrase close by in case she needed it again. "Thank you for the drink, but I've got to prepare for tomorrow. Don't get up," she said as Tillman started to rise. "I can find my way back to my room. Good night."

Emily listened for Tillman's footsteps behind her as she

waited for the elevator. She exhaled in relief when the doors closed and she was alone in the plush car. She punched the button for Hayden's floor and watched the numbers above the mirrored doors as she slowly descended.

CHAPTER SEVENTEEN

The knock on the door was tentative. Hayden set her laptop down on the bed and crossed to the door. The hotel room was the largest she had ever stayed in, and if it weren't for the hospitality of *Good Morning America* she never would have seen it in the first place. If it had been left up to good old Uncle Sam, she would be stuck in a Motel 6 in New Jersey, with a cracker-box rental car. The thick carpet muffled her footsteps and she had to bend down slightly to see through the peephole. She opened the door instantly.

"Hayden, I have to talk to you." Emily looked up and down the hallway as though afraid someone would see her. She walked into the room, her eyes immediately moving across the large king-size bed that dominated it.

"Emily, what is it?" Hayden was worried. This was not the same angry woman she'd left in the lobby an hour ago.

Emily paced the room. Her pulse beat even faster than it had during her elevator ride. "It's Tillman."

"What about him?" Hayden had seen the way he looked at Emily. It was the same way she looked at her, and his obvious interest made her nervous. Had he made a pass?

"He said some very interesting things a few minutes ago, while we were having a drink in the lounge. I thought you should know."

"I'm almost afraid to ask," Hayden said dryly.

"After he'd finished lecturing me on how I need to swoon over you more for being my hero, he asked if I knew you were a lesbian. He also wanted to know if you made a move on me while we were on the beach." Emily felt herself blush slightly.

"And what did you tell him?" Hayden was so angry she could only think in short sentences.

"The truth. I told him that you did not make any unwanted advances toward me."

Hayden cocked her head at Emily's specific words. "Is it?"

Emily didn't understand the question. "Is it what?"

"The truth?" Hayden held her gaze.

Emily's heart jumped. "Yes. You didn't make any *unwanted* advances. I wanted you then, and I want you now." The words surprised her, and her hand flew to her mouth as if to stop anything else from slipping out.

Hayden could hardly breathe. Images flashed through her brain like a slide show, each more intense than the one before. And Emily was here now, in her room. They were alone and she'd just confessed that she wanted her. Hayden was unable to move.

"Hayden?" Emily watched as emotion clouded Hayden's expressive eyes. Fear and compassion. Anger, softness, and desire. It was desire that remained, and it was mirrored in the rumbling through Emily's veins.

Hayden finally found her voice. "How did you leave it? Your conversation with Tillman?"

This certainly wasn't the response Emily had expected. "Um, I told him I was perfectly capable of taking care of myself. I told him I had to prepare for tomorrow and left. I came right here."

"Why?" Hayden could not believe she was asking another stupid question. Emily wanted to make love with her again, and all she had in her repertoire were questions. God, she was pathetic, and by the look on Emily's face she thought so, too.

"Why? Because you need to know. Tillman's after something and we have to be careful."

"But everybody knows you're a lesbian. What do you need to worry about?" That was the crux of the matter here. Emily had absolutely nothing to hide. Hayden, however, did.

"I'm not going to be the one they use to out you. Your association with me is enough to start tongues wagging. And who knows what some horny creep like Tillman would say. You could lose everything if it got out."

And it would kill Emily if she were the cause.

"Why do you care what happens to me?" Hayden felt like she was picking a fight but she couldn't help herself. She was facing a ledge and she needed to know what her fallback positions were if she chose to go over it.

"Hayden, what in the fuck are you talking about? If I didn't care about you, do you think I'd be here? I'd throw your ass to the sharks and sit back and watch the feeding frenzy. I'd laugh as another stupid military regulation blows up in their face. Good God, Hayden, what kind of a person do you think I am?"

Emily was hurt that her motives were being questioned and that Hayden hadn't responded to her unsubtle hint about wanting her. But it wasn't two hours ago that she'd lit into Hayden about her military life, so she could understand her anger.

"Are you going to stand there and gawk at me or are you going to say something?" So far Hayden hadn't answered any of her questions but stood immobile with her hands clenched and her back ramrod straight.

Hayden wasn't gawking, she was feasting on the sight in front of her. Emily's eyes flashed daggers and her breathing was ragged. She was a beautiful woman and Hayden wanted her. Their differences were vast, but in the short time they'd known each other, Hayden had grown to respect her. Emily gave of herself every day for children who might never know a warm smile other than the ones she gave them. She'd gone against the path mapped out for her, to follow her conscience. She had strong beliefs and wasn't afraid to stand by them.

Hayden walked slowly across the space between them and stopped a mere hand's width from Emily. Emily's eyes could not be still, scientist eyes searching for an answer. Flecks of gold surrounded pupils dilated in expectation. Hayden felt her body being pulled as if she were a piece of steel and Emily a magnet. She ached to hold Emily in her arms again, to feel her soft skin, to hear whispers of desire fall from her lips. They were not touching, but Hayden felt as if she were wrapped in Emily from the inside out. She wanted her, desired her, had to have her. It took all her strength to not take Emily in her arms and kiss her.

She stepped back and dropped her eyes from the face indelibly burned into her brain. Emily's touch forever branded her. Her voice was hoarse when she answered Emily the only way she could.

"Thank you for telling me about Tillman."

The silence in the room was deadly. Hayden waited for Emily to respond, and when she didn't she lifted her gaze. Emily was staring at her with an incredulous look on her face. Hayden braced for the worst.

"That's all you have to say?" Emily wanted Hayden to hold her and kiss her and tell her everything was going to be all right. Hayden disappointed her when she did none of those. Shocked that Hayden could be so casual about something so special, Emily said, "You're a coward, Hayden."

Hayden felt the scathing reply as if she had been slapped. She wanted to say more, she wanted to say that she didn't care about Tillman or about her career. That all she wanted was to have Emily in her life. But she couldn't, and she was not sure why.

❖

Emily was halfway down the hall when she heard the door to Hayden's room latch. She pushed the elevator button, impatient and desperate to be back in her room. "Stupid, stupid, stupid," she chastised herself as she jabbed the button for her floor.

Her rebuke echoed in the empty elevator. She leaned back against the mahogany-paneled wall and stared at her bisected reflection in the mirrors on the doors. The image depicted exactly how she felt whenever she was around Hayden. One half wanted her, and the other didn't.

Emily had a corner room with large windows that filled two walls almost from floor to ceiling. The lights of the city floated into the room and would have been spectacular if Emily wasn't so distracted by the events of the entire day. She retraced her steps, kicking her shoes aside before tearing off the security seal on the mini-bar. She was in no mood for food, but the small bottle of Seagram's 7 caught her eye. Grabbing two bottles and a glass, she dropped into the lounge chair facing the window.

The contents of the first bottle burned as it went down her throat, but the second was smooth and warm. She let her mind shift away from dozens of thoughts dashing around in her head. But she could not forget the look on Hayden's face just moments ago. Her eyes were filled with passion and desire, their intensity almost frightening. Emily knew Hayden would never hurt her, but it was almost as if she were a feral cat stalking its prey.

She'd been surprised when Hayden stepped away. Surprised and disappointed. She wanted Hayden to kiss her, and by the look in her eyes Hayden wanted to do much, much more than simply kiss her. But she hadn't. She had stepped away, and Emily's disappointment and frustration turned into anger. Emily didn't want to hurt Hayden, but she had been so caught off guard, she didn't know what to do. She'd lashed out at her where it hurt the most, but her actions gave her no satisfaction.

Emily didn't bother closing the curtains as she stripped and climbed between the heavy sheets. Her room was on the sixth floor and the only people that could see her would have to be using a telescope, and she didn't care. There was a switch by the bed that overrode the automatic lighting system, and when Emily touched it the room fell into semidarkness.

The lights of the city reflected on the ceiling, reminding her of being in Hayden's arms in Khao Lak. Even before they made love, she'd sensed a connection between them that was more than just two survivors of a terrible tragedy. Where was that Hayden now? Where was the woman with the sense of humor and always a kind, reassuring word to say? Did she remain on the beach, or did she come home and have her spark extinguished by the suffocating military life? In the past twenty-four hours Emily had seen glimpses of her, on the observation deck of the Statue of Liberty, buying a hot dog from a street vendor, and at Ground Zero. But she wasn't here now, and she certainly wasn't in Hayden's room earlier.

"And why do I care?" Emily asked the shadows. "Why did I agree to this crazy tour in the first place?"

She knew the answers to her questions. She wanted to see Hayden again and had jumped at the chance to do so. She wanted to be with her and know everything about her. What made her smile, the name of her first grade teacher, did she like going to baseball games, eating peanuts and drinking beer? These were the thoughts that danced in her head as she fell asleep.

Hayden glanced in the mirror above the sink in her hotel room one last time. Dark circles were starting to emerge below her eyes. She hoped the studio makeup would hide the evidence that she had not slept well. She reached for the light switch but paused, examining her reflection instead. The woman staring back at her was the same one she'd seen for years, but as she looked closer she detected something had changed. Sure, there were a few more strands of gray in her hair and a couple of lines had sneaked up around her mouth, but it was her eyes that were different. Gone was the determined, focused look she'd seen every morning since boot camp. In its place was uncertainty.

Hayden sucked in a breath realizing that not only had she wanted Emily last night, but also yesterday, the day before, and even the day she had rescued her from the raging waters. Without even knowing it, she had become a different person on that fateful day in December. Emily had opened a chasm in her life that Hayden had not been aware was even there. She'd thought she was happy. Her life was in order, her future planned and on track. She had explored places all over the world, from Kazakhstan to Heidelberg to Antarctica. She had friends and acquaintances on every continent, some she would remain close to until she died. But this morning, her eyes reflected something that had burrowed its way deep into her chest.

Emily was right. She was a coward. She wanted Emily in her life but had done nothing to make it happen. Emily's presence hung in the room like a thick cloud, choking Hayden with regret. She wanted to take Emily in her arms and kiss her senseless; it was all she'd thought about as she lay awake most of the night. Restless, and disappointed in herself, she got dressed and drank coffee. On the table in front of her lay an assortment of brochures Emily had gathered as they'd toured the city.

Like a child, Emily was fascinated by everything she saw. She wanted to read every plaque and follow every trail on the map of Central Park. It was as if she was afraid she would never again be in New York and had to take it all in on this trip. She had been full of excitement and chatter all day, but when they approached Ground Zero she became silent. They were several blocks from the site of where the Twin Towers had once stood, two huge pillars extending into the air, defining the New York skyline, when Emily's steps slowed and the exuberance left her expression.

On the corner of Vesey and Church Street, she stopped and looked up. The expression on her face shifted from shock to anger, then profound sadness. Hayden didn't know if she was imagining that the towers were still standing or looking into the face of God. Either way, it was a moment Hayden would always remember.

When they arrived at the observation deck Emily stood close and didn't say anything. While others around them were equally respectful, there was a group of four or five teenagers to their left who were boisterous, their voices carrying above the quiet murmurs of respect. Emily glared at them, and when they didn't take the hint she walked over to them, her posture indicating a woman with a purpose. Hayden couldn't hear what she said but the teens lost their bravado and sullenly walked away. When Emily reclaimed her place beside Hayden, she slipped her hand into Hayden's just as she had during those days at Khao Lak. Most of the time, she needed assistance, but that last night, the night they made love under the stars, she had reached out to her in desire.

On the observation deck, Emily reached out, seeking comfort and offering it as well. Hayden didn't know how much she had needed that reassurance until Emily withdrew her hand when they started to leave.

A hard knock on her door accompanied by Tillman's brusque voice wrenched Hayden out of her reflections. With one last check to make sure she had everything she needed, she joined their handler in the hallway. Tillman said something obnoxious. Hayden congratulated herself for not flattening him.

The ride to the NBC studio was unbearably long. Emily had prepared herself to face Hayden this morning, but she had not anticipated the jolt of pleasure that shot through her body when she stepped out of the elevator. It was as if she'd never seen her before. Hayden was impeccably dressed in a uniform Emily suspected had been tailored to fit her perfectly. She'd seen dozens of similar uniforms, but none that looked as crisp as Hayden's. The sleeves of her jacket were the perfect length, revealing just the right amount of the cuff of her shirt. The fit of her pants accentuated her long legs, the hems buckling just enough to cover the tops of her shoes. The gold buttons gleamed from the lights in the lobby. A uniform could easily transform an ordinary-looking woman into a frump, or worse, a dyke. It turned Hayden into the most attractive woman Emily had ever seen.

Hayden sat across from her in the limo, her hands perfectly still on top of her thighs. She never stopped looking out the window. Emily sensed a tension in her that had not been there yesterday, and she suspected it was from their discussion the previous night. She felt bad about what she'd said. Hayden was not a coward, and Emily had no right to judge what she did or didn't do, but it had made her so angry she said the first thing that came to her. She wanted to apologize but so far had not had the chance.

The limo pulled up to the curb at Rockefeller Center and the doorman held the door. Tillman exited first, leaving Emily alone with Hayden for the first time that morning.

"Hayden," Emily started to say.

"They're waiting for us," Hayden replied stiffly, indicating the men standing on the sidewalk.

Hurt by the gruff response, Emily stepped out of the car, Hayden following a second behind her.

The accommodations were similar to those provided for them the previous day. Hayden sat to Emily's left in the makeup chair, the beautician adding touches of powder to her cheeks. Emily watched Hayden's reflection in the large lighted mirror, hoping to make eye contact, but Hayden never looked her way. Emily felt a pang of jealousy when she chatted easily with the makeup artist, who was offering a bird's-eye view of the cleavage exposed by her V-neck top. The second interview was similar to the first, with the host asking general questions before getting into the specifics about the tsunami. Hayden's eye twitched when the host referred to their experience as an adventure. An adventure was a hike in the Grand Canyon or kayaking down the Colorado River. Being washed inland by a thirty-foot tidal wave obliterating everything in its path, without regard to human life, was not what she would call an adventure.

She subtly corrected the highly groomed interviewer. "Like most people who went to Khao Lak Beach, adventure was not what I had in mind."

"And what did you have in mind?"

Hayden's eyes darted to Emily's. "Sun. Relaxation." Her smile was forced.

"Before the tsunami hit, were you finding what you were looking for?"

"Yes." For the first time that morning, she actually felt like smiling. "As a matter of fact, I found more than I was looking for."

She gave up fighting to keep her eyes off Emily. Her hair was down this morning and shimmered like the early morning sunshine. Her dark blue skirt was short, revealing far too much leg to be ignored, and Hayden was tired from commanding her eyes not to look.

As the questions progressed, she answered automatically, impatient for the interview to end. Emily had the last few questions, which gave Hayden an excuse to watch her attentively.

She knew her steady regard was affecting Emily when her voice fractured slightly and she gave a breathless laugh. The interview concluded with a cut to a breaking news item and Hayden unclipped the microphone from her jacket and handed it to the sound man. Emily was struggling with hers.

"Need some help?" Hayden reached out and unclipped the device before Emily had a chance to answer. The backs of her fingers lightly brushed against Emily's chest and she felt Emily stiffen in response. Looking into her eyes, Hayden asked, "Will you have breakfast with me?"

Emily was stunned. One moment Hayden was cold and aloof, the next she was looking at her as if *she* were for breakfast.

Her nipples strained against her bra and her breathing instantly become quick and shallow. Her pride was telling her to refuse the invitation, but her heart and body were saying something altogether different. She rationalized her response with the thought that she should apologize to Hayden for her outburst yesterday.

"All right." Her answer was hesitant, but at this point she couldn't jump in with both feet.

"Fabulous, ladies, absolutely fabulous," Tillman said, clapping his hands. "We have to go. The car should be downstairs. We can have breakfast in the airport."

Damn. Hayden had completely forgotten that they were flying to Chicago for an afternoon taping of Oprah, with other tsunami survivors. They were scheduled to appear the next day on *Good Morning Chicago.*

As soon as Tillman walked away she said softly, "I'm sorry about breakfast. I forgot we had to go right to the airport."

Emily gave her a reassuring smile. "I did, too."

Actually, she'd forgotten everything except the way her nipples tingled under the brush of Hayden's fingers. She shuddered, remembering the sensation. Hayden's eyes grew dark with arousal. Emily wanted nothing more than to kiss her, to be taken in her arms once again, but this was not the place. The smoldering look in her eyes right now told her something altogether different. Tillman called after them again and Emily didn't get a chance to say anything more.

The taping at Harpo Studios took longer than Hayden expected. It was the only show being taped that day, so the crew had the luxury of time. Between warming up the audience and staying for the social gathering after the taping, Hayden was not surprised when she glanced at her watch and saw that the entire afternoon had gone by. They were mingling with the other guests, Tillman never far from her side. When he wasn't, he kept glancing her way as if expecting her to drag some woman out of the room by her hair and ravish her on the hard tile of the hallway floor. She was tired of his constant hovering. He was either right on top of them or close enough to overhear anything she and Emily were saying.

When he stepped between them for the umpteenth time that day, Hayden said, "For God's sake, Tillman. I'm not going to touch her, if that's what you're afraid of." The look on his face confirmed that was exactly what he was afraid of. "You've been hovering around us like an old maid chaperone, and I am tired of it. I'm not a teenager who can't keep her hormones in check."

Hayden stopped when she realized she had practically admitted she was a lesbian. She waited for Tillman to reply, but it was Emily who spoke up.

"I've also had enough, Mr. Tillman. I told you I'm perfectly capable of taking care of myself, so back off."

Tillman looked as though he had been struck. He brought his hand to his chest. "Now ladies…" was as far as he got before Emily interrupted him.

"That's right, Mr. Tillman, we are ladies, and as such we deserve to be treated with a little more respect. Now, I'm going out to dinner with Colonel Caldwell and you are not invited. In fact, why don't you take the car and do whatever it is you would be doing if you weren't our shadow. We'll see you in the morning."

Hayden suppressed a laugh at the look on Tillman's face. He was beet red and looked like he was going to explode. He sputtered a few unintelligible words and walked away in a huff.

"Well, you certainly told him."

"He was making me nuts sniffing around us like a bounty hunter on the scent of a big kill." Emily chuckled. "The funny thing is, he was never going to catch us doing anything by being two feet from us all the time. What an idiot."

"I'm not sure he's ever been talked to like that. When you shook your finger at him I thought he was going to pee his pants." Emily reminded Hayden of her eighth grade teacher who had an annoying habit of pointing at absolutely everything.

They walked toward the exit doors and when they were alone in the corridor. Emily turned to Hayden. "Can he really report you?"

"Yes, he can. Activity doesn't have to be directly observed by a member of the military. Being reported is justification enough to begin an investigation."

Hayden didn't need to define what "activity" was. There were many definitions: conduct unbecoming an officer, homosexual activity, inappropriate behavior, the list went on and on. What she did need to do was thank Emily again for speaking up.

"But thanks, I appreciate it. I really put my foot in it, and that is something I've never done before."

Emily reached out and took Hayden's hand. "There's no need to thank me."

She was going to say something else but the thought drifted out of her head at the look of sheer desire in Hayden's eyes. Her pulse raced and the echo in her ears was her own heart beating. Her breathing quickened when Hayden searched her face as if looking for the answer to an important question. Her stomach knotted in anticipation when Hayden's gaze focused on her mouth. She drew closer.

Hayden had never touched a woman romantically when she was in uniform and had always been on guard, not giving any hint of her sexual orientation, either. The Army frowned upon public displays of affection and she would be in more than her share of trouble if she were caught. But Emily's hand felt good in hers, like it belonged there, public opinion be damned. She did nothing to break the contact. Holding hands with a woman in public was usually out of the question, except when she was someplace no one would know who she was. This was not that place. This was a place where everybody knew who she was, and all it would take would be one person opening the door they'd just exited and her life would never be the same.

Hayden gazed deep into Emily's eyes and what she saw gave her a glimmer of hope. She smiled gently, reflecting that her life had not been the same since she met Emily. If the feel of Emily's hand in hers and the flame in her eyes was any indication, she would be at Hayden's side whatever happened after this. Hayden wanted that possibility, she needed it.

She wanted to kiss her but instead said, "I'm starving."

Emily read exactly what she intended in her statement and her eyes flared with equal desire. "I have quite an appetite myself."

It was all Hayden could do to drag her hand out of Emily's grasp and suggest, "You said something about dinner?"

They changed clothes, took a cab downtown, and strolled down Michigan Avenue, window-shopping and enjoying the early evening. They stopped and went inside Burberry, Louis Vuitton, J.Crew, Tiffany's, and Cartier. Hayden knew the prices were out of her range even though there wasn't a price tag to be seen. They decided to walk to Navy Pier. Emily wanted to have dinner on the Spirit of Chicago cruise.

"The cruise doesn't leave until nine thirty, and it's three hours," Hayden said, reading the information sign on the ticket booth. "The car is picking us up at five thirty tomorrow morning. Are you sure you want to do this? We can get something to eat in one of the restaurants if you'd like."

Emily linked her arm through Hayden's and leaned close. She swept an appreciative look over the gleaming luxury liner, sleek and proud in the water. "I'm game if you are."

Hayden replied by asking the clerk for two tickets.

They chatted easily over dinner of prime rib and crabmeat-stuffed filet of sole. Hayden offered her a taste of the fish and the gesture of sharing the small sample from her fork felt as intimate as the setting in the dining room. The room was dark with the candles on the table and the lights of the city the only source of illumination. They were tucked in a corner of the room, providing them a fabulous view of the city yet almost complete privacy. They sipped wine and shared stories about their childhoods. It was during this time when Emily tentatively asked Hayden about her life in the military. Hayden looked at her questioningly.

"I'm not going to bite your head off. Please, I really want to know." Emily wanted to know what made Hayden tick. Why she joined the Army, why she remained, how it had shaped her character and made her the woman she was.

"I wanted to be in the Army as far back as I can remember," Hayden said. "I don't know if it was what I wanted or if my father drilled it into me so firmly I wanted it by osmosis. It was a given. I would follow my father, and his father, and his father, and go to West Point. It didn't matter that I was a girl."

"Did you have any brothers?"

"No. My father was disappointed that he had four daughters. When I was eight, I overheard him begging my mother to have another child, hoping it would be a boy. She must have put her foot down or cut him off because there were no more babies after that. So, being the firstborn, I'm the son my father never had."

"And what does he think?"

Hayden chuckled. "Well, I outrank him. I'm not sure he likes that, but he gets to brag about me to his Army cronies, so I guess it's all right."

Emily detected a touch of bitterness in her voice but didn't mention it. "Did you ever want to do anything else?"

"No. I actually like the discipline and honor that soldiers have. There is something about serving your country that fills you with a sense of pride like nothing else." Hayden was never able to find the words to describe how those words really felt. "I wanted to have that. To be one of them. It's my life and probably will always be in some respects. It was a natural fit, and up until recently, it was a very good fit."

She was surprised that she'd actually verbalized what she'd been struggling with lately.

"What's changed?" Emily kept her questions brief. This was the most Hayden had talked about herself, and she wanted the conversation to continue.

"Me." Hayden's answer was as simple and as complicated as that. "I was happy going around the world meeting people, making friends, doing what I love for an employer I love until one day I guess I found there was something more to life."

Hayden was looking right at Emily as she spoke. She had said as much in their interview yesterday and was saying so again. Unfortunately she couldn't tell Emily that what she had found was her. That kind of statement was much further out there than she was.

"And now?"

Hayden leaned back in her chair and ran her eyes over Emily's face. Her eyes were bright, her nose just a little crooked, and the flickering candles gave her a soft, sensuous glow. Hayden's hands twitched as she remembered how smooth Emily's hair was and how it felt gliding through her fingers. Every nerve in her body was on fire and she wanted Emily more than she'd ever wanted anyone.

"And now I'm sitting across from a beautiful woman enjoying good food, fine wine, and a stunning view of Chicago. What more could a girl want?"

Emily inhaled sharply as Hayden's desire blazed. "To get off this boat, go back to the hotel, and make love all night," she answered breathlessly.

"You're the one who wanted to go on this three-hour cruise. I would have been perfectly content with a hot dog and a beer,"

Hayden teased. "Oh, and the making love all night part, too." Hayden was rewarded with Emily's laughter filling the air and her hand wrapped tightly in hers.

After dinner they went up on the upper deck to get a better view of the city. Lake Michigan was smooth and the ship passed in front of the Adler Planetarium on their return to the dock. The Sears Tower and the AT&T Building were in the background, floor after floor of lights.

Emily shivered and Hayden put her arm around her shoulders. "Cold?"

"Not really. Just thinking."

"About what?" Hayden enjoyed the casual conversation they were sharing under the stars. A couple very much in love sat across from them in a similar position.

"Your love life."

"What about it?" Hayden wasn't really surprised by the question.

"How is it someone as gorgeous as you hasn't been scooped up?"

Hayden tightened her grip around Emily. "I was never in one place long enough, I guess. Relationships take a long time to develop and even longer to build. I was always off to another place before it got to either point. It was easier that way, too. I saw too many broken hearts and too many cheaters. I wasn't interested in either one."

"So do you have women scattered all over the world?" Emily jabbed her teasingly in the stomach.

"Honestly?"

"Yes, if the number is less than ten, and no if it's not," Emily replied lightly, even though she was very interested in the answer.

Hayden hesitated for a moment, trying to think of the best way to answer the question. "Let's just say that I am forty-three years old and have known I was a lesbian for most of that time."

Hayden had no idea how many women she had been with in the past twenty years. But sitting here beside Emily, she wanted the number to stop increasing.

"Good answer. An evasive one, but good nonetheless." Emily's laughter filled the night air.

They caught a cab back to the hotel and the clock in the lobby struck one as they walked toward the elevator. Silently Hayden pushed the Up button. She wanted to ask Emily to stay with her. She wanted to make love with her in a soft bed on clean sheets, nothing between them but a thin sheen of sweat. They silently stepped into the elevator and turned around. Hayden pushed the button for her floor, and when she went to push the number for Emily's, Emily grasped her wrist and stopped her. Their eyes met in the mirrored doors as and the elevator began to climb. Emily's eyes told Hayden everything she needed to know.

Chapter Eighteen

Hayden's room was dark except for the light coming in through the open curtains. She reached for the light, but again Emily grasped her hand, this time putting it on her breast. Radiant flames danced in her dark eyes and Hayden could feel Emily's heart beat faster against her chest. She cupped Emily's cheek, softly caressing the soft skin the way she had that first time. Emily turned into the caress, kissing Hayden's palm with her lips and tongue. Hayden's legs started to shake. She lowered her head and gently kissed her.

Emily deepened the kiss, sending shock waves through Hayden's body. She wrapped her hands into Hayden's short hair, pulling her closer. Emily's nipple hardened against her palm and Hayden tweaked it, causing Emily to moan into her mouth. A rush of desire shot through Hayden, and she pinned Emily to the door.

In her haste to taste and touch the woman who'd driven her mad the past few days, Hayden's hands and lips were everywhere. She couldn't get her clothes off fast enough, but when Emily's whimper cut through her passion, she forced herself to regain control. Breathing heavily and not certain how long she could restrain herself, Hayden stepped back slightly.

Without a word, Emily knew she was being given the opportunity to step out of their embrace and stop what was about to happen. Hayden was giving her the choice, and in that minute she fell completely in love with her. Hayden was strong but not overpowering, her character was impeccable, and she was confident in what she believed in, but she gave Emily the opportunity to be who she was. She was charming, respectful, striking in her uniform and breathtaking out of it. There was something about her that connected them as more than survivors. They were two strangers who had shared a moment in time. Now they were two women sharing much more.

Hayden broke the spell. "Once upon a time, my life was in perfect order. I knew what was expected of me and what I could expect in return. But then you came floating by and now I don't know who I am, or what I'm supposed to be doing, other than making love to you."

Emily cupped Hayden's face in her hands. She softly kissed her eyes, her cheeks, the edges of her mouth. She pulled away and looked deep into her eyes, confirming without words that she understood and she was also giving Hayden the choice as to where they would go from here. Hayden had much more to lose, and Emily was not about to take her somewhere she was not willing to go.

Hayden teetered on the brink of indecision. If she backed away now, she could return to her regular life. If she kissed Emily one more time, she would be lost forever. She lowered her head, knowing she could never go back and not wanting to.

The intensity of her orgasms was unlike anything she had ever experienced before. Emily knew just what she needed and when she needed it. She spent a lifetime kissing every inch of Hayden's body and Hayden thought she was going to scream from the exquisite sensations. She was amazed with Emily's tenacity and endurance as they made love time and time again. Emily was a fabulous lover, eager yet patient, deliberate one minute, spontaneous the next. She encouraged her with her mouth, sweet words flowing from her lips as soft as the feather kisses that covered her body, all the while making Hayden feel like she was the most desirable woman in the world.

"Touch me," Emily whispered in her ear, bringing Hayden back to the present.

Emily was draped over her like a warm blanket, smothering her with a passionate kiss. Hayden slid her hands down Emily's back and across her tight ass before she shifted and rolled on top of her. She cradled Emily's head with one arm while the other drifted closer to Emily's arching hips. Her skin was soft and warm quivering under her fingertips. Hayden caressed the inside of Emily's thighs, her touch alternating between slow, deliberate strokes and teasing flicks of pressure. She planted soft kisses down the long scar on her leg. Her stomach clenched when she briefly thought that Emily could have died from this injury.

Emily grabbed her hair and pulled her into a fierce kiss. Her tongue danced in Hayden's mouth and her fingers mimicked the movement as they slid into warm wetness. Faster and faster they moved, their breath mixing together as one. She came hard and fast, lifting them both off the bed with the force of her climax.

Hayden tasted blood on her lips when Emily released the viselike grip on her head. She was light-headed and panting from the passion they'd shared. She soothed Emily with light kisses on her cheek, her jaw, her swollen lips. Emily's eyes fluttered open, dazzling Hayden with their brilliance.

They made love into the wee hours of the morning, and caught only an exhausted hour of sleep before the automated wake-up call wished them a great day.

"Time to get up." Hayden dropped the receiver back into the cradle as Emily snuggled closer. "We have a date for coffee with five million Americans."

Getting out of bed was the last thing she was interested in doing. She had just gotten to sleep, and if she was going to be awake with Emily lying naked in her arms, getting *out* of bed was not what she would be doing. Obviously Emily had the same idea because her fingers were already teasing an alert nipple.

"If you keep doing that we we'll be late," Hayden admonished.

Just before Emily leaned in for a kiss, Hayden heard her say, "Then you'd better hurry."

Hayden's heart lurched and she tried to swallow the lump in her throat. "Good morning."

"Yes, it is. I'll have to bring you along anytime I travel. Your wake-up call is much more pleasant than the hotel operator's."

Emily caressed Hayden's cheek. Her heart was bursting, and it was not from their recent exertion. She knew she had fallen a little bit in love with her rescuer during their time together on the beach, but her feelings were well beyond that early crush. Hayden's smile was crooked and her hair a mess, but right now, she was the most stunning woman Emily had ever met.

"Just my luck we're doing interviews in five different cities." Hayden raised her eyebrows mischievously. She was rewarded by another hard kiss that threatened to ignite her passion again. She pulled back reluctantly. "We've got to get up. If we're late, Tillman will come looking for us."

"Damn your military discipline." Emily swatted at her arm.

This time, Hayden detected only teasing in her tone. "I know, I know, but we've got to get going."

Emily looked at her with such longing Hayden couldn't make herself move. She was one touch away from forgetting everything she had learned about duty.

"I can't get up with you lying on top of me." Emily's voice was sultry. She watched as something flickered in Hayden's eyes.

"But I like it here," Hayden responded, lowering her head, fully intending to nibble on the sensitive spot just below Emily's left ear.

Emily pushed against her chest. "I like you there, too, but we have to get up. I have to get back to my room, shower, and get dressed. You"—she poked Hayden affectionately in the chest—"just have to roll into the shower and put on your uniform, which if I haven't mentioned it, you look stunning in. It takes me a little longer to get myself together."

"I would think you're beautiful in anything you wear," Hayden countered.

The seriousness of her comment surprised Emily. "Thank you, but get up."

She was rewarded with Hayden's laughter as she rolled off her and onto her back. The place where Hayden had lain was immediately cool, and Emily fought the urge to crawl back into the warm cocoon of her arms.

Hayden felt surprisingly content. Mornings after were usually awkward at best, but she felt as if she could spar with Emily all morning. She reached over and turned on the light. The room was cast in a warm glow.

"You first," she said, shaking the covers.

"What?"

"I said you first. Go on. Go." Hayden waved her hands as if shooing away a pesky fly.

Emily caught on to her ulterior motive. Hayden wanted to see her naked. Feigning indignation, she said, "Colonel Caldwell, I thought you were an officer and a gentleman."

"I will admit that I am an officer, but I have never been mistaken for a gentleman. Now up."

Emily looked Hayden directly in the eye. Slowly and sensuously, she rose from the bed, all the while maintaining eye contact. She reached her arms above her head and stretched like a cat after a long nap. A soft moan slipped from her lips and Hayden's eyes narrowed. Just as slowly she lowered her arms and walked around the foot of the bed to Hayden's side.

In her most innocent voice, she asked, "Where are my clothes?" She turned her full body from side to side, exaggerating her actions and giving Hayden an eyeful. "There they are." With a quick glance over her shoulder, she bent down to pick up her shirt.

There was no mistaking Hayden's intake of breath and the sound of sheets rustling behind her. She pivoted just as Hayden was about to touch her, and pointed her finger like the teacher she was. "Don't even think about it. We're going to be late."

"I don't care," Hayden stuttered, and she meant it. She would gladly face a court martial for just one more touch of Emily's soft body.

Emily surged with the influence she had over this strong woman. She would never use it against Hayden, but she felt powerful just the same. It was something her analytical mind would have to digest.

"Don't come any closer, Colonel. I may have to hurt you."

"Promise?" Hayden teased but stayed where she was. She picked up Emily's pants and the loafers that had been tossed carelessly next to the bed, then handed them to Emily. "The least I can do is walk you to the door."

Emily zipped her pants and stepped into her shoes. "Only if you put on a robe. It's a bit chilly in here." She studied Hayden's erect nipples.

Hayden felt Emily's gaze travel hotly from her nipples to her crotch but managed to walk to the closet and don the plush terrycloth robe provided by the hotel. "Better?"

"Much. I can't seem to think straight when you're around, let alone when you have no clothes on."

Hayden reached the door before Emily did. Her warm breath fanned Emily's ear. "Thank you for coming last night, and for telling me about Tillman the other day." Emily didn't reply but Hayden could feel her breath hitch.

She opened the door and Emily stepped into the hall. What she really wanted to do was turn around, hang the Do Not Disturb sign on the door, and never come out. She wanted to spend a lifetime in Hayden's arms where she felt safe. She wanted to spend the rest of her life getting to know everything there was to know about this strong, sensitive woman. She wanted to make her laugh, comfort her when she hurt, and listen to her dreams. But she wasn't quite ready to say those things to Hayden. Shit, she was barely able to say them to herself.

What she said instead was "I'll see you downstairs."

❖

"You both look like hell," Tillman said after their appearance on *Good Morning Chicago*, when they were in the guest room removing their stage makeup.

Hayden didn't agree. Emily was stunning in a dark green suit with a cream shell accentuating the long neck Hayden had nibbled on so thoroughly just a few short hours before. She looked for any signs of their lovemaking and was relieved by the absence of marks.

Tillman backed out of the room and Hayden closed the door behind him. "I think you look fabulous," she said, countering Tillman's description.

Emily felt herself blush. She had taken extra care preparing for this morning, knowing Hayden would be sitting across from her. Her hair was up in a French braid and her earrings sparkled in the light. Every time she crossed her legs, Hayden's eyes shot to them and Emily wondered if Hayden even realized she was doing it. The sensation of knowing she had the undivided attention of a woman like Hayden was unbelievable.

"Thank you. You're pretty hot yourself."

"It's the uniform. Drives women wild. Does it every time."

Emily felt the heat from Hayden's gaze and crossed the small room and stopped just in front of her. "That, too. But personally, I like the woman underneath all the buckles and buttons." Hayden licked her lips and Emily's crotch started to throb.

"You know," she began, caressing the gold buttons on Hayden's jacket, "I've never undressed a woman in uniform. How many layers are under there?" She pretended to sneak a peek between the button holes.

"Why don't we ditch Tillman, go back to the hotel, and you can use your amazing fing—powers of deduction and find out." The slip of the words was intentional.

Emily's eyes grew dark. "You make an interesting proposition, Colonel. I just might have to take you up on that, considering I can't seem to keep my mind on anything other than how smooth your skin is just below your breasts. And how hard your muscles are along the back of your legs, and…"

Hayden didn't give Emily a chance to finish. She closed the remaining inches and did what she'd wanted to do for hours. She kissed her. Emily wrapped her arms around her neck and deepened the kiss. Hayden's head started to spin when they were abruptly interrupted by the opening of the door. Thankfully Hayden's back was a few inches from it, giving them an instant to recover before Tillman pushed on it again.

Emily stepped back quickly, adjusting her suit jacket. She glanced at Hayden, who was running her hand through her hair, and she noticed a lipstick smudge on Hayden's lips. Before Tillman had a chance to notice she signaled to Hayden to wipe her mouth and was relieved when Hayden pulled out a handkerchief and used a cough to cover up her efforts.

Tillman rattled on about something that Emily half paid attention to, her mind a jumble of sensations ranging from arousal to passion to fear to relief. She couldn't wait for him to leave so they could finish what they started.

"We're going where?" she asked.

"To Dallas. The producer for the Phil Privett show called. They have a last-minute cancellation and we are booked for his show this afternoon."

Phil Privett was a nationally syndicated talk show host with politics so far right he could see the backs of the people on the left. His show was live and nationally syndicated in over one hundred cities across the country.

Tillman droned on with the details, but Hayden was too engrossed by the look of disappointment on Emily's face to pay attention. She was certain her face displayed her equal frustration at the abrupt change of plans.

"This is huge," Tillman concluded, finally. "Come on, ladies, let's get going. We have a plane to catch."

❖

Emily was between Hayden and Tillman when they entered the lobby of the Ritz-Carlton. Their footsteps echoed on the marble floor as they approached the reception desk. They passed a large rectangular table occupied by vases of various sizes, each filled with fresh flowers. The brass trim around the furniture was polished to perfection, reminding Hayden of how she and her fellow recruits would spend hours polishing their brass prior to inspection. Just a hint of dirt would mean the end of any hope they had for liberty that weekend.

Emily hung back, seizing her first chance to talk to Hayden privately. "I don't suppose it would be a good idea to ask for one room with a king-size bed?"

"I've already thought of that, but the way I feel right now, I don't need a bed. Any horizontal surface will do. Or vertical," she added, passing one of the large marble pillars.

Emily followed her gaze, registering what Hayden was talking about. The thrill that came with knowing Hayden wanted her was indescribable. She practically groaned with desire. "How are you holding up?"

Hayden didn't pretend she didn't know what Emily was talking about. She was wound as tight as a harp string, and one pluck would be all it took to break. "Fine."

"Bullshit," was Emily's reply. A small smile formed on her lips. This playful side had emerged somewhere between their third and sixth time making love last night.

Hayden didn't get the chance to respond. Tillman was calling Emily over to sign the registration form. Hayden's clit throbbed as she watched Emily handle the gold pen. Her fingers were long and skillful and had brought Hayden to orgasm on more than one occasion with their gentle touch. Hayden could still feel Emily stroking her, demanding she receive as much as she was giving. Emily toyed with the pen as she asked the clerk a question, and Hayden thought her knees might give out.

None too soon she was standing next to Emily, the elevator whisking them to their respective floors. Thankfully the doors did not have mirrors like many elevators do, and their position in the confined space gave Hayden the opportunity to drop her hand behind Emily and cup her ass. She was impressed by Emily's self-control when she barely acknowledged her hand other than to tighten the muscle in her well-formed cheek. Tillman was slightly in front of them and oblivious to the activity behind him.

They arrived at Emily's floor first and she stepped out, glancing over her shoulder. Tillman reminded them that they had to be in the lobby in twenty minutes, but Emily's eyes and thoughts were squarely on Hayden. She'd casually inquired about Hayden's room number, giving hers in return, and was rewarded with a sweet smile from Hayden at her ingenuity. She knew that Hayden would come to her room as soon as she could. Hopefully she wouldn't have to wait long.

Emily had just finished her unpacking when there was a light knock on her door. After a quick look through the peephole, she opened the door, dragged Hayden inside, and pinned her against the door, kissing her hard. After several moments Emily began fumbling with the buckle on Hayden's uniform pants.

"You said something about a vertical surface," she mumbled breathlessly into Hayden's mouth.

She was on fire and had to have Hayden now. She slipped

her hand down the front of Hayden's pants, the unopened zipper scraping the back of her hand. Her fingers found what they were searching for and easily slid into the warmth she remembered from the night before.

"God, you feel good."

"No, that feels good," Hayden managed to croak out just as Emily's fingers stroked her clit. "One more of those and that'll be it." Her voice was throaty and shook when she spoke.

"Good, I love it when you come," Emily replied, teasing Hayden just to the brink and then backing off slightly. "I love to feel you get harder and wetter before you explode in my hand. I love it when you're weak with desire and cling to me. I love it when you call my name."

Emily knew she could easily come with Hayden. They'd come together several times last night, a rare feat in her experience. It usually took years of being together to perfect the timing of mutual orgasms. Hayden tensed in her arms and Emily knew her release was just moments away.

"Emily," Hayden whispered in her ear an instant before she shook uncontrollably in Emily's arms.

The sounds that Hayden made when she was on the verge of orgasm were the most arousing she had ever heard. Her moans were deep, her whispers soft, and her cry at the peak was breathless. Hayden's responses were all because of her. Her touch, her caress, her tongue. Emily had never felt so powerful.

Slowly her head cleared and she regained the strength in her legs. Her hand, still deep inside Hayden's pants, was warm and wet from Hayden's climax. She moved her fingers and Hayden shuddered, grabbing her wrist tightly.

"Wait, we can't do this again," Hayden said. "We've got to go." Her words didn't sound convincing.

Emily smiled and kissed her warm neck. Hayden's clit was trapped between her fingers and she could feel its hardness growing again. "Once more. I can feel you. You need this." She punctuated each sentence with a squeeze of her fingers.

Hayden was losing her mind. Emily's hand in her pants, her fingers splayed against her clit, was almost her undoing. But if they didn't get downstairs soon, Tillman would come knocking. He'd almost caught them once. This time it would be harder to explain what she was doing in Emily's room.

Hayden chuckled. "I'm an officer in the United States Army. I am trained to the utmost physical standards. I think I can manage a little arousal."

"A little?" Emily asked, her fingers finding their way to the hard nub.

Hayden tensed and forced her mind to disengage from her body. It was a trick she'd learned in boot camp, when they were forced to stand at attention for hours on end. She made her mind go off into another place to ease the stress her body was under. She had used the same method dozens of times when she was in similar situations, when her body was overriding her mind. It didn't work this time.

"Fuck," she groaned as the force of her second orgasm hit her hard.

Her mind refocused, and when she opened her eyes, she saw Emily's face. She wore a look of smug conceit, as if she were proud of herself for causing Hayden to lose all sense of control. Hayden didn't mind. Emily was the only woman she had let take her like this, when her duty demanded she be somewhere else. And she wanted it to happen again.

"Yes, I believe we did," Emily said, sliding her hands out of Hayden's pants, this time kissing her lightly. She stepped back, releasing Hayden from her position against the door.

Hayden didn't follow her line of thought. "Did what?"

"Fuck."

Hayden's hands froze in the middle of buckling her belt. Slowly she lifted her head and found Emily's twinkling eyes filled with mischief and the promise of more to come.

She raised her eyebrows. "Really? I suppose that's one way to phrase it."

Emily stepped back giving her much-needed space. Her hands shook as she straightened her jacket, the bottom button having come undone the same time she did. She laughed as she stepped into the bathroom to wash her hands. Hayden came up behind her and wrapped her arms around her, cupping her breasts. Rockets shot through her as Hayden nibbled on her left ear.

"You know paybacks are hell?" Hayden asked, flicking her fingers over Emily's already erect nipples.

Locking her knees to prevent herself from falling from the sensation, Emily looked at Hayden in the mirror. "God, I hope so."

The fire in Hayden's eyes flickered brighter and Emily arched her back, pressing her ass into Hayden's crotch. Then she slapped Hayden's hands away and slid out of her embrace.

Chapter Nineteen

"We have about five minutes before you go on."

The look in Emily's eyes took Hayden's breath away. It was the same look she'd seen just before she touched her the first time. Desire, confusion, passion, and fire all mixed together and burned brightest in her eyes. Hayden nearly dropped to her knees when Emily licked her lips.

Five minutes turned into one and they were ushered out onto the stage. The bright lights were hot, and Hayden didn't need any additional heat on her already inflamed body. Emily looked cool and composed sitting next to her on a hard-backed chair as the sound technician adjusted their microphones. He seemed to spend a little too long near Emily's breasts and Hayden fought the urge to grab his hands and tie them behind his back. None too soon they were being peppered with questions.

According to Tillman, Phil Privett always warmed up his guests with some innocent chatter before he eviscerated them. He started with Emily, asking her what the tsunami looked like.

"Awesome, breathtaking, frightening," Emily said softly.

"We've heard reports from other survivors that there was absolutely no sound."

Emily nodded. "When I first saw it I would say there was an eerie silence, kind of like the calm before the storm. Then as it came closer, the roar was unbelievable."

"Colonel Caldwell, what about you, where were you?"

Lying on top of a beautiful woman, my tongue half way down her throat, my hand on her breast and my leg between her thighs. "I was on the beach. My back was to the ocean and when I heard the screams I turned around. The wave was about fifty yards from me."

"What did you do?"

Hayden smiled. "I ran. I grabbed anyone I could but we couldn't outrun it. The water was so powerful it knocked me off my feet."

"What did you think about when you saw Ms. Bradshaw coming toward you?"

"I was up a tree by then and I don't remember thinking anything. She needed help and I just reacted."

"How about you, Ms. Bradshaw? What did you think when you saw the colonel reaching down to grab you?"

"All I remember was her hand grasping mine. She was telling me to hang on. One minute I was terrified and the next I was hoisted in the air."

"Ms. Bradshaw, I understand that you didn't know who Colonel Caldwell was until you saw her at the base where you were protesting."

Emily wasn't sure if that was a question or not but she replied anyway. "That's right. We only exchanged first names on the beach and we lost contact after the rescue. Needless to say I was quite surprised to even see her again, regardless of the situation."

"Colonel Caldwell, how did you feel to see the woman whose life you saved protesting at your base?" Privett asked, digging into the juicy part of the story. "Protesting the very training that saved her life?"

Hayden was ready for this. She didn't need the scripted answers of her handlers to talk about this. "Like Ms. Bradshaw, I too was surprised. I never expected to see her again. I did think about her and the children from time to time." Hayden saw Emily's head turn in her direction. "I wondered how they were doing and how they'd recovered from the experience."

"But how did you feel when you saw her waving a placard?" Privett asked.

"Surprised and glad that she was all right," Hayden answered vaguely.

"It didn't make you angry?"

He smelled blood and Hayden was not about to give it to him. "No, I wasn't angry at her or any of the other protesters. That's what's great about our country. They have a right to voice their opinion, and members of the armed forces live and die every day to protect that right."

"What about you, Ms. Bradshaw?" Privett asked. "Why were you protesting at the base?"

If any other military figure were sitting beside her, she would have let loose with everything she had against the institution and its policies. But it was Hayden beside her now, the woman who had saved her life. The woman Emily couldn't get out of her mind. Hayden had a lifetime invested in her career. Emily was not going to attack her.

"Like many Americans, I don't believe we should be fighting another country's war," she said. "I showed my loathing by demonstrating. We were a peaceful group exercising our right to protest."

"But your hero is a very big part of that policy you claim to loathe."

Emily remained calm and chose her words carefully. "First of all, I can't thank Colonel Caldwell enough for what she did for me and the two children. She didn't have to risk her life for us but she did. I hardly know her, but I suspect it was the training she received in the Army as much as her own sense of doing the right thing that made her act. I would be a hypocrite if I said otherwise. Now, nothing against the colonel, but I seriously doubt the president asks for her opinion about military policy. Colonel Caldwell has a job to do just like you or I." Emily could feel the tension Hayden was holding in check.

"What was the first thing that went through your mind when you saw her again?"

Emily chuckled and looked at Hayden. She was focused on their host and did not look at her. "Well, considering that we last saw each other covered in mud and God knows what else, wearing clothes that didn't belong to us, and we hadn't slept in two nights, it took me a few minutes to recognize her. She was in her uniform, all pressed and starched and official. I don't know for sure what it was, maybe the way she was standing or the way she carried herself. But suddenly I just knew it was her." Emily remembered the punch in her gut as if it were yesterday.

"How did that make you feel?"

"I guess I'd describe it as surprise, shock, joy, confusion all rolled up into one. But the thing I remember the most is a sense of relief that she'd made it back home safely."

"I'm sure Colonel Caldwell means a lot to you," Privett concluded slickly.

Jesus Christ, this guy is an asshole, Hayden thought to herself. Phil Privett thought he was the second coming of Larry King, but with the tact of Nancy Grace. His set was similar, down to the microphone in front of him. His hair was too black to be natural and had enough gel in it to withstand his own tsunami, and instead of suspenders he wore a bow tie. Hayden thought he looked ridiculous. She willed herself not to sweat, but the hot lights of the studio and the probing questions made it difficult. The camera over Privett's right shoulder glared at her like it could see into her soul. The pressure of Emily's leg against hers was reassuring.

She didn't like the direction Privett's questions were going. He had obviously seen the original photo in the *Bugle* and was circling around the issue, just one question away from the big one. She didn't have to wait long.

"Tell me, Emily, is it true that you are a lesbian?"

Emily felt Hayden stiffen beside her. She looked Privett squarely in the eye. "Yes." She'd learned long ago that if you made something a big deal, it became a big deal.

"And you had a girlfriend you left behind when you went to Khao Lak?"

"She decided not to go, at the last minute. She had an unexpected conflict with her job."

"And you went without her?" Privett leaned forward in his seat. "Is it because your relationship was on the rocks and you were going to meet Colonel Caldwell there?"

Emily was surprised at this question but remained calm. She hoped Hayden didn't jump to her defense, it would only make it worse. "No, Mr. Privett. I went because it was a vacation planned well in advance and I was not going to miss it just because she wasn't able to come. And to address your insinuation, I did not know Colonel Caldwell until she risked her life to save not only me but two children from certain death."

"What about you, Colonel? Are you a lesbian?" Privett practically spat out the word.

Hayden was ready. "Mr. Privett, I don't know what this has to do with the destruction and death caused by the tsunami."

"You didn't answer my question, Colonel."

"And I'm not going to," Hayden replied solidly.

"Why not?"

Hayden clasped her hands in front of her on the table. "Because it is none of your business."

"Don't ask, don't tell doesn't apply here."

Hayden tensed at his comment but felt Emily's leg offering support. "Mr. Privett, I'm fully aware of the policy in this country against gays in the military. I don't tell because it's nobody's business. Not the Army's, not yours, and certainly not your viewers'. I'm more than willing to talk about anything that has to do with the tsunami and the rescue, but that's all."

Privett leaned back and crossed his arms over his chest.

"She doth protest too much," he said snidely. "Are you married, Colonel?"

"No, Mr. Privett," Hayden replied, composed.

She was not going to be goaded into revealing anything about herself, especially when it concerned Emily. She had enough training to know that silence was an effective interrogation technique, and calmly waited for him to ask the next question. Under pressure, most people became uncomfortable with silence, and Privett was no exception. He had everything to lose if he could not get conversation out of his guests.

"Have you ever been married?"

"No."

"Why not?"

"I've never found someone I love enough to commit to marriage."

"Have you ever been in love?" When Hayden didn't answer, he goaded her. "Come on, it's a simple question."

"Yes, it is a simple question, but it has nothing to do with the tsunami." Hayden saw Tillman out of the corner of her eye trying to get her attention. She knew she was going to catch hell from him and probably General Foreman over her behavior during this interview. She didn't care. The questions Privett was asking were not appropriate.

"Were you and Emily intimate after you rescued her?"

Emily spoke up this time. "Mr. Privett, what are you getting at?"

"The truth, that's all." Privett held his hands palms up as if he were showing he had nothing to hide. "Is there something you're trying to keep the nation from knowing?"

"As Colonel Caldwell said, we're here to talk about the tsunami. You, however, seem to be on a wild goose chase or a witch hunt, and I will not participate while you try to disparage the character of the person who saved my life." Emily's knees shook but she made sure that was the only outward sign of her nervousness. Thankfully her legs were out of camera range.

They broke for a commercial, and Privett slid out of his chair and went over to talk to the stage director. Tillman was beside Hayden the instant the red light went out on the camera. "What in the fuck are you doing?" His teeth were clenched so hard his jaw bulged.

"He is totally out of line and you know it." Hayden kept her voice down but she knew the microphone was probably transmitting everything they were saying to the control room. "I am not answering any questions that don't have to do with the rescue."

"You are a representative of the United States Army, and as such you have a responsibility—"

"Don't you dare tell me what my responsibility is, Tillman. You've never served your country a day in your life."

"I don't have to have served my country to know what my job is," he snapped back.

"And I know mine." Hayden's voice was tight with controlled anger. "I also know that I will not be humiliated, vilified, outed, or whatever in the hell this asshole is trying to do. I am not his puppet in some ratings game. And I will not allow Emily to be, either."

"I thought the general made it clear to you that I work for him and I speak for him." The expression on Tillman's face was sinister and the message he conveyed clear.

"I don't take orders from you."

"Yes, Colonel, you do."

Privett chose that moment to return to his place at the desk. He adjusted his mike and fussed with his already perfectly straight tie. There was a satisfied look on his face that indicted he'd heard every word spoken between them. "Ladies, are we ready? We're on in fifteen seconds."

"Hayden." Emily placed her hand on Hayden's forearm.

Her touch was soothing and just what Hayden needed to regain her balance. The probing questions from Privett and Tillman's sanctimonious attitude were almost her undoing. She held Tillman's eyes, reflecting a blank stare back at him. When he didn't move, the set director practically dragged him out of camera range as he counted backward from five. The red light over Privett's shoulder turned on and he recapped, then returned his attention to Emily, asking, "Emily, have you seen Colonel Caldwell since your return from Thailand?" He emphasized the word "seen," inferring something more than the two women simply seeing each other across the room.

"We've spoken since we returned." Emily carefully avoided answering a direct yes. If she did, Tillman would have pounced on it as an admission there was something more to their relationship.

"And what did you talk about?"

Emily felt like she was on trial. Tillman had briefed them that Privett had been a practicing attorney years before he became a talk show host. "We talked about a lot of things. How our injuries had healed, how we were adjusting to everyday life again. That sort of thing."

"Did you tell her about your girlfriend?"

"I've already said that we talked about a lot of things." Emily was being careful not to be sucked into his vortex.

"How many times did you two meet?"

"Mr. Privett, I don't think your viewers are interested in how many times the colonel and I had coffee in the past six months."

"I beg to differ with you, Emily. The questions I'm asking *are* things my viewers want to know about," Privett answered smugly.

"Really? I thought your viewers were highly educated middle- and upper-class professionals concerned with the economy, global warming, and the struggles in the Middle East. I was not aware they lived in trailer parks and had an annual subscription to the *National Enquirer*."

Zing! That was one for the good guys. Hayden's respect for Emily soared anew. She was handling this jerk like he was a badly behaved student in her classroom.

"Now who's being ugly, Emily? I think you just insulted forty million viewers."

Tillman squirmed to her left. Emily tossed her hair back with her hand. "Not at all. Your viewers need to have a roof over their heads and entertainment. I just speculated as to where they lived and what they did for fun. Why not watch your show?"

"Emily, I'm beginning to think you don't like me. Why are you so upset?"

Emily saw the fine beads of sweat forming on Privett's upper lip. She watched him brush them away when the camera was live on her.

"I'm not upset." She laughed. "When I was about to be gang-raped by a bunch of thugs I was upset. When I saw a mother barely alive still holding on to the handle of her child's stroller buried in mud, I was upset. When I had to wear clothes taken off a dead man, that was upsetting. This, Mr. Privett, is not even close to 'upset.'" Sometime in the past few minutes the absurdity of arguing with this man became clear. He wasn't worth that much emotion.

"Then what would you call it?"

"Tolerance. I'm tolerating your questions, knowing that sooner or later you'll ask something interesting or your viewers will change the channel."

The flash of panic in his face was worth the past few minutes. Privett was insecure. His paycheck depended on how much people liked him and how often they tuned in. His show was like a beauty contest, and tonight he was the second runner-up. He broke for another commercial and left the desk paler than when he arrived a few minutes ago. For the second time Tillman dashed to where they were sitting. This time his tirade was directed at Emily.

"Do you have any idea how much trouble you are going to be in, Ms. Bradshaw?"

"Shut up, Tillman." Hayden didn't raise her voice, but her tone made him stop. "You will not speak to her like that. She is not your lackey. She is a thousand times smarter than you and could run circles around you so fast you'd be screwed into the ground. This is our interview, not yours, so I suggest you go back and stand in your little spot." She turned away, effectively dismissing him.

"Thank you," Emily said.

Hayden met her eyes. "He's an ass. I'm tired of him sniffing around and acting like he owns us."

"Is what he said true? Are you going to be in trouble with the general?"

Hayden had certainly not endeared herself to Tillman. Emily hadn't either, but she had nothing to worry about. Hayden could lose everything.

"Probably," Hayden answered more nonchalantly than she felt.

Tillman himself was no threat to her, but Foreman could be. She had enough service to retire with a full pension, but any hint of impropriety would jeopardize that. At her previous base she knew a man who was outed after thirty-two years in the Army and was dishonorably discharged on some trumped-up charges. As a result he was ineligible for any retirement benefits.

Hayden didn't know what she would do if she were in a similar situation. Being in the Army was all she knew. It was the only job she'd ever had. It was a way of life for her. To have it all taken away would be a blow she wasn't sure she would ever recover from. And she had just put herself in that position. No one was to blame for this but her. If she lost it all, it would be because of something she'd done. Her hands started to shake.

Privett was pretty demure after Emily had taken him down a notch or two. His questions were benign and within minutes, they were off the air. Hayden could not recall spending a worse thirty minutes of her life. Not only was it painful at the time, but the aftershocks were already echoing around her.

No one said anything as they exited the studio and entered the limousine. Emily was beside Hayden. Tillman faced them, and his hard stare told Hayden that she would have some serious questions to answer when she returned to her base. Hell, he was probably on the phone to Foreman the instant the director yelled "cut." She was surprised he wasn't wearing a smug, satisfied look.

The car crawled through the late-afternoon Dallas traffic. The chill in the interior of the limo was colder than the air-conditioning that blew out from the vents strategically placed in the ceiling of the big car. They pulled up in front of the Ritz. Before the doorman reached the limousine, Tillman had the door open and was on his way out. He finally spoke. "Tomorrow we go home. Our flight is at eleven fifteen. Be in the lobby by nine."

"I guess this means he won't be joining us for dinner," Hayden remarked wryly.

Emily was surprised at her flippant remark. She had been silent the entire ride and had kept her hands flat on her thighs. The tension in the rear of the car was so thick it was stifling. There was a sense of fear coming off Hayden that was far heavier than the anger from Tillman.

"That's good, because we need to talk." Or at least she needed to.

Hayden exited the car next and without thinking held out her hand to assist Emily. She stopped when she realized what she looked like to anyone passing by. She was in full Class A uniform and she was holding the hand of a beautiful woman in a fabulous suit. She looked at their intertwined hands, then at Emily, and reluctantly released her grip.

"How about room service?"

"Your place or mine?"

Hayden shrugged, indicating it didn't matter, and they rode the elevator to Emily's floor in silence. Once inside, Hayden removed her coat and tie and tossed them over a chair. She loosened her collar, and with nothing left to do, put her hands in her pockets and looked around. The room was large, but not as large as the Drake in Chicago the previous night. The bed was a queen and set off to the left of an intimate seating area complete with two chairs, a small table, and a reading lamp. The drapes were open and Hayden walked across the room and gazed out the window.

She didn't hear Emily come up behind her until she asked softly, "Are you all right?"

For the first time in her life Hayden didn't know who or what she was. She had always been confident and sure of her next steps, but now she wasn't sure what to do the very next minute. She was adrift, a sensation she'd never experienced before. Her course had been set years ago, and through her skilled navigation and a bit of luck she'd always headed in the right direction. Nothing other than a minor course correction was ever needed. But this was very different.

"What are you thinking?" Emily asked.

"Nothing."

"Hayden, please talk to me." Emily tried not to plead. She wanted to wrap her arms around this strong woman but was afraid she would be rejected.

"No, really, I'm not thinking about anything. That's just it. Absolutely nothing." Hayden's hands were still in her pockets and she had not moved from where she stood in front of the large bay window. The Dallas skyline was in front of her, a plane low in the sky on its final approach to the left. "I have to figure out a few things. I'll be faced with some difficult decisions in the next few days and I have to be prepared."

Emily's heart ached for the position Hayden was in. She was partly to blame, but there was nothing she could do other than to offer her support. "What can I do to help?"

"I don't know," Hayden replied.

Emily's tender expression shot straight to her heart. She needed Emily to help her sort this out, to help her make sense of the last six months of her life. Hell, she needed to make sense of the last twenty-three years of her life. It had always been so clear, even as a little girl. She would progress through the ranks and retire as a colonel, or maybe even the general her father never was able to be. He would look at her, beaming with pride. He would salute her, but she would never be able to stop calling him "sir." The habit was ingrained in her, just like the Army and all its rules and regulations.

But if things got ugly, she would be on her own for the first time ever. She had gone straight from high school to college to the Army. Wherever she lived, whatever apartment or house she occupied, she was never alone. The brotherhood and sisterhood of the Army was always with her. But right now she felt bereft of that constant in her life. Isolated and uncertain.

Emily sensed Hayden's struggle. "Come lie down with me. Let me hold you. I need to hold you."

When Hayden finally turned around, the look of anguish and confusion in her eyes tore at Emily's heart. She had fallen for Hayden the minute she rescued little Jake and Victoria from the water. The last few weeks had simply solidified her character, her integrity, her place in Emily's heart. She reached up and cupped Hayden's face.

"Come lie down with me," she repeated softly.

In a daze, Hayden did as she asked. Emily helped her out of her clothes and they slipped between the cool sheets, Emily on her back with Hayden wrapped in her arms. She just held her tight, her hands in her hair, gently rubbing.

From across the room Hayden heard the familiar chirp of her cell phone indicating she had a voicemail message. She didn't have to think too hard to know it was either her father or Foreman. She was surprised it had taken either one of them this long to call, and she didn't know which she would prefer.

She was sure her father had watched the show. Hell, he'd probably recorded it to play over and over to his cronies. She could almost hear him now, reaming her about her answers to Privett's questions. His face would be beet red and his eyes bulging as he used every profanity he knew to tell her just what he thought of her performance. Her father she could deal with.

She would simply ignore him. Foreman, on the other hand, had probably waited this long to call because he was putting the final nails in her military career.

He was just the kind of man who would enjoy signing her transfer papers, shipping her to some godforsaken place where the temperature never fell below 110 degrees or got above freezing. Worse yet, he could keep her right where she was and make her life a living hell. He could push to have her dishonorably discharged, and she would walk away from twenty-three years of service to her country with a black mark and absolutely nothing.

"I'm sorry." Emily's soft voice finally broke through the silence.

"For what?"

"For touching you that night. If I had just kept my hands to myself, you wouldn't be in this position." Emily was lost in her own thoughts as well. She had taken the initiative with Hayden, had made the first move, and this was the result. The realization of what she had done, what they had done, hit her hard. Hayden might be forever scarred because she couldn't control herself.

"That's ridiculous and you know it." Hayden wasn't about to let her take the blame for her current situation. "I'm a big girl. I knew exactly what I was doing."

"But not with who you were doing it with," Emily said. "A protester."

Hayden disengaged herself from Emily's arms and moved on top of her. This was a serious discussion and she wanted to look in Emily's eyes when they talked. "It wouldn't have mattered if you were the biggest supporter of the president's policy. The fact is, they're looking for a way to distance the Army from even the hint of impropriety and scandal. Parading us around like a dog-and-pony show is how they want to do it."

"But—"

"But nothing," Hayden interrupted. "Do I wish that Tillman and Foreman didn't have my career by the short hairs? Of course

I do. But if it wasn't this it probably would have been something else. Foreman has been out to get me from the day I set foot on his base." She shifted so her full weight was not on Emily and caressed her face with the back of her hand. She erased the worry lines from her forehead and around her mouth, stunned at how much she felt for her.

Emily had been there for her. Her viewpoint was different, but she had defended and supported her when she needed it most. And here she was, trying to assume the blame for what Hayden was going through. No one had ever done that for her, and Hayden never expected anyone in her life would. She was proud to know Emily and to be with her.

"You are not to blame for any of this. Do you understand? I wanted you so bad in Khao Lak. I wanted to touch you, feel you move against me, kiss you. But I was afraid you would think I was taking advantage of you. We were in horrendous conditions and the last thing on my mind should have been sex, but it was all I could think of. I felt like a dog, like I couldn't keep it in my pants, so to speak. You deserved better than a romp in desperation."

Emily smiled. "I meant what I said. I have no regrets."

"I don't regret what we did then or what we're doing now, for one second," Hayden said. "What I do regret is that we were thrown together in horrific circumstances and didn't have the chance to meet in the park or on a calm beach."

Her declaration tugged at Emily's heart. She very easily could have let Emily take the fall for her behavior, but she didn't. She wouldn't let her. She had too much integrity to do that. It was at that moment Emily realized that she was deeply in love with Hayden. She, of all people: an anti-war protestor, a military-loathing woman had fallen in love with a career soldier in the U.S. Army.

Her brain scrambled to accept the idea. Hundreds of thoughts and questions bounced around in her head, each more confusing than the one before it. By loving Hayden, was she being disloyal to herself and her beliefs? Did everything she believed in have to change? Was she going to become a different person? Did she want to?

Hayden must have read the confusion on her face because she smiled and gently kissed her on the lips. "What are you thinking about?"

"Just how much you stand to lose because of us. I don't know how you do it every day. It's like you have to have two lives. I thought we were so far past that." Emily was out with her family, her job, her friends. It was difficult to imagine what life would be like if she could not talk freely about her life and those who were important to her.

"Yeah, well, the Army may have the most sophisticated military technology, but it's still in the Middle Ages about some things. It's not that bad. Those of us that are gay know who we are, and those that aren't gay also know who we are. It's the worst kept secret on any base in any branch of the military. We have more important things to worry about than who is sleeping with whom. As long as nobody is getting hurt, most people look the other way."

"Except people like Tillman."

"And my boss, General Foreman. He's a throwback who should have been retired ten years ago. He must know where the bodies are buried to be able to have the position he does."

"Would you like to have his job?" Emily knew that wasn't quite the way people got promoted in the military, but her question still made sense.

"I've always thought General Caldwell had a nice ring to it," Hayden said.

The room was dark, but Emily could see the pride and dream in Hayden's eyes when she said "General Caldwell." She'd once had a dream like that, to achieve the pinnacle of her career. She still did, but instead of standing on the Nobel Prize podium she wanted to be standing on a podium with her first graders.

Emily ran her fingers up and down Hayden's bare back like she was stroking the keys on a piano. She could feel Hayden's heart beat faster with every stroke, and it wasn't long before the smoldering look of passion returned to her eyes. Emily surged with joy that she was the one to put it there. There were hours to go before the sun peeked over the horizon, and she was going to enjoy every one of them.

CHAPTER TWENTY

"I don't know who you've been fucking, Caldwell, but you were either very good or very, very bad."

"I'm not following, General." Her father had not disappointed her in his criticism of the Privett interview, but Hayden had no idea what General Foreman was talking about. He had been uncharacteristically quiet since her return from Dallas. She'd gone about her business for three days, her ear to the ground waiting for the other shoe to drop. Once inside Foreman's office she didn't have to wait long. He started in on her the minute she crossed the threshold. For fifteen minutes he critiqued her performance, ranting and raving about what she'd said at which interview, how she'd said it, and how she looked. Finally he stopped and tossed a tan folder across the desk.

"This," he spat out. "Your orders. You leave in a week. Now get out."

Hayden was stunned. She had not put in for a change of assignment, nor was she due to be moved. She picked up the thick folder, executed a perfect about-face, and walked out of Foreman's office. She didn't stop walking until she was behind her desk. She sat down heavily in her chair, placing the folder in the middle of her desk. She sat there for several minutes looking at the file as if she could see her future through the thick cover. Her hands shook as she slid the contents onto her desk.

The word "Afghanistan" jumped off the first page and lodged in her throat. The room started spinning. She could hardly read the rest of the information on the page. She was going to Afghanistan for a three-year assignment. She couldn't think. She couldn't breathe. She dropped the paper, grabbing the edge of her desk for support.

She was going to Afghanistan, she repeated to herself several times, hoping that it would sink in and become real. She had been sent many places in her career, including some difficult, dangerous ones, but her reaction to this destination surprised her. She'd wanted an assignment to the Middle East, but the Army, in its infinite wisdom, had chosen to send her to Fort Tanner instead. She should be thrilled to have this opportunity to do what she was trained for, and do it in one of the most difficult situations in the world. Normally she would have been, but the room started closing in on her.

She grabbed her car keys and told a surprised Corporal Stone that she would be back later.

Hayden drove to the park and sat on the same bench she was sitting on when she saw Emily and her kids. The sun was high in the sky and a light breeze kept the day from being too hot. A man with a scraggly beard was pushing a child on a swing. A dog barked happily at his feet. Hayden glanced at her watch. She had an hour until Emily would bring her class to this park after lunch.

Emily was why she was sitting here. Hayden didn't question or hesitate over accepting any of her assignments, but she was different now, and Emily was the reason. She had purposely kept her life free of romantic entanglements for just this reason. She had seen her fellow soldiers break the hearts of the ones they left behind. Too many marriages failed under the strain of absence. She didn't want to subject anyone to that, including herself, and she'd succeeded so far. Until now. Until Emily.

She had fallen in love with an anti-war protester. She wasn't sure if it happened the minute she saw Emily in the water, or when she was struggling through knee-deep mud carrying a sleeping child, or when she kissed her the first time. It really didn't matter. She'd come back from Thailand a different person than when she left because of Emily. They had a shared destiny. Why else would they have met again under such bizarre circumstances?

Emily had called her a coward. It felt like a lifetime since that quarrel. Emily had challenged Hayden over not making love to her. She'd since been proven very, very wrong. At least a dozen times wrong. But what about now? Hayden didn't feel afraid. She had a decision to make and she was going to weigh her situation very carefully.

She'd finally read her orders from start to finish. With her deployment was a promotion to full colonel, but only if she accepted the duty. Judging by Foreman's comment, he wasn't the one that recommended her for the increase in rank, and she didn't think her father had the clout to pull it off. So that only left someone higher up who wanted her quiet and out of the public eye. What better way to accomplish both than to give her the promotion she'd dreamed of as the lure to get her away from the scandal, the cameras, and Emily.

Hayden smiled. She could certainly live without the publicity. But Emily…

Hayden stepped inside the front door but she was too distracted to notice the shades of tan and brown, the immaculate décor or the highly polished wood floors. "Sorry I haven't been able to see you for a couple of days. I had some things to think about."

Emily's heart slammed into her chest. Hayden's entire demeanor echoed the hollowness in her voice. "Hayden, come sit down." She led them into the living room and sat beside her on the couch. She wanted to take her hand but was afraid. "What is it?"

"I have orders to go to Afghanistan." Hayden had rehearsed what she was going to say, and this was not it. The look of alarm in Emily's eyes was exactly what she'd hoped to avoid, but she watched with pride as Emily fought to maintain control. "I'll be promoted to colonel effective my first day in country."

Emily didn't know whether to cry for herself because Hayden was leaving or for Hayden because the promotion brought her closer to her dream. Either way she felt the prickling of tears behind her eyes. She didn't want Hayden to see her cry over this. She swallowed the baseball that had lodged in her throat.

"I don't know what to say. Congratulations on your promotion, I know it's what you've always wanted. But I'm afraid for you in Afghanistan." Afraid didn't even begin to describe what she was feeling.

"I'm not going." Hayden was barely able to say the words.

"What?" Emily couldn't be sure she'd heard her correctly.

"I'm not going." This time her voice was stronger.

"Why not? My God, Hayden, you're going to be a full colonel." Emily knew she should be thrilled that Hayden wasn't going to a war zone, but she could not understand her decision.

Hayden looked at Emily for the first time since she came in. "I'm not going because I don't want to leave you."

Hayden's words didn't immediately sink in and Emily asked, "But if you don't go you don't get the promotion, right?"

Hayden nodded. "That's how it works."

"Oh, I get it. Is that the way they get you to go to godforsaken places? Dangle a promotion over your head?"

Emily gasped and put her hand over her mouth. What she'd just said was despicable. Hayden deserved more respect. She waited for Hayden to tear into her for the absurd comment, and when she got a soft smile instead she was totally confused.

"I said I don't want to leave you," Hayden repeated. "I want to see you every day. I want to be with you every day, not once a month over a scrambled video link. I don't want to worry about you here, and I don't want you worrying about me. At least I hope you'd worry about me." Hayden's smile quirked. "I love you, Emily. I'm not going because I need to be with you."

The impact of Hayden's words hit her and she was stunned. Hayden was giving up her dream for her. Emily couldn't let her do that. She loved her too much to let her do that. "No, Hayden, I love you. I want you to go."

"Emily," Hayden began.

"No." Emily held up a hand. "Let me finish before I change my mind. Over the past few weeks I've come to realize how much being a soldier means to you. It defines you. It's who you are inside. I could never take that away from you."

"You're not."

"Then why aren't you going?"

Hayden smiled calmly. Emily was having the same difficulty with her decision as she had. But the weight of the world was lifted off her shoulders when she looked into the dark eyes staring at her.

"Because I love you and I want to be with you now, today, tomorrow, not three years from now. I'm tired of hiding in plain sight. I want to be able to walk down the street holding hands with my girl and not have to worry if I'm going to face a court martial or not. I can't help but think that fate brought us together for something good. Why else would we have kept running into each other? Why else would we be beamed into millions of people's homes? We're meant to be together, and I want to be with the woman I love."

"What are you going to do? The Army is your life." Emily was starting to believe what Hayden was saying. She wasn't leaving. And she loved her.

"You are my life now. I don't know what I'm going to do, but I know with you by my side I can do anything. If you'll have me."

Saying the last few words was the scariest thing Hayden had ever done. She'd always been strong. Through her childhood, West Point, and her career. Never once showing any sign of weakness until now. She needed Emily, and she was not afraid to show it. She'd been shot at and survived all the other dangerous situations the Army put her in, but nothing was more frightening than laying herself open before the woman she loved.

Emily's heart soared. Hayden loved her and wanted to spend the rest of her life with her. They were so different, had so many challenges to face, but she wanted to face them together. What Hayden had said was true. With Hayden by her side, she could do anything. "Was that a proposal, Colonel? Because if it wasn't, you had better get your U.S. government–issued butt out of here until it is."

For the first time in days Hayden started to relax. "When we were in Chicago you said something to me that I'll never forget. It was when we were deciding if we were going on the dinner cruise. You said, 'I'm game if you are.' Well, Emily, I'm game if you are."

"And I remember you asking the clerk for two tickets after that. Well," Emily said softly lowering her head closer to Hayden's mouth. "I'll take two tickets to paradise."

About the Author

Julie Cannon is a native sun goddess born and raised in Phoenix, Arizona. Her day job is in Corporate America and her nights are spent bringing to life the stories that bounce around in her head throughout the day. Julie and her partner Laura have been together for sixteen years and spend their weekends camping, or lounging around the pool with their two kids.

Julie has selections in *Erotic Interludes 4: Extreme Passions* and *Erotic Interludes 5: Road Games*. She is the author of *Come and Get Me*, *Heart 2 Heart*, *Heartland*, *Uncharted Passage*, and *Just Business* (2009), all published by Bold Strokes Books.

Visit Julie online at www.juliecannon.com.

Books Available From Bold Strokes Books

truelesbianlove.com by Carsen Taite. Mackenzie Lewis and Dr. Jordan Wagner have very different ideas about love, but discover truelesbianlove is closer than a click away. (978-1-60282-071-5)

Justice at Risk by John Morgan Wilson. Benjamin Justice's blind date leads to a rare opportunity for legitimate work, but a reckless risk changes his life forever. (978-1-60282-059-3)

Run to Me by Lisa Girolami. Burned by the four-letter word called love, the only thing Beth Standish wants to do is run for—or maybe from—her life. (978-1-60282-034-0)

Split the Aces by Jove Belle. In the neon glare of Sin City, two women ride a wave of passion that threatens to consume them in a world of fast money and fast times. (978-1-60282-033-3)

Uncharted Passage by Julie Cannon. Two women on a vacation that turns deadly face down one of nature's most ruthless killers—and find themselves falling in love. (978-1-60282-032-6)

Night Call by Radclyffe. All medevac helicopter pilot Jett McNally wants to do is fly and forget about the horror and heartbreak she left behind in the Middle East, but anesthesiologist Tristan Holmes has other plans. (978-1-60282-031-9)

Lake Effect Snow by C.P. Rowlands. News correspondent Annie T. Booker and FBI Agent Sarah Moore struggle to stay one step ahead of disaster as Annie's life becomes the war zone she once reported on. Eclipse EBook (978-1-60282-068-5)

Revision of Justice by John Morgan Wilson. Murder shifts into high gear, propelling Benjamin Justice into a raging fire that consumes the Hollywood Hills, burning steadily toward the famous Hollywood Sign—and the identity of a cold-blooded killer. Gay Mystery. (978-1-60282-058-6)

I Dare You by Larkin Rose. Stripper by night, corporate raider by day, Kelsey's only looking for sex and power, until she meets a woman who stirs her heart and her body. (978-1-60282-030-2)

Truth Behind the Mask by Lesley Davis. Erith Baylor is drawn to Sentinel Pagan Osborne's quiet strength, but the secrets between them strain duty and family ties. (978-1-60282-029-6)

Cooper's Deale by KI Thompson. Two would-be lovers and a decidedly inopportune murder spell trouble for Addy Cooper, no matter which way the cards fall. (978-1-60282-028-9)

Romantic Interludes 1: Discovery ed. by Radclyffe and Stacia Seaman. An anthology of sensual, erotic contemporary love stories from the best-selling Bold Strokes authors. (978-1-60282-027-2)

A Guarded Heart by Jennifer Fulton. The last place FBI Special Agent Pat Roussel expects to find herself is assigned to an illicit private security gig baby-sitting a celebrity. (Ebook) (978-1-60282-067-8)

Saving Grace by Jennifer Fulton. Champion swimmer Dawn Beaumont, injured in a car crash she caused, flees to Moon Island, where scientist Grace Ramsay welcomes her. (Ebook) (978-1-60282-066-1)

The Sacred Shore by Jennifer Fulton. Successful tech industry survivor Merris Randall does not believe in love at first sight until she meets Olivia Pearce. (Ebook) (978-1-60282-065-4)

Passion Bay by Jennifer Fulton. Two women from different ends of the earth meet in paradise. Author's expanded edition. (Ebook) (978-1-60282-064-7)

Never Wake by Gabrielle Goldsby. After a brutal attack, Emma Webster becomes a self-sentenced prisoner inside her condo—until the world outside her window goes silent. (Ebook) (978-1-60282-063-0)

The Caretaker's Daughter by Gabrielle Goldsby. Against the backdrop of a nineteenth-century English country estate, two women struggle to find love. (Ebook) (978-1-60282-062-3)

Simple Justice by John Morgan Wilson. When a pretty-boy cokehead is murdered, former LA reporter Benjamin Justice and his reluctant new partner, Alexandra Templeton, must unveil the real killer. (978-1-60282-057-9)

Remember Tomorrow by Gabrielle Goldsby. Cees Bannigan and Arieanna Simon find that a successful relationship rests in remembering the mistakes of the past. (978-1-60282-026-5)

Put Away Wet by Susan Smith. Jocelyn "Joey" Fellows has just been savagely dumped—when she posts an online personal ad, she discovers more than just the great sex she expected. (978-1-60282-025-8)

Homecoming by Nell Stark. Sarah Storm loses everything that matters—family, future dreams, and love—will her new "straight" roommate cause Sarah to take a chance at happiness? (978-1-60282-024-1)

The Three by Meghan O'Brien. A daring, provocative exploration of love and sexuality. Two lovers, Elin and Kael, struggle to survive in a postapocalyptic world. (Ebook) (978-1-60282-056-2)

Falling Star by Gill McKnight. Solley Rayner hopes a few weeks with her family will help heal her shattered dreams, but she hasn't counted on meeting a woman who stirs her heart. (978-1-60282-023-4)

Lethal Affairs by Kim Baldwin and Xenia Alexiou. Elite operative Domino is no stranger to peril, but her investigation of journalist Hayley Ward will test more than her skills. (978-1-60282-022-7)

A Place to Rest by Erin Dutton. Sawyer Drake doesn't know what she wants from life until she meets Jori Diamantina—only trouble is, Jori doesn't seem to share her desire. (978-1-60282-021-0)

Warrior's Valor by Gun Brooke. Dwyn Izsontro and Emeron D'Artansis must put aside personal animosity and unwelcome attraction to defeat an enemy of the Protector of the Realm. (978-1-60282-020-3)

Finding Home by Georgia Beers. Take two polar-opposite women with an attraction for one another they're trying desperately to ignore, throw in a far-too-observant dog, and then sit back and enjoy the romance. (978-1-60282-019-7)

Heartland by Julie Cannon. When political strategist Rachel Stanton and dude ranch owner Shivley McCoy collide on an empty country road, fate intervenes. (978-1-60282-009-8)

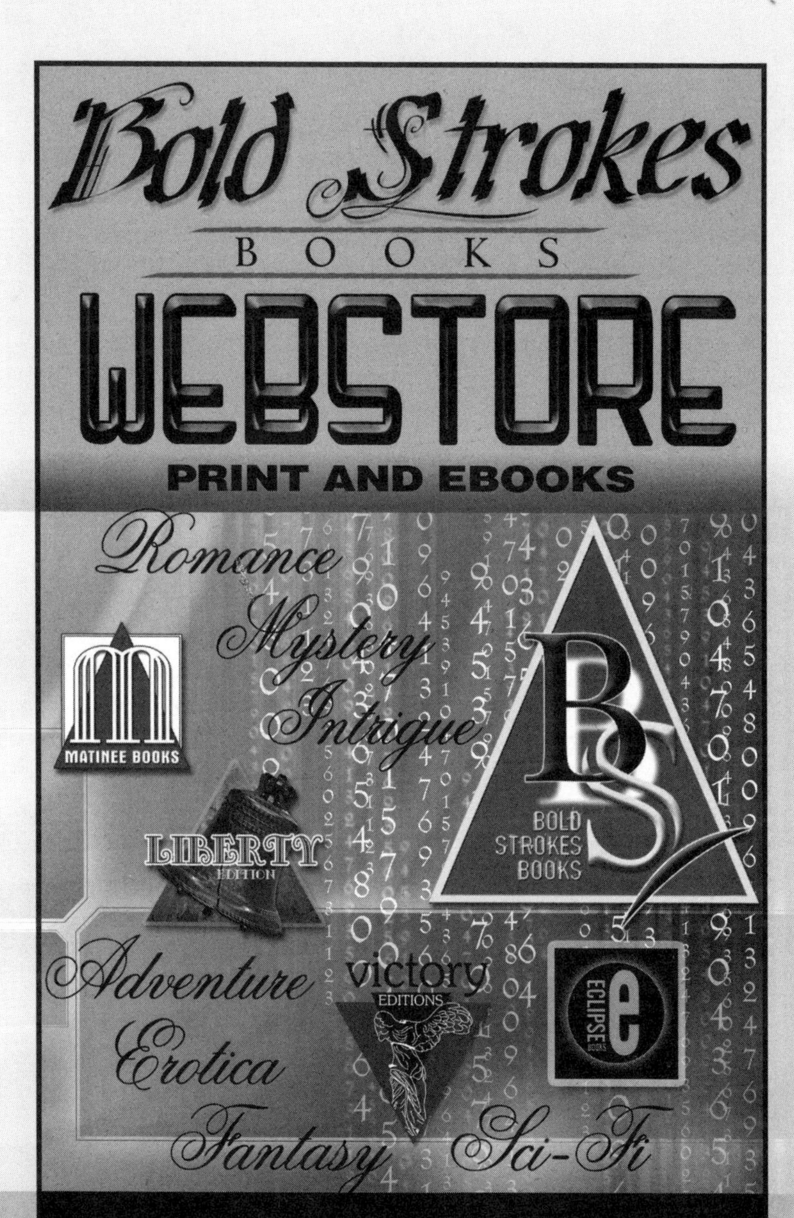

Bold Strokes
BOOKS
WEBSTORE
PRINT AND EBOOKS
Romance
Mystery
Intrigue
MATINEE BOOKS
LIBERTY
EDITION
BOLD
STROKES
BOOKS
Adventure
victory
EDITIONS
ECLIPSE
Erotica
Fantasy
Sci-Fi
http://www.boldstrokesbooks.com